Praise for Phyllis Richman's Delectable Mysteries

Who's Afraid of Virginia Ham?

"Like its predecessors, it features a lot of juicy, inside information about various genuine Washington, D.C., eateries, as well as generous dollops of humor."
Washington Post Book World

"Contains fascinating insider information that might astonish the average diner."
Santa Fe New Mexican

"Takes us on an insider's tour of both the newsroom and the restaurant scene.
New Orleans Times-Picayune

Murder on the Gravy Train

The Butter Did It
Agatha Award-Nominee

Also by Phyllis Richman

THE BUTTER DID IT
MURDER ON THE GRAVY TRAIN

Who's Afraid of Virginia Ham?

PHYLLIS RICHMAN

AVON BOOKS
An Imprint of HarperCollins*Publishers*

AVON BOOKS
An Imprint of HarperCollins*Publishers*
10 East 53rd Street
New York, New York 10022-5299

Copyright © 2001 by Phyllis Richman
ISBN: 0-06-109782-9
www.avonmystery.com

First Avon Books paperback printing: April 2002
First HarperCollins hardcover printing: May 2001

Avon Trademark Reg. U.S. Pat. Off. and in Other Counties,
Marca Registrada, Hecho en U.S.A.
HarperCollins® is a registered trademark of HarperCollins Publishers Inc.

Printed in the U.S.A.

10 9 8 7 6 5 4 3 2 1

For Bronx Bob

Acknowledgments

Whom can one thank for inspiring a villain? I'll leave them unsung. But I gladly herald those who influenced my heroes and otherwise helped me along my way. First of all, the late Dr. David Rall. While at the Centers for Disease Control and NIH he undoubtedly helped save countless lives; he had the wit and humor to dream up the perfect murder weapon for me. Anna Rentz, without even knowing the plot, suggested the most apt title. Quintin Peterson, of the D.C. Police Department, offered advice on procedural issues, while Judge Howard Chasanow weighed in on the legal and moral ones. For guidance on the details of restaurant finances, I thank Mark Furstenberg and Bob Kinkead, the man with the magic calculator. Many friends at the *Washington Post* have listened and debated and informed my thoughts regarding this fictional newspaper world, particularly

Lloyd Rose on theater and Tom Frail on journalistic ethics. For generously lending an ear to matters of fiction-writing, I'm grateful to Anne Tyler, Jody Jaffe, and Jeff Deaver. And for shepherding me through the labyrinth of publishing, it's been my great good fortune to have Bob Barnett as my agent, Carolyn Marino as my editor, and cookbook editor Susan Friedland as my friend.

My children, Joe, Matt, and Libby (unlike Chas Wheatley, I have three), are generous with their inspiration and appreciation. No mother could wish for better. And mostly, I thank Bob Burton: my reader, my cheerleader, my supporter in every way—my very home.

Who's Afraid of Virginia Ham?

1

"St. Mary's County stuffed ham was the most pathetic murder weapon of the twentieth century."

Ringo Laurenge wore an avuncular early Walter Cronkite smile as he lectured me on the peculiar Southern Maryland specialty of country ham slit in a dozen places and packed to bursting with chopped kale, cabbage, wild cress, scallions, and celery, spiked with red and black pepper, then wrapped in a clean T-shirt and boiled for hours. It's a Chesapeake Bay church-supper mainstay—at least it was until 1997, when stuffed hams at an annual fund-raiser were responsible for one death and more than seven hundred nonlethal cases of salmonella poisoning.

Ringo's sermon on ham making rang with authority. His was a face you trusted, and his deep, young voice sounded thick with concern for victims and cooks alike. It had a resonance that drew attention, while his just barely handsome looks—soft, friendly cheeks strengthened by bushy eyebrows and deep, sympathetic eyes—kept you riveted.

Everyone in the newsroom at the *Washington Examiner* agreed that Ringo Laurenge was a brilliant new hire, an exciting and talented addition to the Financial Desk staff. The best thing to come out of Los Angeles since *Casablanca*. Indeed, those who didn't speak of him as a budding Walter Cronkite compared him to Humphrey Bogart. Or Robert Redford. Sometimes Woodward *and* Bernstein. Ringo mania had hit Washington.

Call me jealous, but I wasn't buying it. Here was a Californian who'd just arrived in Washington, where I've been food critic for more than ten years. And he was telling me about our local stuffed ham. He'd even thought St. Mary's County was in Virginia until I corrected him.

"A life could have been saved if those Virginia churchwomen had used my recipe," he expounded.

"Maryland. St. Mary's County is in Maryland," I interrupted. "Just because it's south of D.C. doesn't mean it's Virginia."

"Did I say Virginia? I meant that in my recipe I use Virginia ham. Exclusively."

I was beginning to think that Ringo was the most irritating reporter our managing editor, Bull Stannard, had ever foisted on this newspaper. And the competition for such honors in the newspaper world is fierce.

He was also the youngest windbag I'd ever encountered; until now I had thought it would take
more than thirty-two years to develop full windbag capacity. But despite his youth, Ringo had
learned to harrumph like the most senior member
of the U.S. Senate.

While Ringo droned on about his recipe for
stuffed ham and how he'd adapted it to kitchens
in Rome and Saigon when he was on assignment,
I let my mind wander. I began to imagine him as a
stuffed ham or, given his youth, a suckling pig
awaiting an apple for his mouth. Why did I have
to put up with this harrumphing know-it-all? My
boss would answer that Ringo was here to save
our paper's future.

I suppose, in a way that turned out to be true
for the *Examiner*. But the cost was too great. It was
Ringo's death, more than his life, that brought
worldwide attention and thousands of new readers to the paper. And for the rest of my years I'll
blame the victim, Ringo, for goading someone I
cared about into committing murder.

The groundwork for the events that led to Ringo's
death, you might say, was laid by the news business itself. Newspapers are in big trouble. Everyone knows that. Nobody feels confident that they
are going to survive the twenty-first century, not
when the younger generation is being reared on
television and the Internet. Even older adults increasingly turn to electronic media for news.

Newspaper editors everywhere, particularly those in three-newspaper towns like Washington, are on a desperate mission to attract young readers.

That's why Bull had set about hiring Ringo Laurenge. He was a big catch. His coverage of the O. J. Simpson trial written in the form of a rap album had launched him as a media celebrity. Ringo had been drafted to cover that trial halfway through the testimony, only after his paper's lead reporter committed suicide, yet even though he'd been writing from that disadvantage, Ringo's pieces were brilliant. Creative. He hadn't just reported the news, he'd become news. That qualified him as Bull's dream writer. Bull saw him as our messiah. So did dozens of other papers, but Bull had snagged him because our newspaper came up with an offer more interesting than just a lot of money. Bull promised Ringo syndication of his best stories and what was considered a groundbreaking project as well: Ringo was going to cover business as a Lifestyles beat. I didn't quite see that as sufficient reason for Ringo to choose a second-rung newspaper, but I figured that this ambitious reporter recognized that Washington is a top-notch platform for an up-and-coming newspaperman, and I'd heard rumors that the *Post* wouldn't hire him. I also assumed that Bull had sweetened the deal in ways that the rest of us would never know.

At some newspapers, the other reporters would have felt threatened by the arrival of such a golden boy. The *Examiner* is different. It's smaller than other big-city dailies, and newer. Hardly more than a decade old, the *Examiner* is feisty, aggressive, and challenging—to other papers, not to its coworkers. Inside the newsroom, we tend to maintain the rare feeling that we're all on the same side. As soon as he was hired, Ringo became One of Us.

I felt like a traitor for resenting the guy.

I'd almost forgotten that Ringo was still talking about stuffed ham. "If the church had been lucky enough to have my recipe, the disaster never would have occurred. The safeguard would have been the pepper. With a sufficient level and the precise balance of red and black pepper, the ham never could have become lethal. And, as I said, I use only Virginia hams for mine. Once you've tried the recipe with a Virginia ham, you'll consider every other version mediocre."

Virginia ham? For Southern Maryland's oldest and dearest cooking tradition? The man was suggesting heresy. While I imagined him being placed in the stocks in the St. Mary's town square, he rattled on.

"As it is, that deadly stuffed ham has set church fund-raising back a decade. I'm glad to say it might be given another chance after I finish writing about how just a few more red chilies could have averted the disaster."

Bullshit. Enough pepper to keep the moist kale stuffing from spoiling and thus becoming toxic would have scorched the mouth of anyone who ate it or maybe even burned a deadly hole in the gut. The St. Mary's church food poisoning was tragic carelessness, and in its wake churches around the country had reviewed their food-handling practices. I thought it was callous for Ringo to stir up once again the pain of that poor, devastated community.

At least, I told myself, I'd never have to eat Ringo's blistering stuffed ham. On the other hand, if he went on much longer, I mused, a quick death might seem attractive.

That was then. Now I'd feel differently about it. Now that I've seen someone die right in front of me, I no longer consider death something to joke about.

I'd had enough of stuffed ham. I was ready to tell Ringo I was on deadline, a statement every journalist accepts as a legitimate order to get lost. Instead, Ringo was astute enough to change the subject.

"What are you working on, Chas?" His question seemed innocent enough, a friendly gesture.

"I'm writing Bull a proposal. It's a project for my syndicated column," I answered, admittedly throwing in the syndicated column mention to pull rank just a bit.

"I like that little column of yours," he said, maddeningly patronizing despite his being nearly two decades younger than I. "What's your project?"

"I'm looking into why expensive restaurants cost so much and whether their prices are warranted."

"Interesting. I have considerable experience in this field, of course. Feel free to pick my brain any time you need to."

Sure, if I could use an ice pick. Ringo's words sounded generous, but the tone was one of the master chef addressing an apprentice. On second thought, maybe I was being too defensive. Ringo hadn't actually done anything to offend me except sound more pompous than I thought any thirty-two-year-old had any right to be. I decided to give the boy more of a chance.

"I may need to tap your expertise later in the project. Thanks." What did it cost me to sound appreciative? "At the moment, I'm working up a budget and a schedule. I'm starting with the most expensive restaurant in the country, Ginza Sushiko. The fixed-price dinner is $300, and a couple of people I know blew a couple grand there on a fugu dinner. Without major wine."

"In Los Angeles? Gosh, Chas, it's a good thing we talked. I'm already doing a story on Ginza Sushiko. Fascinating story. I'll be glad to show you my notes if they would help you."

So much for meeting a colleague halfway. This interloper was stealing my story. His mouth seemed to wiggle and squirm as his words ate holes in my plan for a California trip. Nor did he stop there.

"I've lived most of my life in L.A., so I know

Ginza inside out. First-name basis with the sushi master there. I'd be glad to give you an introduction."

I tried to maintain a neutral expression. People really do see red, I discovered at that moment. At least I saw red when I heard Ringo stomping on my territory. Restaurants are my beat. He's got plenty of other businesses to write about without stealing my ground. I didn't want to let him know how outraged I felt, but I couldn't muster a calm word.

It didn't matter. Ringo was the kind of person who listened only to his own voice. He continued as if I weren't tongue-tied. "I'm new, so I don't know how things work around here. Do you think Bull will swing for you to visit Ginza Sushiko, too, after I've just done it?"

Of course Bull wasn't going to send both of us to California and foot another $300-a-person dinner bill so that two reporters could write about the same restaurant. Bull fancies himself a foodie, even bakes fancy cookies for his office from time to time. But he worships his budget above all. Damn, I wished I hadn't postponed this story idea for so long.

I took care not to show my dismay to Ringo. This man was born to exploit vulnerabilities. I kept my face bland and stuffed my anger into a corner of my mind for the moment. I covered my tracks with, "I wasn't sure Ginza was the right restaurant for me to start with anyway. It's already a bit overexposed, don't you think? Actually, there's another, more expensive and totally unknown restaurant I had in mind, but it keeps its phone number unlisted and swears its patrons to secrecy. I was proposing Ginza in case I couldn't track down my source, a sommelier who used to work there."

"You know, I'm an honorary member of the sommelier society. I'm sure I can help you. What's the man's name?"

"I've got it in my files. I don't want to make you wait while I go through that mess. I'll get it for you later."

"The name of the restaurant might do. I have a list of sommeliers on my computer."

"I always get it wrong. Very complicated spelling. It's somewhere in a stack of papers I was just about to tackle."

Ringo had lost interest by now. "Duty calls. I just saw Bull head into his office, and he's been trying to get in touch with me all morning."

Ringo hefted himself off in the direction of Bull's office, at last leaving me a chance to breathe fire and wish him a salmonella-infested batch of stuffed ham. I'd been dreaming for months of California's most luxurious sushi, and if the *Examiner* was going to underwrite a world-class raw-fish tasting, the opportunity should go to the restaurant critic, not to a business writer.

I'd have to find another outlandishly expensive restaurant for my story. I'd made up the one with the secret phone number and the ex-sommelier, just to have something to taunt Ringo with. Now I'd have to fill in the blanks with a real place. This time I'd get Bull's approval for the trip before I told Ringo about it.

2

I love eating with my hands. It makes me feel closer to the food, and brings in another set of senses to appreciate the textures. On the tongue, food tastes better to me without a metal fork or even a wooden chopstick intervening. I draw pleasure in thinking of those whole countries—Ethiopia, India, Saudi Arabia—where it is considered perfectly normal to use only your fingers to convey food to your mouth.

That's the main reason I review Ethiopian restaurants as often as I can. But there are other attractions: I crave the tangy fermented taste of *injera*, those floppy, spongy pancakes that look like oversize napkins and serve for Ethiopians as plates and utensils.

Dinner in an Ethiopian restaurant arrives on a tray covered with pancakes. Each stewy dish—

chicken and boiled egg in a thick yellow sauce, lamb in a brick-red paste, chopped cooked kale, a puree of mashed chickpeas—is mounded separately on the injera until the tray looks like a painter's palette. A pile of folded injera is placed alongside.

Few meals could be more fun—or more sensual. You tear off a piece of injera and use it to scoop up a shred of chicken and sauce, a smear of vegetable, a chunk of meat. You eat that, tear off another few inches of injera and go back for more, tasting each of the stews on its own, then trying them in combination. The seasoning is simple and often hot, depending on how much *berbere*—red pepper paste—has been used. You cool down with a hunk of potato or a wad of yellow lentil puree. *Tej*, the sweet honey wine, also helps, but I prefer beer.

Something about this food, these seasonings, the sour and yeasty pancakes, makes it impossible to stop until I'm utterly stuffed. It's food for a lingering evening and an intimate conversation.

It's food that Dave Zeeger and I feel equally passionate about. I have no trouble persuading him to join me if I'm dining at Addis Ababa, Demera, Entotto, Meskerem, or Zed's.

Dave and I feel equally passionate about each other, too, at least since we've gotten back together after a trial separation that, fortunately, didn't work. Dave is an investigative reporter at the *Examiner*, and our relationship has taken

years to arrive where it is now: publicly acknowl-
edged, deeply committed, serious and fun,
though still a tiny bit wary. Despite our intimacy,
we remain a little too polite with each other,
afraid to rock the boat.

For instance, I'm always anxious about finding
restaurants Dave will enjoy with me. He hates
wearing a jacket and tie, says he's allergic to
French food, and feels much more comfortable
eating a ten-dollar meal than a seventy-dollar one,
even if the *Examiner* is paying. Therefore, I save
the temples of gastronomy for other friends, and
lard my workweek with enough down-to-earth
restaurants that I won't risk going more than a
day or two without dining with Dave.

Addis Ababa, with its clattery chairs and frayed
plastic tablemats, is absolutely Dave's kind of
place.

In honor of the suffocating Washington summer evening waiting just outside the door, we
started our dinner with one of my favorite hot-
weather dishes, a tomato *fitfit*. It's a toss of diced
raw tomatoes, onions, hot green chilies, and injera, though in this case the pancakes are torn into
pieces the size of tortilla chips and combined with
the vegetables so that they absorb the tomatoes'
juices and flavor. It's a distant relative of Italy's
panzanella or Middle Eastern *fettoosh*, coolly refreshing and pepper-fired at the same time. It
suited the fire-eating mood that had clung to me
since my encounter with Ringo.

And since I was feeling so aggressive, I ordered *kitfo*, a kind of Ethiopian steak tartar made with chilies and pungent melted butter. I felt like living dangerously.

Dave not only shied away from the raw meat, he tried to quench my internal fires.

"Chas, dear one, you're overreacting. Ringo is no threat to you. You're one of the main reasons our readers buy the *Examiner*. The straight news they can get in the *Post*. But they can't get you there, which means that everyone who loves food has to read the *Examiner*. Nobody's going to mess with your turf. Bull would never allow it."

I was scooping up the raw meat as if it were an antidote to my anger. Instead, it was making my lips burn. "Nobody is going to be safe with this vulture around. He think he knows everybody's job. What's a business reporter doing writing about sushi?"

Dave pushed the plate of injera away from his side of the table, signaling that he'd eaten enough. He sat, lazily sipping his beer. That fired me up more; I feel guilty when he stops eating after just a modest portion and leaves the rest. I'm addicted to scraping plates clean, his as well as mine. I fumed and ate. He talked and sipped.

"What does Sherele say about Ringo?" Sherele is not only my best—and wisest—friend, she is the *Examiner's* theater critic, the first African-American theater critic in a major metropolitan daily newspaper. Her desk is next to mine, but these days it might as well be across the city, for all I get to see her.

"We haven't exactly had time to discuss it, with all the new plays opening this season. And even when we do talk, these days Sherele has bigger problems."

"You mean the New African Theater Company?"

"Exactly. Its campaign against her is pretty much all she can think about, and I don't blame her."

"I didn't consider her reviews of its first two plays all that bad."

"They weren't. But killing the messenger is a time-honored way of dealing with failure. Besides, mounting a public tirade against Sherele has given the theater company plenty of publicity. Sherele understands the motivation, of course, but it's still painful, being called a racist by your own people. Black self-hatred, that's the accusation that really upset Sherele."

"Her situation ought to help you put your problems with Ringo in perspective. He's merely an irritant to you. Unlike a theater company maligning Sherele, he's not going to affect your job much, except for maybe this one little California trip. Besides, you're looking at him all wrong," he argued. "You're seeing Ringo only in relation to yourself. In the long run, he'll turn out to be good for you because he's good for the paper. Face it: the *Examiner* needs every bit of competitive edge it can finagle. And this guy is a winner. He's going to be a big draw. A star. God knows, the *Examiner* can use some higher wattage."

"He's a blowhard."

"He's confident."

"He's grabby."

"He has far-reaching ideas."

"He's conniving."

"He's aggressive. He's tenacious. He's just what a pace-setting reporter needs to be."

I shoved my plate away. I couldn't win any moral arguments with Dave while I was pigging out on butter-doused raw meat. Dave rewarded me with a dab of his napkin on my mouth and a smoldering look as if via the napkin he had just kissed me.

"Lovey, it doesn't become you. You're too good, too worthwhile to feel threatened. You needn't take Ringo's aggressiveness personally. The guy's a little clumsy. He doesn't know how to hide his IQ, and that makes you see him as a show-off. But there's more to him than that. Get to know him. He's got a powerful mind, original ideas, and a real ear for writing. You and he should be on the same team."

The next morning, when I woke up sweaty in my brass bed with my arm stretched against the cool metal, I felt buoyant for two reasons: first, my other arm was wrapped around Dave, and second, I felt no signs of salmonella, *E. coli*, or any other raw-meat threat.

I was also glad we'd come home to my Seventh Street loft last night rather than to Dave's ramshackle Adams Morgan apartment. I keep whole coffee beans and an espresso maker in my kitchen; at Dave's, it's instant.

In honor of my good fortune, I defrosted two Amernick Danish. Even Dave has learned to appreciate these real-butter, properly flaky old-world pastries, which I buy whenever I can make a Saturday run to Wheaton. The man, the pastry, the coffee: what could be wrong with such a life?

I was ready to reconsider Ringo Laurenge in a more favorable light, if only because Dave was backing him so vehemently. By the light of day, I thought I understood why Dave cared so much.

I've only known Dave for a decade, and when we first met he was a well-established and mellow reporter past forty. I could imagine, though, how aggressive, and possibly arrogant, he must have been in his twenties and thirties when he was propelling himself to the top of investigative journalism. That field was as competitive in the wake of Watergate as the Internet is today. Any ambitious boy who didn't aspire to be a rock star or a quarterback aimed to topple presidents with newsprint (it was still pretty much a guy thing in those post-Nixon years). For Dave to have nailed the kind of job that would put him in position to undertake Pulitzer-level reporting, he had to be pushy. No time for insecurity; self-doubt would have drained valuable emotional resources. He had to be sure, demanding, and ruthless in his pursuit of information.

I would have hated him.

By the time I got to know Dave, his rough edges had smoothed. He had a Pulitzer in his résumé and knew he was as capable as the best. He didn't need anyone else's reassurance that he was a good reporter, and he didn't need to remind those around him that he was a success. Most important, he'd learned that there were plenty of stories to go around. He didn't have to hog them all.

Ringo, I reminded myself, was still a puppy, albeit one who looked like a grown dog.

Lost in thought, I took a carton of milk from the refrigerator and shook it. It felt like enough for my two cappuccinos and Dave's American coffee, light. Then I smelled it. Luck held. This was a rare morning when I had milk for my coffee, and it hadn't spoiled. I celebrated with my first cup.

As I sat staring out my kitchen window at the street below, which was beginning to bustle with delivery trucks, I shifted the focus of my thoughts. I lectured myself silently. The questions I was posing in my head, I realized, shouldn't be about Ringo, but about me.

The main question: since I have one of perhaps the five best jobs in the world, and have held it for more than ten years without a hint of disapproval from my editors, why am I worried about protecting my turf? Furthermore, Ringo doesn't want my job. It wouldn't be considered serious journalism by him, and he'd much rather stand on the side-lines criticizing the critic. No, Ringo wasn't a real threat; he only wanted to grab a few of my perks.

Well, there are enough of those to go around. I shouldn't be so grabby myself. Even more impor-tant, if I am so easily worried about my position, then I am not enjoying it as much as it deserves. What a waste, to spend my time feeling suspicious.

As if rewarding me for thinking brave thoughts, Dave kissed the top of my head. I turned to hug him, and found my face buried in his hairy bare chest. He ruffled my hair and I looked up to see his sleepy grin.

"Been up long?" Dave reached to feel my coffee cup, nodding when he found it had grown cold.

"Long enough to think about what you said last night. About Ringo."

"That's not the guy I'd hope you'd be thinking about this morning." Dave took a sip of my cold cappuccino and grimaced. He's all-American when it comes to his coffee. It's the only thing in life he prefers weak.

"That's not like you, to let your insecurities show," I countered. "A good weak cup of coffee is what you need." I rose to brew him some walnut-colored water, knowing that he'd definitely prefer instant. I warmed him a Danish while he rinsed out the glasses—one of calvados, one beer—from our return home last night. He also prefers drink-ing his beer from a bottle, but he is scrupulous about adhering to niceties in my apartment.

Dave knows that he can be overbearing, and takes pains to squelch those tendencies around me. He probably couldn't have done that at Ringo's age.

"I think I'll invite Ringo to dinner," I announced as I brought Dave's Danish to the table.

"What, no bran muffins left?" It's a running joke with us, ever since I did a little research and found that the city's most popular bran muffins have more calories than these Danish, and only a shade less fat.

"You want to go?"

"What, to dinner?"

"Of course, to dinner."

"Where will you take him?"

"This is not a guy you take to an Ethiopian restaurant. It's got to be someplace fancy, or he's going to feel he's been put on my B list. He'll care about that."

"I guess the guy ain't so smart after all."

"No, he'll probably want to drink wine, too."

Dave grimaced. "Well, I'll go anyway. Just don't make it French."

We both settled into reading the papers: the *Washington Post*, the *New York Times*, the *Wall Street Journal*. One of the advantages of working for a newspaper is that this extravagant expenditure of morning hours is considered work.

I quoted Dave a few lines from one of the *Examiner*'s business stories. He leafed through the *Times* to show me how differently it had been approached by that paper. We agreed that ours was better. Sometimes we agree, just as readily, that the *Times*'s, or the *Post*'s story is smarter or clearer or has a stronger lede. Our reading isn't boosterism, it's honing our skills. It actually is work, just more pleasant and more applicable to real life than most work. That's one of the benefits of being a journalist.

I don't take enough advantage of my opportunities, I thought as I ate the last of my Danish and wiped my sticky fingers on my napkin. I work in one of the most interesting offices imaginable, with people who are among the brightest and most stimulating anywhere, and I don't make nearly enough effort to get to know them.

"I'm going to invite more people from the *Examiner* out to dinner."

"With Ringo?"

"No, that's not what I meant. Separately. I get too lazy, always go to dinner with the same people—Sherele, Homer, Lily, you know. I should expand my horizons." Homer is more than a homicide detective I've occasionally dealt with professionally, he's the love of Sherele's life and practically my surrogate brother-in-law. Lily is my daughter. I tend to keep my dinner invitations in the family.

"I like your horizons." Dave picked up my hand and licked the sugar from my fingers. Bran muffins aren't much good for that.

"Fine. I'm going to develop more of them. I'm

going to make a list of people in other sections of the paper I'd like to get to know better, and invite them."

"Bull will appreciate that, too." Dave is the leading expert on our managing editor's unfathomable mind-set. Never have I known such a basically good man to camouflage his more admirable instincts as Bull does, but Dave understands better than any of us what's below that hard crust. "He'll like using your expense account to feed more of the staff. It's as if you're giving them each a little bonus, on him."

"Then I won't tell him. No sense making Bull happy unnecessarily."

Dave went off to the courthouse for one of his favorite activities, browsing through legal documents. I headed to the office.

The *Examiner*'s entrance was disappointingly quiet. Until recently, I'd have had to thread my way to the front door through a phalanx of picketers and protesters. Sometimes I've had to duck TV cameras. The *Examiner* was perpetually in the local news. It was always being accused of doing too much of one thing, not enough of another. You could count on taxi associations, real-estate developers, medical insurers, hair-coloring manufacturers, almost any group, at some time, to express outrage about a story we'd written. Bull really loved it when they went beyond letters to the editor, especially when they threatened lawsuits. He was happiest when picket lines ringed the building. What he craved on behalf of his newspaper was attention. Any kind of attention.

These days, except for an occasional passerby who happened to look up, nobody was paying attention to the *Examiner* building. We hadn't had a sit-in for months. No sandwich boards. No floppy posters on splintery wooden posts. Not even any gaunt, wild-eyed loonies handing out leaflets indicting us for the impending doomsday.

I'd heard that Bull had taken to driving past the *Washington Post* at odd hours to check whether it had any sidewalk protesters. I could readily believe that, but I dismissed the rumors that he'd tried to bribe some to come to our end of town.

The *Examiner* just wasn't making enough noise. Maybe Dave was right, maybe a loudmouthed, irritating Ringo Laurenge was just what we needed.

I usually come to work early, which in the newspaper business means before ten A.M. Today, having dawdled with Dave until eleven, I found the newsroom full. Instead of aiming directly for my desk, I decided to take a few detours—to the mail room, the water fountain, the library, and the vending machines. The destinations weren't what motivated me; I wanted to saunter past as many desks as possible, gathering mental notes for my list of dinner companions.

"Well, if it isn't Ms. Wheatley. I was just going to send you a message to thank you for steering me to that new Iraqi restaurant. I thought it was great."

"You're peeking at my advance directory again, Hank."

"You don't actually mind, do you? I hate to have to fight those crowds after your reviews come out."

"No, not as long as you're discreet, which I know you are. But in return, one of these days I'm going to pick your brain about the congressional election. I'm having a hard time this year distinguishing the good guys from the bad guys."

"What makes you think that there are good guys in this election?"

I would definitely enjoy an evening with Hank.

By the time I got to my desk, I had a long mental list of possible dinner partners, and felt excited about the evenings to come. Why had I let myself get into a social rut, with all these potentially fascinating companions around me?

Settling into the day's work, I turned to my notes on restaurant pricing to figure where I should go next on that story. I started with what was going to be the greatest fun, researching the most expensive restaurants in the country, looking for an alternative to Ginza Sushiko. I decided to focus on those with fixed-price dinners.

The Inn at Little Washington, in Washington, Virginia, was charging $128 per person for its fixed-price dinner, but that was only on Saturdays. Fridays and Sundays, dinner was $108, and during the week $98. Sure, that's enough money to feed an entire public-school classroom at Mc-

Donald's, but in haute-cuisine terms, it probably wasn't the pinnacle.

Lespinasse in New York might be considered more reasonable at $110 if you dined there on Saturday, but on weekdays it out-priced the Inn, and certainly it took the single-dish prize for its $35 leek-and-potato soup (albeit garnished with white truffles and langoustine).

Moving west to Chicago, I logged in Charlie Trotter's dinners at $100. Not a contender. If you booked the kitchen table, though, so you could watch the chefs go through their paces, you could get to spend $150 a person. Then I recalled the Herbfarm, in Fall City, Washington. Weekdays, the fixed price was $135, Saturdays it was $155, and if you signed up for special dinners or special reservations you could spend $250 per person, including wine but without tax or tip.

Along the way I picked up rumors of higher price levels to come. If I stretched this story out long enough, I could hold out for France's most-starred chef, Alain Ducasse, to open in New York with lunches and dinners starting at $160—without wine. His fifty-dollar appetizers and five-hundred-dollar-a-person check averages promised a new round of soul searching among diners and critics.

As if the thought of a more extravagant boondoggle had summoned him, Ringo was heading right for my desk. Despite my new commitment to give the guy a chance, I quickly stored the restaurant prices I had on my computer screen and brought up an innocuous restaurant list. No sense tempting fate. Or greedy eyes.

"My dear Miss Wheatley, how very kind of you to invite me to dinner." If I'd closed my eyes, I'd have thought the man addressing me was three or four decades older than this young ham stuffed into a striped shirt. Was he joking, or did he construct such pompous sentences sincerely?

My attitude was slipping. I shored it up.

"I thought it would be nice for us to have a chance to get to know each other," I said, trying to sound enthusiastic but probably only being wordy. "And maybe I can show you a part of Washington you haven't had a chance to see yet."

"I'm quite certain you can. And in exchange, I will be glad to offer you my insights into our meal. I've done a little restaurant reviewing myself, in case you didn't know. In Asia. And my sister works for Paul Bocuse."

Sure. Bocuse is the most chauvinistic French chef on the planet. His sister's probably the pot scrubber. I made a mental note to check her out with my sources in France.

There's nothing more bothersome than one of my guests at dinner telling me what I should think about our meal. But I decided to assume that Ringo meant it generously. As a fellow professional. So, instead of informing him that I would be fully capable of reviewing the restaurant without his expertise, and that he would be there just to chew and swallow and keep me company, I stretched my mouth into a smile.

"Let's pick a date. How's tomorrow?"

Ringo studied his Palm VII and eventually determined that he was free.

Dave was going to have to come with us, even if we wound up wearing black tie to a four-hour dinner at the Willard Room.

3

Like an alcoholic bolstering herself with a little drink before her AA meeting, I immediately corralled Sherele for dinner that night. I needed a cozy meal shared with a trusted friend to shore up my self-confidence so that I could make it through tomorrow's dinner in a gracious mood.

Getting Sherele to go to dinner with me was no easy task. As the *Examiner*'s theater critic, she's out working many nights; and on the other ones, Sherele, like me, is grateful for a chance to stay home. She'd been planning to read through a stack of new plays this evening.

But as her best friend, I know how to exploit Sherele's weaknesses. Like most thin women, she's a fool for desserts. I, being on the more rounded side, much prefer things salty and crunchy, though I understand those dessert cravers. I promised to take her to the Morrison-Clark Inn for lemon chess pie. It would fit into a column I was planning on the Southern dishes of Washington.

Once we were at the restaurant, I persuaded Sherele that she'd be doing the lemon chess pie an injustice if she didn't precede it with a good meal, so she tucked into bunny-and-bourbon, which was chef Susan McCreight Lindeborg's glorious and witty grilled rabbit with pecan-bourbon sauce, accompanied by spoonbread, while I ventured into grits soufflé and crayfish étouffée. A bottle of very un-Southern pinot noir bridged the gap between shellfish and white meat, even seemed companionable with the bourbon sauce. Morrison-Clark Inn was in its heyday; Chef Lindeborg has since left and opened the Majestic Café in Alexandria.

"I'd say you're jumping the gun, except that I try not to use clichés," Sherele said when I finished outlining my complaints about Ringo. "You haven't given our new media star much of a chance, particularly since, with his history, he's undoubtedly learned to always come to a new job with both guns blazing."

"Jumping the gun? Both guns blazing? What's with the weaponry? Not to mention the clichés."

"I'm working on a new attitude, and I don't quite have it in order yet," Sherele answered, though she was in no hurry to explain. First she broke open a biscuit and looked closely. Its texture met with her approval, so she took a tentative bite.

Sherele is a biscuit purist. She quickly ate the rest, then was ready to continue.

"I'm trying to make anger my ally by tempering it with pity. The pity part allows me to stop feeling sorry for myself. Thus I've decided to see the New African Theater as a tragic antihero; I'm not all that good at playing the victim, so I'm reassigning that role to the theater board. You might try the pity mode with Ringo, and see how it works. Dave's got a good point: Ringo's new here and just learning his way around."

"What did you mean by Ringo's history making him wary in a new job?"

"It's that suicide thing—when Ringo got the O. J. Simpson assignment because the reporter who had the job killed himself. Imagine how receptive his colleagues must have been to Ringo's stepping into those still-warm shoes. Had to develop a thick skin. Had to prove himself in a hurry."

"I see your point, and Dave's. But I'm just telling you how I feel about Ringo. I'm not saying I'm justified in feeling that way."

"How you feel about Ringo isn't the crucial part. The important thing is how Ringo makes you feel about yourself." Sherele found the last bit of biscuit and used it to swipe up the final streaks of étouffée from my plate. When Sherele eats, she really eats. But her lean figure tells you she must not eat very often. Either that or she has some miraculous kind of metabolism that would be worth a fortune if you could replicate it.

"I feel threatened. Why wouldn't I feel threatened when somebody parks his fat butt on my desk and tells me that he knows more about food than I do, and then beats me to an out-of-town assignment I assumed was mine? Of course I feel threatened. It's normal to feel threatened when you are threatened. You, of all people, should know that." I clasped my hands in my lap to remind them not to reach for another roll to punctuate my point.

"It's not normal for people to feel threatened. It's only normal for women to feel threatened. Men don't get all nervous and scared when some other guy ambles into their territory. They clap him on the shoulder—hard enough so he'll feel it every time he wakes up for a week—and give him a friendly nudge that propels him right back out of their territory. They do it with a smile. Not a whimper."

"Easy for you to say. You're the best in the business. And you've mastered the technique."

"I may look invulnerable, girl, but I wasn't born this way. No African-American is. But if I took every attack as a chance to feel insecure, I'd never be able to crawl out of bed in the morning."

"I'm sorry, Sherele. I was being insensitive."

"Now, don't go all apologetic and insecure about this, too, Chas. I'm not complaining about you. I'm just trying to remind you of how we, especially we women who've been successful, got where we are. It wasn't by letting our hurts show.

Women nowadays don't sleep their way to the top—if they ever did. They wrap themselves in armor and stride to the top, pretending that nobody, no way, can take them down. Certainly that's necessary for African-American women."

"You make me feel as if I don't understand because I'm white."

"You don't."

"If you believe that, how can you have me as a best friend?"

"The same way you can have Dave as a best friend, even though he is a man. You don't have to understand everything about a friend, as long as you understand enough."

"We never talk about race, Sherele. Do you think it's an issue between us? Is it hard for you to have a white best friend?"

"Sure it is. I don't even know what it means to you that I'm black."

"I kind of forget it unless something like the New African Theater brings up the issue. No, it's not exactly that, it's that I don't even think of the physical you unless something reminds me about it. I catch the way some guy looks at you, and I am reminded how beautiful you are. You get up from a chair and stand next to me, and I recall how tall you are. And sure, sometimes, especially when I see somebody cut in front of you as if you weren't there, or treat you in some other dismissive way, I'm made aware that you're black and you're treated differently because of that."

"In good ways as well as bad ones. One difference between us is that I can never ignore my identity. I can't forget for a second that I'm black."

"Maybe you're more aware of it than you need to be."

"Not a chance, sister. I'm black, we're women, that's always the main point in identifying us. Nobody says, 'See that person over there?' It's always, 'See that woman?' if it's you, or, 'See that black woman?' if it's me. Gender, race, ethnicity, they shape our experience of the world, and the world's reaction to us. To the world, we are our genes, not our achievements."

"I don't agree. Take me, for example. I'm a quarter Jewish."

"So am I."

She was right. I suddenly saw her differently.

I didn't get a chance to explore that at the moment. Here we were, Sherele and I, a little stunned and sizing each other up in a new way, wondering how come neither of us knew about this link until now. And before either of us said a word, a harrumph interrupted our concentration.

"What a nice surprise, Wheatley. And the rapier-witted Ms. Travis. I can see that I've been steered to dine at the right place if I encounter the two of you here." Ringo must have planted a homing device on me. I wished he'd get beeped back to his desk by Bull.

Sherele threw me a complicitous glance of irritation, but it wasn't to last long. This was a new

Ringo standing before our table, at least a Ringo I
hadn't seen before. His eyes fixed on Sherele as if
they'd been starving and she were a sizzling
steak. He quoted a line from her last review—
from the middle, not just the lede or the kicker. He
expressed such intelligently reasoned admiration
for her that Sherele grew taller by the minute and
gleamed as if she were brass and his voice were a
chamois cloth.

It was quite a performance. I grew uncomfortably warm with jealousy and felt nauseated by the
idea that I could be jealous of Ringo's attentions.
No doubt about it, the guy was masterful.

He only stayed about three minutes, but they
seemed like a week to me. And when he kissed
both our hands and took leave to meet his dinner
guest—the CEO of Martin Marietta, no less—
Sherele and I were a thousand miles from the intimacy of our interrupted conversation.

"Of course I'm wary of him," Sherele explained
to me the next day, when we began to talk about
how awkwardly our evening had ended. "He's
smooth, too smooth. But he's also truly smart.
And well read. There aren't many Renaissance
men in this day and age. So you don't want to
miss out on a dazzling mind just because you're
scared by his ambition. Even his avarice is something you can learn from."

She was being co-opted. A few clever phrases
and a bucketload of flattery had wormed their
way through Sherele's armor, and now my two

dearest friends thought my distaste for Ringo was petty. I had two options: I could sulk or I could re-think my stand.

Sulking's more fun.

Mine got a boost later in the day. Vince Davis, our most deliciously cynical business reporter, walked by my desk, which isn't on his normal route. As he said hello in passing, he crooked his finger discreetly to signal me to follow him.

Pretty mysterious, I thought. When he was five desks ahead, I got up and sauntered in his direction. We met in the stairwell.

"Didn't want to seem I was tattling, Chas."

Vince doesn't waste words. He'd already said hello.

I hadn't, though. "Hi, Vince. Why all the secrecy?"

"Big ears in the newsroom. Never know who's on whose good side, or wants to be."

"You can't mean Sherele. There's nobody I'd trust more than Sherele."

"A lot of ex-wives once said that about their husbands." I started to protest, but Vince held up his hands in apology. "No point getting into that. I just wanted to make sure you know what's what around here."

"You've always been a big help to me that way. I owe you already. What don't I know that I should know, this time?"

"It's that new guy. Laurenge."

"Oh, Ringo. Yeah, I've met him."

"Ringo. Why would a guy go through life with a name like that? You'd think he'd at least change to initials." Vince shook his head. I assumed he'd run out of words, that he'd just wanted to warn me to be wary of Ringo. But he had more.

"You been planning a trip to L.A.?"

"Sort of. But it turned out to be wishful thinking. I'd hoped to do a story on the country's most expensive sushi restaurant."

"Ginza, right?"

"I didn't know you were up on such things."

"Not me. But your boy, Ring-Oh."

"Yes, that's the problem. He'd already gotten approval from Bull for a story on Ginza Sushiko."

"Gotten approval, eh? He told you that?"

"Yes, a couple of days ago."

"Since when do we need duplicate approvals around here? I heard him just yesterday proposing such a story to Bull, with a travel form in his hand ready for a signature."

"You mean he lied about having approval already?" I was seeing red again, vermilion this time. "The guy is unbelievably smooth. Didn't miss a beat, just slid right in with a full-blown fabrication."

"Never seen one smoother in all my days. He even managed to slide a trip to Richmond out from under me. I'm amazed anyone would squander such chicanery on Richmond."

"You're taking this more coolly than I can."

"It's only Richmond. And truth be told, it was kind of fascinating, watching him operate. Me, I'm at the end of my career and just marking time here. But in all my years I've never seen such a fierce empire builder. This Ring-Oh has the biggest Rolodex in the business and massages it daily as if he were a concert pianist working out on his Steinway."

I was grateful to Vince for warning me, and I told him. Cynic though he is, Vince had gone out of his way for me once again. Not many colleagues would bother.

"You're not the only one he's going to be crossing wires with around here, you just watch. The guy is shrewd. Some people wondered why, ambitious as he is, he settled for a beat in Business. It ain't Congress. But those of us who look below the surface know how smart that was."

I'd rarely heard Vince string together so many words at once. Another accomplishment of Ringo. But I wanted to hear more.

"I wondered myself why he'd settle for a business beat. What did I miss?"

"Chas, think about what Business is. It's not a subject, it's an approach. It is nothing less than a way of looking at everything in the world. Politics. Sports. Entertainment. Education. Choose any section of the paper, and you can connect it to Business. The White House. Foreign. Health. Home Design. They're all justifiably part of Ringo's turf. You, Sherele, even the movie critic would be remiss not to watch your backs."

Investigative reporters, too? I didn't ask Vince.

I didn't get much more work done that day, at least not the kind of work I was supposed to be doing. I had Ringo on my mind. His presence still irritated me and his past lured me. I had a couple of hunches and was compelled to follow them. Though I felt a twinge of discomfort about taking work time to dig dirt, especially on a colleague who'd been nice to me lately, obsession won the day. First I called France. It took no time to be assured that Paul Bocuse's Lyon restaurant had never had a California woman on its staff. So much for Ringo's boast that his sister worked there.

Next I combed Los Angeles obituaries until I found the reporter whose suicide had propelled Ringo to stardom. Edwin George Lansing was his name, generally known as E. G. His newspaper's obit didn't exactly specify that his death was a suicide; it was called an accidental drug overdose. Follow-up stories in journalism journals and on the Internet were more revealing. The death was officially being listed as accidental, but unofficial questions were raised about how a couple dozen sleeping pills could be swallowed accidentally. I wondered whether Ringo had an answer to that. I'd find out somehow.

4

"Why can't we go to Pizzeria Paradiso instead? It's got classy food. You could impress Ringo with a *bottarga* pizza."

Dave was just putting up a token fight so I wouldn't worry that he was sick or something. At normal times, he wouldn't even give Paradiso a second glance. He doesn't believe in minimalist pizza. His has to be oozing lots of oil from the tomato sauce and slithering with stringy cheese. Paradiso applies its toppings with restraint and, even more alien to Dave's style, it stocks only the best mozzarella, aged parmesan, and nutty pale-green olive oil. Its toppings include that rare tuna roe called bottarga, as well as sliced potatoes or gorgonzola. Its wood-fired oven turns out dough so good it doesn't even need toppings. All of those qualities interfere with Dave's man-of-the-people pose, not to mention that he ordinarily refuses to wait in line for his dinner.

We were climbing the iron steps next door, to paradiso's sibling restaurant, Obelisk. Despite its name, it's the most pure Italian restaurant in Washington, not at all Dave's idea of dinner. The owner, Peter Pastan, the son of a poet, picks his ingredients as carefully as his mother chooses her words, and he puts them together as simply and deftly.

I chose it not just because it makes me feel serene, but because its fixed-price menu offers only three or four choices for each course, so there'd be little chance of Ringo one-upping me or sabotaging my ordering, should he be into playing such games.

He was already seated, even though Dave and I had arrived a few minutes early, at my insistence. What's worse, Ringo had a bottle of wine open on the table. It was a Brunello di Montalcino, a wine considered so important that the Riedel crystal company designed a special glass for it. I didn't have to look at the maker or the vintage to know that Bull would hit the ceiling if I charged such an extravagant bottle on my expense account. What's more, it's a wine to drink with hearty food, not one to sip while poring over the menu. Ringo had ordered this as an act of aggression.

"Good evening, Ringo," I said as I picked up the bottle to examine the label. "What an original idea. Did the sommelier suggest this?"

Ringo struggled to his feet, bumping the table as he did. It was fortunate I was holding the bottle; Dave barely rescued Ringo's glass of red wine before it was wasted on the tablecloth.

"I've had quite a nice talk with the owner about this wine," Ringo said, not taking notice of the havoc he had caused. "Like most Americans who've spent time in Italy, he thinks he knows all there is to know about Italian wine and food pairings, but he came around to my way of seeing it and ultimately approved my choice. I also explained to him that you love brunello, which I'm sure you do."

"You told him I was coming tonight?" I nearly missed the seat the waiter had pulled out for me. I was infuriated. Ringo would know that a restaurant critic never announces her visit ahead of time. Even if she's likely to be recognized when she arrives, she doesn't want a restaurateur to have time to prepare for her.

"I certainly would not do that. He just happened to notice your name when I was showing him how the 'Schedule' function works on my Palm VII. It could hardly matter anyway, Chas. Every restaurateur in town recognizes you by now, I'm told. It's even said that when you show up, the restaurateur calls all his friends to tell them that they're off the hook for the evening."

"That wine looks very good. I think I'll try some," Dave interrupted, probably anticipating that a volcano was about to erupt beside him.

"Chas, let me pour some for you." He was trying so hard to defuse my impending explosion that he didn't even venture to order a beer.

Ringo, too, must have noticed my fury. He immediately turned contrite, showed me still another face.

"I do hope you like this wine, Chas, because I ordered it as a gift for you. It was so kind of you to invite me to what I hear is one of your favorite restaurants, that I didn't know how to thank you except with a taste of something close to my heart. I feared that if I waited until after you arrived, you wouldn't let me pay for it."

I'd been watching Ringo's mouth move, trying to figure out why it reminded me of Walter Cronkite even when I didn't trust a word he said, so it took a moment for his words to sink in.

"You're paying for this wine?"

"Why, of course. You don't think I'd presume on your generosity this greatly, do you?"

"No, it wouldn't have crossed her mind," Dave chimed in, nudging my knee with his, secretly telling me, "I told you so."

Ringo did it. I felt a little chagrined to have to admit it, but he charmed me that evening. He told witty and hilarious stories about being sent to follow an American rock group on a tour of Italy and of trying to cover news in Hollywood. He flattered me. He displayed his humble side, wondering what I thought accounted for the pasta's unusually sheer texture and where the chef might have found veal with so much flavor. He asked questions about Washington restaurants in a way that led me to think about them in a fresh light. He even made me feel that, despite my being old enough to have been his teenage mother, he found me devastatingly attractive, and he made sure Dave knew it too.

The food helped to soften me for my conversion. Even Dave, like most men a beet hater, loved his beet-and-tongue salad as much as I did. Ringo insisted I eat the last bites of his extravagantly simple and pure fettuccine with fresh peas. We paused before dessert for a leisurely nibble of grainy aged parmesan as we finished our wine—I bought the second bottle, a considerably less expensive one. And, while we shared all the desserts, the men conceded to me the lion's share of the biscotti with vin santo, since that was obviously my favorite.

Ringo brought out the best in Dave, sought his war stories and expressed his admiration without fawning. By the end of the evening, a little giddy from the wine, I was laughing so hard that I hardly looked at the bill, just added a tip and waved it away.

I didn't notice until the next day, when I sobered up and filed my expenses, that the bill was so high that the restaurant must have mistakenly charged me for the brunello. I decided it would be shabby of me to remind Ringo, so I just deducted a hundred bucks from the bill I submitted to the *Examiner*, and chalked it up to a surprisingly pleasant evening.

My after-dinner chocolates came the next day. Obelisk isn't the kind of restaurant that pampers you with tuiles and truffles at the end of the meal, I was thinking as I wrote up my notes the next morning. But almost as if he'd read my thoughts, and just as I was checking my watch to see how long I'd have to wait until lunch, Ringo stopped at my desk, holding before him a small white box rimmed in fuchsia.

"Chas, that was a grand evening. You can't know how much it means to me, being so new in town, that you included me. I couldn't hope to repay you, but let me at least introduce you to something you should know about. Have you ever tried Wittamer chocolates?"

I hadn't even heard of them.

"They're Belgian," Ringo said as he opened the box. "Been in business since 1910. Still run by three generations of Wittamers, everything done by hand."

The candies inside were beautiful, each one a meticulous pyramid, or a leaf, or a trio of interlocked disks. Some looked like printed floral fabric, several were two-toned. They were among the prettiest chocolates I'd seen.

"Try one. Here, the passion-fruit ganache." He pointed to a dark square with tiny pink flecks. It turned out to be a jolt of bitter with an undercurrent of sweet and acid, flowing and creamy in my mouth.

"This is fabulous. Where did you get them?" I looked at the box hungrily.

"You've got to try this pistachio fresh-cream filling." Ringo picked another from the box and put it on my desk. "And the ginger. The nougatine praline. Fresh chocolate mousse. This one's made with Earl Grey tea." He reached to the second layer for a flat little rectangle stamped "THÉ" in the same fuchsia as the package.

I tasted it and was suffused with fondness for Ringo. A person doesn't part easily with such treasures as these. I'd probably have squirreled away the whole box and never breathed a word to anyone else. These were chocolates as deep and velvety as any I'd ever known.

"You're my kind of hero, Ringo," I gushed. "How did you get these from Belgium?"

"The Internet. I'm doing a story on the luxuries being sold on the Internet. These little masterpieces cost a mere $95 a pound."

I choked on the pistachio cream.

Fortunately, Sherele didn't arrive at work until I'd finished the last of my chocolates. I'd have had to share them.

"You're looking happy this morning," she said as she pulled a brown paper bag from her briefcase and dangled it in front of me.

"What's this?" I reached for the bag.

"Pecans. The first of the season, from my uncle

in Georgia. Couldn't eat them all without sharing
them with my best friend."

I know how much Sherele values this annual
windfall from her uncle, and I'm ready to concede
that they're the world's best pecans. At the moment, though, my excitement was tempered by
guilt. The only thing Sherele loves more than
pecans is chocolates. I hadn't saved her a single one.

"Go ahead, dig in," Sherele urged.

"Thanks. It's really nice of you. I'd better save
them for later." I positioned the bag on my desk to
cover the fuchsia-rimmed Wittamer brochure
Ringo had left with me. And I vowed to blow a
hundred bucks on a full pound of them for
Sherele's next birthday.

"How was last night?"

"As usual, you were right." I was feeling mag-
nanimous toward Sherele, so I exaggerated my
new assessment of Ringo. I still had reservations,
but Sherele—and Dave—had been way ahead of
me in seeing his virtues.

Never have I gotten so much mileage out of taking someone to dinner. In the following weeks,
Ringo seemed to be making himself my new best
friend. He sent me a copy of an amusing article on
dining in America from the *London Observer*. He
begged me to be his guest at a wine tasting of the
Commanderie de Bordeaux, apologizing that the
organization still doesn't think to invite women to
its events. He sent me the address of his favorite

mail-order lamb from New Zealand and of a mom-and-pop fish-smoking operation outside of Seattle. One Sunday afternoon he showed up at my apartment with a bouquet of flowers he'd bought me at the Dupont Circle farmers' market.

Nor was his largesse limited to me. Dave said that Ringo had recommended him for a TV documentary on the future of investigative journalism, and persuaded the producers that it made more sense to have Dave representing Washington newspapers than the *Post* reporter they'd planned to invite. Ringo stopped by Sherele's one Saturday after an estate sale where he'd bought her a century's worth of Broadway playbills he'd found at throwaway prices. Other reporters, too, were talking about what a helpful colleague Ringo turned out to be. The guy was trying so hard to ingratiate himself, it was a wonder that he had any time to write.

But he did. I've seldom witnessed such productivity. He was doing quick news reports and long features. His stories were appearing in every section, though mostly on the front page. What particularly surprised me, he was not hogging space or taking all the credit for the stories. Ringo was cooperating with reporters in every department and sharing bylines. Few reporters, especially young ones, are willing to do that.

Nobody works hard in Washington in the summer. That made Ringo's performance all the greater a surprise. Some reporters file from the beach, others just let the news happen and then write it up, waiting for fall to pursue the big stories. Yet Ringo spent those months writing up a storm and making his stories sound like important stuff. He stayed in the city the entire season and brought so much life to the *Examiner*'s pages, you'd have thought it was October in an election year.

The mood of the newsroom, usually lethargic in summer, was energetic. Desks were filling up earlier and emptying later than they usually do in hot weather, yet nobody seemed tense or pressured, just busy. Lighthearted, too. There was an unusual amount of backslapping, given that newspapers are more habituated to backstabbing.

Most important, the *Examiner* was experiencing a spurt in sales, an unprecedented summer event. Bull celebrated by treating the newsroom to ice cream, to pizza, and one Friday afternoon to beer— also unprecedented. I've never seen Bull happier.

The ultimate measure of our success—or Ringo's—came when we heard that the *Washington Post* was looking for a business reporter to cover popular culture. It was creating what sounded like Ringo's beat. The sincerest form of flattery.

The *Examiner* was on a roll.

Since it was summer, my plan for inviting colleagues to dinner proceeded slowly. I was reminded after a few false starts that it's tricky to schedule dinners with reporters in the months when schools are recessed. On the nights they are in town with no plans, people want to go home and take their shoes off, dine on nothing more than a salad and a gin-and-tonic. Three-course restaurant meals are hardly appealing even to me in the Washington heat, so I understood my colleagues' pleas for a rain check—or a heat check.

I was reduced to writing a column on breakfasts, that fallback subject that saves restaurant critics when they're desperate. Breakfast is a meal one can eat alone without drawing a second glance, the menus are limited enough to cover in a few solo visits, and a big breakfast doesn't kill the appetite for dinner as a big lunch does.

Another advantage to reviewing breakfasts was added that summer. My daughter, Lily, is a musician who makes her living by giving concerts in the schools during the fall and spring semesters. For the interim she had a job playing piano in a hotel lounge.

I'd been uncomfortable about her taking any job related to restaurants, fearing it would be seen as a conflict of interest for me as a restaurant critic. But since her last name—Boucheron—is different from mine, and she was scrupulous about keeping her relationship with me out of the equation, I had no grounds for objecting.

What really bothered me about Lily's summer job, though, was that it kept her occupied at dinnertime. Breakfast solved the problem. One perfect morning I met Lily to review the breakfast at Teaism's branch near the White House.

The marble table felt cool under my elbows as I

watched the foot traffic outside the window. Swishing flowered skirts, khaki pants both long and short, sneakers and sandals, loafers thick-soled and thin, pigeons darting in between feet to peck at muffin crumbs, the debris from Washington's breakfasts-on-the-run.

I didn't register Lily's arrival at first, because I'd been watching for something long and flowing. Instead, she was in a miniskirt topped by a skimpy T-shirt that clung. I was astonished. Lily never dresses in anything form-fitting. She tends to clothe herself like a slightly mysterious sprite.

My face reflected my thoughts imperfectly.

"You don't like it?" Lily asked as she leaned down to kiss me.

"You look great." I truly thought she did. "It's just that I'm not used to your being so . . . un-wrapped."

Lily laughed. "That's exactly how I feel. Or plucked. But it's kind of fun. I may even get used to it. The outfit's a present from Brian." That's her boyfriend, who's a waiter, which is another conflict-of-interest issue that makes me uncomfortable. But I like Brian, and even if his job makes me vulnerable to censure, I certainly can't tell my daughter whom to love.

"What's the occasion for the gift?" A shirt and skirt seemed an extravagant gift for a waiter struggling with summer's meager earnings.

"It's my prize for not criticizing him for a week."

"Sounds like a small price to pay."

Lily's mouth drew into a sour pucker, at which I immediately backpedaled. "Bad joke," I offered, as I rose to signal that it was time to choose our breakfast from the counter display.

Lily played it safe with a candied-ginger scone and a plate of tea-cured salmon, two specialties that practically built the restaurant's success. For me, herbed scrambled eggs and grilled chicken sausage. We both drank sweetly spiced, milky *chai*, since coffee isn't in this tearoom's repertoire.

"Do you think I'm too critical?" Lily asked as she broke off half her scone and cut her salmon in two to share with me.

"Of the food?"

"No, of people. Am I too critical of people?"

"What people? Me?"

"Mamma, don't be so self-centered."

"Lily, don't be so critical."

I knew I was releasing a safety-catch in our conversation, and sure enough, Lily shot back at me, "I knew it. You do think I'm critical. Mamma, why do you always have to find something wrong with me?"

"Once again you've turned your question into an accusation. You started by asking if you were too critical, and now you're criticizing me for responding to your question."

"I can't follow this. Sometimes you're impossibly hard to talk to." Lily reached over to my plate and took a piece of sausage she'd turned down before. I felt a stab of regret that even my lean health-fanatic daughter would use food to try to sweeten a bitter moment.

I'm the mother, I reminded myself. To Lily, I said, "Let's start all over. You introduced the word 'critical' into this conversation. What's really happening, Lily? Why are you feeling so touchy?"

Her face fell. "I don't know. I don't know exactly. But it has something to do with Brian. He said I'm too critical of him, and I took it to heart and was careful all week not to be. And I thought I did a great job. I even *felt* less critical of him. I liked him better."

She came to a full stop and stuck her fork into another bite of sausage.

I finished her thought for her. "Then he gave you a present that you took as a criticism from him, as if he doesn't like the way you dress."

Her face changed as if a cloud had floated past and left it in full sunshine. She put down her fork and sat back in her chair. "You saw that? It's not just my own little paranoid reaction?"

"Well, maybe it's just that you're the daughter of a paranoid, but I'd feel exactly the same way if Dave bought me some sexy little outfit that was a U-turn from the kinds of things I usually wear."

"I couldn't quite figure out why it made me angry. He meant to be nice. And he spent a lot of money. But I couldn't help feeling it was a gift with a hidden agenda."

"I understand how you feel, and you're not wrong. But you're not completely right, either. I think Brian's not necessarily criticizing, but just suggesting variety. I've seen how he looks at you when you walk into a room wearing your usual layers and scarves. It's not the look of a redecorator. His eyes smolder—you can almost see smoke. But with this gift he's just adding something new, a twist, a touch of adventure. The fact is, it looks great on you. No greater than what you wore last time I saw you, but different."

Lily was ready to hear this. My new Lily, the one who'd learned that closing your mouth to criticism might open your eyes to appreciation. She learned things so much faster than I ever had at twenty-three.

"I've got to think about this. You have a point, Mamma."

"I've had my own lessons to learn about being supersensitive," I confessed. I told her about Ringo, how I'd been so insecure that I'd overreacted to his having something to say about restaurants. I admitted how defensive and territorial I'd been, and how he'd proved to be such an asset to the paper. I realized as I spoke that I, too, was trying to be less critical of the people in my life, though I hadn't set it as a specific task, as Lily had done.

"I remember hearing about Ringo from a rap singer I know on the West Coast," Lily said. "From what he had to say, your first reaction was probably the accurate one. He'd tell you to watch your back."

At first I wondered why Lily hadn't mentioned him before, then I realized I'd been so self-conscious about my resentment of Ringo that I'd postponed talking to Lily about him.

"How did Ringo offend your singer friend?"

"He didn't offend him personally, but when my friend heard Ringo had moved to Washington, he e-mailed me a couple of secondhand stories that made Ringo sound like someone to avoid. There was a rap song, as I recall, that Ringo lifted from another singer or something. He changed it only slightly and ran it in his newspaper under his by-line. Made a big splash with it, but didn't give the original one credit. There was more, too, something about a suicide."

I felt we were playing *Six Degrees of Separation*. Here was a new lead, right at my own breakfast table. "I'd like to hear more about this. At least to protect the *Examiner* from rumors. How would you feel about me calling your friend? Would that make you uncomfortable?"

"Quite the contrary. He's a big fan of yours. Sometimes I think the only reason he calls me when he comes to Washington is because he hopes I'll invite him to dinner with you."

When we walked out into the sun-fired oven that was Washington, Lily looked at her watch. "What have you got to do for the next hour, Mamma?"

"Why are you asking?"

"I want to take you shopping."

Sauntering belatedly into the newsroom two hours later, I felt a little awkward. I'd never shown so much thigh this far from a beach. I kept wanting to tug my skirt to make sure it wasn't riding obscenely high. I've probably never walked with my spine so straight in my life; in fact, I was almost leaning backward to make sure my ass was covered.

"Hey there," Dave said as I stopped in front of his desk. "Look at those gams." His eyes rode up and down me as if he were speedreading my body.

"You like it?" The newsroom felt hotter inside than the summer sun had outside.

"I love it. Excuse my slobbering."

While I enjoyed his making my body blush head to toe, I also felt the ambivalence Lily had expressed. "You don't like the way I usually dress?"

"Honey babe, I love that, too. But sometimes even a set-in-his-ways old guy like me gets a hankering to vary my pepperoni-pizza diet with Genoa salami."

"Good. A food metaphor. You sure are the man who knows the way to my heart."

Dave spent a few more minutes reassuring me that I looked drop-dead great in my new outfit, that the skirt wasn't too short for a newsroom, and that I also looked drop-dead great in my usual, more decorous wardrobe. He invited me to come over for a Genoa salami pizza that night, and even volunteered to pick up some espresso beans on his way home for tomorrow's breakfast.

I felt reassured enough to continue on to my own desk rather than flee out the door and run home to change. In fact, I decided that the outfit Lily had wheedled me to buy had been money well spent.

The odd thing was, it made me feel more comfortable talking on the phone to a rap singer.

"Cool. Is this really Chas Wheatley? Real cool."

"Lily tells me you're interested in food." I had to start somewhere.

"Cooking's my life, man. I mean, after music."

We exchanged a few words about sea-urchin sushi and the honey-roasted peanuts on airplanes, then I got down to business.

"You know, we have a new reporter here at the *Examiner* who used to work in your town. Lily says you used to know Ringo Laurenge."

"Know him? Not anymore. I *knew* him. Glad to have it in the past tense."

"What did he do to you?"

"To me, nothing. But the man is a thief. Probably a murderer, too, in a manner of speaking."

"In what manner of speaking?"

"You heard about how he got his job here on the O. J. trial?"

"Yes, I heard that another reporter committed suicide."

"That's the word on the street. But I've got a friend who was tight with E. G.—E .G Lansing, that's the dead guy—and he said Ringo was right on his heels from the beginning, ready to push him out any way he could. Pretended to be buddies, but sabotaged him every which way."

"Are you saying Ringo drove him to suicide?"

"Can't say that exactly, but events made people who knew them very, very uncomfortable about your new colleague."

I would have invited Lily's friend to dinner anyway, but promising a free meal made it all the easier for me to ask if he'd find out whether the dead reporter's friend would be willing to talk to me.

Food is big in L.A. Within a half hour, E. G. Lansing's friend called me.

"You're a living legend, Ms. Wheatley. I can't eat soft-shell crabs without appreciating you for teaching me about them in your columns."

I silently gave thanks to syndication and the Internet for spreading my words, while for a few minutes we talked about rockfish and East Coast vs. West Coast oysters. Then he got down to business.

"I hear you're looking into E. G. Lansing's suicide. What's that about?"

"We've got Ringo Laurenge working here at the *Examiner* now, and rumors have followed him. I just wanted to try to sort them out."

"Unofficially?"

"Unofficially. Off the record. Just between us."

"Well, I don't know many journalists I'd trust as much as you, so fire away."

What the story boiled down to was that E. G. Lansing hadn't seemed depressed, worried, or upset, at least no more so than any other reporter covering a big trial, but one day he swallowed a bottle of sleeping pills. My informant, who asked that I tell nobody his name, was the one who found him dead. Actually, it was more complicated that that: my informant was Lansing's lover, and had come back from a trip late at night to find Lansing sleeping. Or so he thought. Since Lansing had told him on the phone earlier that day that he was coming down with a cold, my informant decided to sleep on the couch. In the morning, he tried to wake Lansing, but it was too late.

"Where was the bottle of sleeping pills?" I wondered why he hadn't noticed it earlier, unless Lansing was such a tidy suicide that he screwed on the top and put it back in the medicine cabinet.

"It was in the bathroom. On the sink."

This was tough, but as long as I was probing: "How come you didn't notice it? Did you have separate bathrooms?"

"No, I saw the bottle before I went to bed. In fact, it was open, and there were only a few pills in it. But I didn't think they were sleeping pills. They were in a vitamin C bottle."

"Was that where Lansing usually kept them?"

"Not that I knew. I wish I had known it. I've re-lived that sequence of events a thousand times in my head."

"And what was Ringo's role?"

"Nothing. Nothing that I could put my finger on. But he'd been badgering E. G. in a low-key way ever since the Simpson trial started, and he'd been stepping up his pressure lately. Making him feel insecure, pointing out errors and small ways he was being scooped. I always thought E. G. should dump the jerk, but he said Ringo was useful in keeping him on his toes—better from inside the paper than someone from without."

"And you think Ringo drove him to suicide?"

"Sort of. Well, not really. But I can't help feeling that was a factor. Mostly I resented the way Ringo took over E. G.'s place at the paper, as if he'd been waiting and wishing for it, which he was."

"The death was ruled an accident."

"That's because the pills were in the wrong bottle. But nobody really thought it was an accident, not after E. G. had swallowed dozens of them."

Dozens did sound like a lot of vitamin C pills. Maybe.

"What was the dosage?"

"Huh?"

"The dosage of the vitamin C. How many milligrams?"

"The usual, I suppose. A thousand. He always bought thousand-milligrams and took one a day."

"Are you sure?" Nobody would take twenty-four thousand milligrams of vitamin C, even to ward off a cold.

"You mean you want me to check?"

"I'd be curious."

I explained why.

5

Since I owed Vince for his being so protective about Ringo stepping on my turf, I looked for a chance to take him for a good meal—and a reality check. I was particularly curious to hear whether he'd revised his assessment of Ringo since we'd talked. I wanted to test Dave's complaint that I was overreacting to Ringo's faults, so I took care to keep my feelings from influencing Vince's response.

By now I knew that Vince's taste ran to bottled water and foods that have little seasoning and not enough calories to count. I took him to Kaz Sushi Bistro, figuring that even if he didn't fancy raw fish, he could find there cooked shrimp, a grilled fish, a great green salad and, if all else failed, a bowl of plain rice.

I'd chosen well. Squeamish as Vince is, he actually grew enthusiastic over Kaz's modernized sushi roll of smoked trout and asparagus. After all, it was composed of cooked fish and a vegetable that was familiar—though he peeled away the wrapper of black seaweed to bare the rice packed around the fish and vegetable. As he ate, he cut each of the six pieces into tiny bits. My pace of eating, I calculated, was four times faster than his. At least.

"It's an amazingly successful summer for the *Examiner*, don't you think?" I asked as I took a minuscule bite of yellowtail-belly sashimi, trying to slow my pace a little rather than eating the whole piece at once. I belatedly noticed that Vince put down his fork when he talked, which further stretched out his meager meal.

I tried to do the same with my chopsticks, but I began to feel deprived if there wasn't a piece of raw fish on its way to my mouth. At this rate I was going to overstuff myself just to keep Vince company. The only solution that came to mind was to reverse the proportion of talking. I decided to stop asking him questions and to talk more myself so he'd have time to eat.

"Bull says the circulation figures are higher than they've been since the late eighties, and most of the gains have been among the post-baby-boom generation," I began my monologue. "It's every newspaper publisher's wet dream, he says—Bull's words, of course. I've never seen him so happy. Most of the front office, he told me, gives Ringo credit. You shared a byline with

Ringo yourself. Terrific story. Did you find him a good team player? It's a relief that he's worked out so well for us all, isn't it . . ." I ran out of steam as I realized that Vince had put his fork down anyway and was staring at me. He'd hardly eaten anything.

"Are you done?" I ventured, taking a big swig of my beer to hide my embarrassment.

"Yes. Are you?"

My plate was empty. "Obviously."

"No, I meant blathering."

I hit a new depth of embarrassment. "Aw, c'mon, Vince."

"Look, Chas, I like you. In fact, you're one of the few people in the newsroom I do like. I think you're smart, and a scrupulously honest critic, and there aren't many like you."

That was a remarkably wordy speech for Vince, and he wasn't finished.

"But hard as you are on restaurants, you're too soft on people. I'd expect all the others to be taken in by Mr. Ring-Oh Superstar, but you ought to know better."

"I'm glad you have such confidence in me, Vince, but I've been worried about being too harsh on Ringo. I've been trying to reexamine my first reaction. Maybe you and I made up our minds too early and ought to admit all the new evidence into our deliberations. Didn't your story with Ringo go well? It was a great story."

"Yes, it was a great story. And I have no problem with sharing the credit for it. Laurenge is a talent. I've never denied that. The guy might even be a fucking genius. But just because he knows how to use the right fork in public, don't think he doesn't eat with his hands in private."

"Huh?"

"I was just trying to state it in your vocabulary."

"Maybe I'm not as smart as you think. Spell it out for me. What do you see as the problem with Ringo?"

"He's setting us all up. It's an old story. Pied Piper. He's worked damn hard this summer to get everybody's trust. Doing the scut work, playing humble, being the cheerleader, and laboring like a dervish. Like I said, he's an amazing talent. But none of this has been natural to the guy. It's an act. Now that he's lulled everybody, he's gonna pounce. There's a glint in those eyes that he can't totally hide if you're looking carefully for it. Just don't forget Ginza Sushiko. And if you do, at least remember the guy who warned you that he was digging in your turf."

"If I didn't know better, Vince, I'd say you've been eating too much raw flesh. A touch of cannibal in you."

Vince sat back and patted his hollow stomach as if he'd pigged out on a big meal. "The thing is, Chas, I know how I sound. I'm just no good at public relations. I've never been able to smooth these rough edges, and people tend to take me as a crank."

"An awfully nice crank." I felt like patting his hand, which I knew would send him fleeing. Instead, I, too, sat back, posing as if we were just two friends relaxing together.

I've always kind of admired Vince's crankiness, seeing it as the dash of Angostura bitters, the classic touch that saves a cocktail from being cloying. Sometimes, I must admit, I was the only one of his colleagues to see anything beneath the bitter edge. Maybe I'd only imagined the sweetness.

No, now I was going too far in the other direction. I knew Vince's kindly side. He just didn't boast about it.

Vince—like me, as I secretly admitted—needed more time to recognize the value of Ringo. At least that's what I told Dave later. Dave didn't buy it; he thought Vince reveled in being a stubborn crank and would never modify his view no matter what Ringo did. In other words, Dave thought I was being soft on Vince.

I wasn't sure that this exchange with Dave was really about Vince. First Dave had complained when I was hard on Ringo. And now Dave saw me as soft on Vince. Which did I mind more? Why did I mind either?

Fortunately, the next night I was dining with Linda, one of those rare reporters who can find even the Prince George's County bureau exciting. Prince George's is the poor relation to Maryland's other county that borders on Washington, Montgomery. While Montgomery County has a new superchic restaurant opening every week, in Prince George's, menus are still stuck in the surf'n'turf era. Though Prince George's has pockets of colonial charm and scenic beauty, it's mostly a county known for its old poverty and new wealth, a suburb that went from farmland to tract housing so fast that much of its history and culture were bulldozed in the process. What's more, the county has become the catchall for whatever urban dysfunctions are being squeezed out of the city. Only in the last few years has Prince George's begun to take pride in its historic buildings, its bucolic countryside, and its new ethnicities. Linda, alone among journalists, loves the county and is devoted to promoting its best features for our readers.

In addition to faithfully covering the county council and the courthouse, she'd unearthed some award-winning feature stories. I, of course, was most fascinated by the Vietnamese farmers who are growing vegetables and herbs never before seen in the mid-Atlantic, and who have started manufacturing bottled fish sauce—the Vietnamese and Thai equivalent of China's soy sauce—to sell nationwide.

She's steered me to those rare Prince George's restaurants that could attract diners from across county and state borders—the Chinese noodle parlor, the tacky roadhouse that serves fabulous giant crab cakes, the Greek fish restaurant that unfortunately didn't last long enough for me to re-

view it. This time she took me to the College Park
Days Inn, close enough to the University of Maryland to serve as a no-tell motel for students with
uncooperative roommates in crowded dorms.

It was the last place I'd expect to find a Korean
restaurant, but there was Yi Jo, its pink-and-green
dining room packed. Men and women in power
suits, their industrial-strength briefcases standing like sentinels beside their chairs, were chat-
tering loudly over the sizzle of meat and whoosh
of exhaust fans. Everyone looked like a Korean
middle manager whose hard day of work was being wafted away in the smoke from tabletop
grills.

Linda and I started with a seafood-scallion pancake as big as a Domino's pizza (which was undoubtedly what everyone else in College Park
was eating that night). The golden pancake was
crunchy to the first bite, but its thick insides were
soft and starchy, a cross between pudding and
dough. I could taste squid, scallops, oysters, and
shrimp, threaded with sweetly cooked scallions. I
intended to eat only one wedge, given that grilled
short ribs were to follow, but when Linda reached
for a second piece, I found that wishes overlapped
with obligation. I didn't want to leave Linda eating alone, nor could I resist more of that briny,
oniony crunch for myself.

"It took years for this restaurant to turn a
profit," Linda was telling me as she knocked back
another inch of *soju*, Korea's answer to vodka.

Here was a woman who could drink any other reporter under the table.

"But it's full, and on a Tuesday night. A lot of downtown restaurants would envy its business." I sipped my soju.

"It wasn't always full. In fact, for the first year or two it was empty on most weeknights. This restaurant's owners needed excruciating patience to build its word-of-mouth business. I wondered how a restaurant could survive on so little business, and this one taught me a lot."

"What was the answer?" Linda was detailing what I knew only vaguely and by hearsay. She had good sources in immigrant communities, and could probably help me with my restaurant-finances story.

"It's the same tale with most successful immigrant restaurants. First, a restaurateur keeps his debt low. He doesn't go to a bank for a loan, at least not for such a small shoestring operation as this one. The interest rates would kill his chances. He borrows from relatives. They scrape up every bit of savings they can, and support each other in starting a business. When one thrives, the profit from that business is used to help the next in line. I'm sure the earnings from this restaurant are now being plowed into a relative's new venture."

"Even so, it needs plenty of capital for its carrying costs until it can break even."

"The relatives count there, too. Restaurateurs such as these hire as few employees as possible.

Mother, father, children, aunts, uncles, and cousins all pitch in. New arrivals from Korea can depend on relatives for room and board until they're self-sufficient, and those relatives expect the newcomers to help in the restaurant in between jobs, classes, whatever."

"It's a world away from a McDonald's, isn't it?"

"In all except the prices. Bite for bite, this wonderful seafood pancake is probably no more expensive than a Big Mac."

Our conversation took a break while the waitress draped thin slices of soy-sauce-and-garlic-drenched beef on the cooktop, and arranged on the table small bowls of kimchi, pickles, fried fish the size of straight pins, bean sprouts, and marinated spinach. We concentrated on cooking the beef and, once it was frizzled crisp, folding it into lettuce leaves.

"You've had a busy summer," I said between bites. "Those were impressive stories you did on the culture of crime. You and Ringo seem to have made a good team."

"Thanks. They required a lot of late nights, but I'd been wanting to do this series for a long time."

"I'm glad you finally got around to it."

"It wasn't a matter of me getting around to it, Chas, it was getting the editors to agree to let me do it. I'd pretty much given up on that."

"What made them change their minds?"

"One word: Ringo. The guy is gold. If he suggested a story on 'Monica Lewinsky: What Lipstick Is She Wearing Now?,' they'd hail it as groundbreaking." Linda's tone would have curdled milk.

"Why so bitter? At least you had the ear of someone who has their ear. Once-removed is better than out-of-the-loop altogether."

Linda and I had finished the meat and were scraping up the crunchy bits that clung to the grill. Thus we hadn't been looking at each other. Now we did.

"Chas, you know, I didn't even notice how bitter I'd become."

We both put down our chopsticks, and the air seemed still despite the exhaust fans. Linda's face slowly changed, and this tough, hard-drinking reporter began to look as if she might cry.

Instead, she knocked back the rest of her soju.

"Maybe you're concentrating too much on the process and not enough on the product," I said. "However it came about, the series was a big success, and that has to help your image with the front office. Did Ringo pull his weight on the reporting?"

"He was better than I expected. Didn't grandstand, got his hands dirty. I'd say, yes, the series was better for having him on it. Once I got into the research, I realized it was a huge project, too much for one person unless the *Examiner* would give me six months to work on it. So I was grateful to have a partner. No doubt, Ringo is a pro. He knows where to dig up the dirt and how to make an interview work. He didn't do anything I couldn't have done, but he shared the burden fairly."

"So why are you complaining rather than celebrating?"

"It's what Ringo's doing with it now."

"What do you mean? The series is done."

"I forgot, you don't watch much television. You're always out to restaurants, aren't you? With those Sunday brunches you probably never even get to see *Face the Nation* or *Meet the Press*."

"I can't remember the last time."

"Ringo's turned our culture-of-crime series into a major embarrassment for the county. Every Sunday this month he's been on one show or another, and he always manages to squeeze in something about crime becoming an accepted form of business, using Prince George's County as his example. And that wasn't what the series demonstrated; it's a gross exaggeration. He has not only infuriated the local community, he's destroying my sources. Nobody will talk to me anymore. People feel betrayed, by me as much as by him. I'm at the point where I think I've got to ask for a transfer. I'm having a hard time being effective on this beat. After years of building confidence, I'm no longer trusted."

"Linda's overreacting." That was Dave's conclusion when I told him about my dinner, and it made me all the more relieved that I hadn't confided in him about my calls to California trying to link Ringo to a suicide. Dave was stretched out on the sofa, where he'd been watching baseball and waiting for me to come home. As usual, he'd saved me a piece of pizza, and as always, he polished it off when I demurred.

"Linda's tough. It's not like her to overreact," I countered as he searched the pizza box for stray nubbins of cheese.

"I'd say you're right about that, but in this case Ringo has touched on three very sensitive nerves that would set off any reporter."

"Like what?" While we'd been talking, I'd been roaming my loft, filing my menu and receipt, changing from restaurant duds into an oversize T-shirt and washing a fish-sauce stain from my dress. Now I was ready to relax. I removed the pizza box from beside Dave on the sofa and took its place.

"First, Linda is still pissed, and rightly so, that Ringo could get a green light for this story when she couldn't."

I could see that. I could also see some luscious curly hair peeking out of Dave's half-unbuttoned shirt. I touched it just to make sure it felt as good as it looked. Then searched for more.

"Second, even if Linda appreciated Ringo's help, she had to be a little disappointed to be sharing a story that she'd planned to do herself, all the more because it was her regular beat and he didn't even know where Prince George's County was." Dave was returning the favor, even though I have no chest hair.

"Third, after this had been her idea and her

beat, Ringo winds up with all the national attention because he's already a talk-show regular. She becomes just the anonymous coauthor, as far as the world outside the *Examiner's* readership knows. She's bound to be supersensitive to everything he says on television. I would be, too. And so is the county; nobody likes his hometown's problems aired in public. But Linda's reaction is temporary. Things will cool down, and in the long run she'll have a more balanced view of what Ringo helped her accomplish."

I didn't want to talk about Linda anymore.

Dinner with Linda had inspired me. Or maybe it was the night with Dave. In any case, the next morning I revved up my restaurant-finances research. I went over the list of sources I'd been developing, which by now included realtors, food and wine wholesalers, lawyers, interior designers and architects, growers, bankers, and the Restaurant Association of America, which has its headquarters in Washington. I wanted interesting numbers to start my imagination working. So I began with equipment.

A restaurant-size mixer: $5,000.

A chair: the sky's the limit, but $80 is probably the bottom for a white-tablecloth restaurant.

A napkin for a luxury restaurant: $2.50 to $3. It is expected to last through 250 meals, but once you add the laundering costs, it will run twenty to thirty cents per use.

One supplier told me that table linens alone can cost a restaurant thirty thousand dollars a year. The cost varies enormously, depending on whether the restaurant owns them and launders them-in-house or has a linen service, on whether placemats or top cloths are used to protect the underlying cloth. It became obvious why a restaurant might opt for decorative laminated tabletops that require no coverings.

I had tablecloths on my mind that night when I met Lily at the new Two Views restaurant in Georgetown. I found myself taking care not to drip red wine on the white cloth, nor to let my fork or knife touch it after they'd been used. I was trying to save the restaurant a dollar or two in laundering costs, hoping this tablecloth could be used for two or three seatings. Once Lily dripped her borscht on it, though, I relaxed. It would need a laundering no matter how meticulous I was.

Two Views was the ideal choice for Lily and me. Judging from the packed tables, plenty of other diners felt the same way. Its theme was so clever, I wondered that it hadn't been done before.

Most obviously, the name referred to what could be seen from its windows. This was the first rooftop restaurant in Georgetown, indeed the only rooftop restaurant in Washington with a view of the Potomac. It also had window walls on the opposite side to provide a panorama of the city, at least of the old Georgetown streets and the spires of the university.

That would have been a feat enough to ensure a restaurant's success. Even more, though, the restaurant catered to two views in food. It was half steakhouse and half vegetarian. All those couples with one carnivore and one herbivore now had an exciting place to share a meal. I'd also heard that the steaks were aged in-house and that the vegetables were organic. The advertisements featured an ever-changing variety of couples: He in boots and cowboy hat, she in hippie tie-dye. She in a leather power suit, he in beard and sandals.

Lily isn't really a vegetarian, she just likes to behave as one. Her eyes go right to the salad section of the menu, whereas I start out at the meats and fish. Eventually we meet in the middle—at potatoes—and, ultimately, Lily eats more of my meat than I do. Her ordering preferences are a matter of self-image more than reality.

The main reason Lily jumped at the chance to dine at Two Views was that her boyfriend, Brian, had recently started as a waiter there. The management didn't know about his connection with me, at least so far. I hoped it never would. And I would have preferred to be assigned a waiter other than Brian so I could see what the rest were like. But I didn't want to raise any questions by asking for a change once we happened to be seated at one of his tables. I'd have to take pains to observe the service at other waiters' tables and try to get seated elsewhere when I returned. Maybe I could time my next visit for Brian's night off.

Lily, of course, felt that luck was on our side in the table assignment; I assume Brian did, too. They were considerate enough to be discreet, though, and behave like friendly strangers.

Given that I'd had no control over the situation, I decided to calm down and take advantage of Brian's presence. He advised us which dishes we should try and why—or why not. We got all the inside dope on what was going on in the kitchen and what was being done differently because the staff knew I was a critic. When the maitre d' came by to check on us, Brian turned impersonal. And every time one of the two young owners came to ask how everything was, Brian managed to stutter a bit or make his hands shake as he swept crumbs from the table. He'd supposedly just learned that he was serving a critic. The guy's a competent actor as well as a charmer.

Lily, to make it feasible for Brian to spend a lot of time at our table, placed constant demands on him. She must have dropped three forks during the dinner, and her napkin had a habit of slipping from her lap every time Brian's hands were empty.

"This would be a good place to examine for my restaurant-finance story," I told Brian and Lily. "A rooftop restaurant, with its elevator access adding bother and expense, would be an interesting case study. I'd have to wait until after I reviewed it, of course. I wonder if the owners are so savvy as to understand that even if the story reveals some secrets they'd rather keep to themselves, it's useful publicity. And they'd have to be broad-minded enough that they wouldn't mind that my review had found some faults with their operation." Halfway through my first meal I knew I'd have plenty of good things to say about Two Views. It might even warrant a rave. But I'd spotted some flaws, too.

"I'm not surprised you'd want to feature this restaurant. It would make a first-rate story," Brian said as he leaned over me to arrange the condiment dishes for my steak.

"This kitchen is serious, and the owners are willing to spend whatever it takes for a quality product," Brian continued the next time he approached our table.

"I expect they'd be glad to show off their extravagance on behalf of the customer," he added a few minutes later as he refilled our wineglasses. He was pouring just an inch at a time so that he'd have to refill them often. Even so, it made for an extremely choppy conversation.

"Give me a couple of weeks, and I'll have a better idea of what their sensitivities might be." That came with our dessert menus.

Brian's timetable suited me fine. I'd have loved to start right in to interview the restaurateurs I was going to write about, but lining them up was going to require time because anyone I chose would require some softening up to the idea. So I was prepared to proceed slowly.

Brian could see I was trying to rise above my impatience. As he delivered Lily's three-plum Brown Betty and my zinfandel cheesecake, he muttered quietly, "I'll give you a preview, Chas. Chew on this one for a while. You like the flowers?"

I nodded enthusiastically. Two Views had hardly needed to decorate, with all the twinkling lights of the river and city creating a sparkling kaleidoscope through the glass. Nevertheless, someone had placed dramatic bouquets of flowers strategically, so they could be seen from all parts of the dining room yet not block the sight lines to the windows. In addition, each table had an arrangement that looked as if it had been gathered from the backyard of an inspired gardener.

"They look good enough to eat," I told Brian as he brought a pitcher of thick cream for Lily's dessert. "The flowers, I mean." Indeed, they included pansies and nasturtiums, both of which appear on plates these days.

"Do you like them $2,500 worth?"

That caught my breath.

"That's how much they spend a week here on those posies." He delivered a calvados that I hadn't ordered, but he knew my taste. Besides, it gave him another reason to swing by our table.

I did a quick calculation. "That's probably a couple of bucks per diner."

"Only if every table does at least two covers a night." Brian fiddled with our table's flower arrangement. He meant that each table would have to turn twice—be used for two or more seatings every evening.

Brian had hoped to appease me with this snippet of information, but he was wrong. Those details excited me, made me all the more eager to dig further. I'd have to rein myself in.

Brian brought the check. "The *Examiner* is certainly doing its part to help pay for those flowers." He placed the folder in the exact center of the table, as if he didn't know whether Lily or I would be paying the bill.

"Our check's not that high," I said, opening the smooth, costly leather envelope to look at the total.

"I didn't mean just you. A number of your colleagues have come for dinner already." I am often among the last to try a new place, since I wait until it's worked out the kinks. "And one has become a regular. At least at the bar."

"Who's that?"

"The new guy. The one who's on all the talk shows. You know, he looks like a a cross between Walter Cronkite and Peter Jennings."

"Ringo Laurenge?"

"That's the one. Trying to make the maitre d' his new best friend."

People do that. They try early on to be identified as a regular at a new, fashionable restaurant in hopes of getting special treatment when it becomes more popular and reservations are scarce. They're like investors buying a newly issued stock in hopes of a run on it. Two Views, I predicted, would be seen as the Yahoo! of the Washington restaurant scene, a reservation becoming ever harder to wangle. The maitre d' was going to have more best friends than he'd ever imagined, and people would be claiming to be close pals of Mr. View in hopes of getting preferential treatment.

But Ringo didn't need to work so hard for that privilege. His name and the *Examiner*'s would be enough to qualify him for VIP treatment. I wondered what his angle was. I'd have thought he was too busy, and the restaurant too far from his home and office for him to just hang out at the bar. That kind of behavior has to have a goal.

Lily and I walked home arm in arm, musing on the future of this new restaurant, and I wondered aloud about Ringo's motivation for making Two Views his hangout. Lily stopped short.

"Where was my head tonight? Having Brian formally serving me turns my mind to jelly. I totally forgot the connection."

"Connection?"

"Ringo. That's the one my musician friend told me was a scumbag, right? The one you were worrying about, then you decided it was too dangerous to dig in his past?"

"He's the one we discussed, the one who was believed to have stolen somebody's rap song. And maybe even had something to do with another reporter's death. The very same guy hanging around Two Views. But what makes you think I was afraid to look into his past?"

"Your e-mail."

"What e-mail?"

"The one you sent . . . I forgot when . . . a couple of days after we had breakfast. The one where you said you'd decided it wasn't wise to snoop into other people's private business, that it might get you into trouble. You know, the one where you warned me about walking around Dupont Circle alone at night?"

"Me? Worried about walking at night? Afraid of getting in trouble for asking questions? Why would I write such an e-mail?"

"I thought it sounded a little weird. But I just attributed it to your writing it in the midst of a frazzled workday. You do get a little wacky when you're on deadline or something. So I ignored it."

When I insisted I'd never written such a note, Lily promised to e-mail me a copy at home that night if it was still on her server. Once it arrived, I scrolled through it with chilled fingers and a thumping heart.

It had been definitely sent from my office e-mail address. It was from me to Lily. The message told her I'd decided it would be too dangerous to continue digging into someone's past. And it expressed concern about her walking alone at night.

I knew only one person who could have sent it. What I didn't know was how Ringo had sent a message from my e-mail address, since I'm careful to sign off when I leave my desk. I supposed I could have forgotten from time to time, and that he'd watched for that opportunity.

More worrisome was how he knew I'd been asking questions about him. And what disturbed me most was that the message had made it clear that he knew my daughter walked alone at night around Dupont Circle.

The man was clever. He'd sent a warning that nobody but me would recognize, and managed to make it untraceable to him. He also understood that I'd be most vulnerable to a threat to my daughter.

But he had an idealized view of close-knit mother-daughter relationships. He didn't know that we don't always tell each other everything. Lily hadn't bothered to respond to my message, so his threat had never hit home. I'd continued digging. And now I knew that the message was all bark and no bite. So far.

6

Ordinarily I feel as sympathetic to our food editor, Andy Mutton, as I do to frozen fish sticks, but this morning I cringed on his behalf. He's a shambling porridge of a man who wears his lunch stains on his necktie and his breakfast stains on his shirtsleeves. I try not to cross paths with him after work, so I don't know where he finds room for his dinner stains. Andy is mewling and territorial, suspicious and lazy. What more could you want in a rival? I wouldn't consider him a competitor, except that once in a while we're vying for the same expense-account dollars or for space in the paper to cover the same food event.

I'd rather eat at Arby's than encounter Andy. Today, though, I had compassion for the poor slob. It's embarrassing to a reporter when his story has an error that requires the newspaper to run a correction, but once in a great while that happens, even to the best. A reporter then apologizes, looks into how the error occurred, and learns a lesson from it, then moves on. That's the way with a normal correction, which runs on the second page of the newspaper. Once or twice in my life I've seen worse: a correction placed on the front page. That's big. That's humiliating. That's job-threatening. That's what happened to Andy Mutton this morning. And it was a restaurant story, one that I might have done if he hadn't gotten the information first.

"I didn't know it wasn't nailed down," he sniveled. "I swear on everything I hold sacred." I couldn't imagine what that would be, but I reminded myself that I was here to listen, not to judge. Andy was sitting in a sea of empty desks, as if nobody'd remembered to tell him that the building was being swept for mines. When he saw me coming his way, he burst into blubbery incoherence.

"I checked. I had it nailed down. Somebody must have been lying." Andy hadn't gotten to the lesson-learning stage yet.

"I'm truly sorry, Andy. If there's anything I can do to help . . ."

"You can believe me. That would help."

That might be more than I could manage. "I'm certainly willing to listen."

The issue was that Andy had reported the sale of a restaurant that hadn't been sold. Maybe that doesn't sound life-threatening, but restaurants are like the stock market, vulnerable to rumor and dependent on being considered hot, at least the expensive ones. They are desperate to keep their image untarnished, to be seen as in demand. Success breeds success, popularity encourages more popularity.

Thus, if word gets around that a restaurant has been sold, its customer base can dry up in a day. People stop going because they're afraid it is no longer the "right" place to be seen, or because they expect it to be changed and don't want to be caught eating in an off-brand restaurant. As soon as Andy's story appeared, the restaurant's phones stopped ringing, then they started again, but largely for cancellations. If the restaurant hadn't been failing before, it was now.

"Tell me about it," I urged him. I might have a lesson to learn in this, too.

"It came from a tip. Some guy called and gave me the details, right down to the price and the phone numbers of the principals."

"But you checked it out." Any reporter would, of course. I was just encouraging Andy to keep talking. I write about the restaurant world, too, and wouldn't want to fall into a similar trap. "Somebody must have been lying, right?"

Andy looked as if a bomb had been found, and he was sitting on it. I'd seen that look on Danny Glover's face in one of those *Lethal Weapon* movies.

"Yeah, but I'm not sure just who."

"You mean you checked two sources and they differed?"

"Chas, I gotta be able to trust you on this. This is off the record, for your ears only, not to be shared with anybody, and I mean anybody. Do you promise?" He must have been desperate to talk if he was willing to trust a nemesis like me. "The second source wasn't exactly firsthand. But please don't tell anyone. It would be worse if people knew how really stupid I've been."

I couldn't imagine his looking more stupid than he already did with that front-page apology, but I held my tongue on that. "I promise. Just between us," I reassured him.

"After the phone call, Ringo came by to check out a story he was doing, to make sure it wouldn't conflict with anything I had working. He said he'd already cleared it with you."

Not that I could remember. "What story was that?"

"It was this one. The restaurant being sold."

That was puzzling. I'd never heard about the purported sale until Andy's story appeared, and in light of the aftermath, I was glad I hadn't. I didn't want to divert Andy from telling me his side of it, so I just muttered a noncommittal "hmmm."

"I told him it was my story, that I'd already been working on it."

"Which wasn't quite true," I couldn't resist

chiding him. For once, Andy was getting his comeuppance for being territorial.

"Well, it was sort of true. I had the tip. And I was ready to work on it. Besides, restaurants are my beat more than his."

And my beat more than yours, I didn't say out loud. "He just let you have the story? Caved in? That's not like Ringo." In fact, I thought it was rather generous of him.

"I didn't even have to fight him on it. He kind of insisted I do it, said that he had too much on his plate anyway."

Andy had even greater feats of generosity to report. "He was so nice about it, I felt ashamed I'd been so selfish. He even gave me his notes."

"So he'd been lied to, too?"

"Apparently." Andy's eyes were darting around as if he were looking for an escape route.

I was fascinated by now. It was odd that both Ringo's sources and Andy's would lie about the sale, since the information was so specific as to price and date and other details that had made the story seem unshakable. One source, maybe. But two sounded like a conspiracy. Andy'd been taken.

"Why would the owner lie? That's the most puzzling part. It was against his own self-interest."

"He says he didn't."

"But you had the notes."

"He says nobody ever talked to him."

"You did, though. Why would Bull believe a scumbag like that rather than his own reporter?"

"Ringo's the one who talked to him. It was in his notes."

"Then who was your source?"

"Just the guy on the phone. He said he was the new owner. I figured that between Ringo and me, we had the two required sources, and all the details were identical."

"Ouch. What did Ringo say?"

"He said I got it wrong, that he never told me his notes were from interviewing the owner, but that he got them from a telephone tip that must have been the same as mine."

Andy had no recourse. It was lazy of him to depend on Ringo's notes and not check the story further on his own. He looked as if he wanted to stand up and let the imaginary bomb blow him to bits. I didn't blame him.

"The worst part, Chas . . ." He was saying this reluctantly.

"What?"

"When I thought back on that phone call, the guy had a funny way of pronouncing 'restaurant.' "

"Funny in what way?" I didn't see the point.

"He enunciated every vowel. Rest-oh-rahnt. You know, the way Ringo does."

I was dying to march right into the office of Helen, the Lifestyles editor and the paper's conscience, to settle in my mind whether Andy was paranoid or Ringo was evil. But I'd promised Andy I'd tell nobody, and I take such vows very seriously, as I do commitments to keep information off the record. Any journalist who can't be trusted with secrets isn't likely to turn up many good stories.

My next conversation was even more alarming but also off-the-record.

"It took more digging than you could imagine, but I finally found a crime-scene photo of the vitamin C bottle." It was E. G. Lansing's lover, who hadn't even paused for a hello.

"What's it show?"

"I had to use a magnifying glass, but it was 250 milligrams. The drugstore must have run out of the stronger pills."

"So now do you think it was an accident? E. G. thought he was swallowing 6,000 milligrams of vitamin C?"

"I would, since he took as much as ten thousand when he thought he was getting sick. But if he'd put his sleeping tablets in his vitamin C bottle for some reason, he would have remembered. E. G. had a very orderly mind."

"You think somebody else switched them."

"I do."

"And you've told the police?"

"Not much point in that. There's no way to find any proof, never was and certainly wouldn't be now. The police might respond by making me a suspect."

"What are you going to do?"

"Nothing. Just continue grieving. For now."

I felt sick as I hung up the phone.

As my mind went over and over the implied accusation by E. G. Lansing's lover, I vowed I wouldn't simply let it go. I'd find out more about my dangerous colleague. And I had an idea how I might do it.

"Ms. Wheatley, I'm here to solicit your opinion on a very important matter."

I jumped at Ringo's voice. I'd been so absorbed in mulling over my plan.

My first reaction to someone seeking my opinion is to feel flattered, but in this case it was smothered by revulsion—and wariness. My fingers hit the "Close" command and I stored the column on my computer before I turned to answer him. I hoped he hadn't overheard my phone conversation.

"Ringo. What can I do for you?" I searched his eyes for signs of cold steel.

"What's your view of Two Views?" He paused and watched my expression, which apparently wasn't what he'd hoped it would be. I didn't smile. "Lame joke, I apologize. But I understand you've dined there already, and I always like to go straight to the best source. There's no point listening to anyone else's opinion on restaurants now that I have personal access to yours."

"You've been to the restaurant, too, so you must have your own opinion." I wondered why he was asking, since he's the kind of blowhard who doesn't give credence to what anybody else thinks anyway, unless it reinforces his own convictions.

"I'm just an amateur. I'm seeking the wisdom of a professional."

As I watched his firm mouth, his concerned eyebrows, his intent eyes all add up to an expression that promised trustworthiness, I still couldn't decide whether he was being friendly or devious. I decided to honor my instinct for caution.

"Aw, Ringo, you say the nicest things. But seriously, I haven't tried Two Views enough to venture much of an opinion yet. It's certainly a promising restaurant, but you know us critics— we need a lot more evidence to make up our professional minds than just plain customers do. Come back after I've paid it a couple more visits if you want anything that might pose as wisdom."

Ringo didn't look disappointed. He just swung Sherele's empty chair to face me and settled himself into it. Apparently it was time to get to the real reason for his visit. "Do you think your opinion can make or break a restaurant?"

"Hardly. It's just one factor among many that hurry a restaurant along toward its fate."

"But if you really tried hard to influence that fate, couldn't you have a major impact?"

This was a peculiar subject for two journalists to discuss. The impact of our work has already been talked to death by the time we've been on the job as long as we have. It's a topic that's predictable, it's trite, and it makes us feel either uncomfortably powerful or disappointingly ineffectual. I consider it a waste of time. "I suppose I could influence a restaurant's success, if I really campaigned for or against it. But that's not the point of my job. In fact, it sounds unethical. I can't imagine why I'd do such a thing."

"How would you go about it, though?" Ringo was invading my personal space as his chair edged closer. The man had no sense of boundaries, and he looked as if he were chewing up all the air and not planning to leave any for me.

"I wouldn't, as I said."

That didn't work. He decided to answer the question himself.

"If I were a restaurant critic and wanted to promote a restaurant's success, I'd simply mention it as often as possible. I'd drop its name into other columns and compare other restaurants to it when I was critiquing them."

His smugness drew me in. "That's obvious, just as, if you wanted to sabotage it, you'd mention it negatively at every chance."

He still didn't go away. "But don't you think the quickest way to destroy a restaurant would be to spread some dirty story about rats in the kitchen or food poisoning?"

I rose to the bait. "Or start a rumor that it was being sold?" Ringo didn't flinch, not a glimmer of recognition. Maybe Andy was the crazy one in today's drama. "But that's not something I would do. In fact, none of this is."

At just the right moment, my phone rang. I looked at the caller ID, which was a number I didn't recognize, but still said to Ringo, "Sorry, this is the call I've been waiting for. See you later."

He had no alternative but to find some other colleague to plague.

"Enough of Ringo already."

Dave was right. I tend to chew a subject to unappetizing mush. And Dave's not much of a gossip. Nor one to accept speculation and guesswork as sufficient evidence. He's a two-sources reporter, through and through. I needed Sherele to be my sounding board about Ringo. He was becoming my morbid fascination of the year, and I'd been spouting off to Dave only because Sherele was way too busy with the opening of the fall theater season. Reluctant as my mind was to stop gnawing on Ringo, I realized it was time for me to file away that subject for the evening.

I had better uses for Dave. I removed the overstuffed, oily Italian hoagie from his grasp and took a big oozing bite. Now we were onion-and-garlic equals. I settled his sandwich back in its greasy white paper and wiped my mouth, then Dave's. He looked at me as if I were undressing him. I was about to.

He gave me a long, salami-drenched kiss.

"We've got far better things to discuss," he said when he broke away about a month later, or so it seemed.

"I'm sure we do. Got some ideas?"

"I vote that we start planning our wedding."

Oops.

My body must have shrunk back along with my thoughts. Dave's face looked as if he'd just encountered a jalapeño.

"Too soon, huh?"

This was an old, never-healing sore in our relationship. Dave, a widower, was always wanting to lock me into a new marriage. I, a divorcee, had planned never to officially tie the knot again. For me, there was no better world than one that offered the joy of a loyal lover and the freedom of legal independence.

"It's probably not too soon to talk about it again," I conceded, beginning to understand that some disagreements in a relationship need to be aired from time to time even if they were never going to be resolved. "I haven't changed my mind, but then again, I haven't gotten tired of your proposing to me. In fact, I rather like that. As long as you don't get fed up with my saying no." I touched his cheek and traced his eyebrows with my finger. "Are you okay?"

"Chas, dear one, I don't want to crowd you. But I do reserve the right to ask the question every once in a while."

"If the question includes an unspoken one— how much do I love you?—I am glad to answer it any time it occurs to you. I love you greatly ... enormously ... monumentally ... and I plan to do so forever and ever."

Dave smothered me in a hug and enveloped me in another kiss. This one seemed to go on until spring. At least I felt like a blossoming tree.

"But let's talk about why you want to make it official," I said when we came up for air.

Dave settled his head in my lap and looked directly and thoroughly into my eyes. "One: I want the whole world to officially recognize how much we love each other."

I nodded.

"Two: I want to throw a big party to celebrate that we are a couple and always will be."

"Stop right there. A pizza-and-beer party?"

"Caviar and champagne, if you like."

"You'd hate it. That wouldn't be your kind of party. Even if I agreed that we should get married, we'd spend the rest of our life trying to figure out what kind of party would fit the wedding fantasies of each of us."

"I'd leave it all in your hands. You could plan whatever kind of three-star bash you wanted."

"That's not the point."

"Let's talk about that part later. Here's the really important reason. I find it a drag to have to figure out all the time what to call you."

" 'Chas' will do. Or 'Hot Lips,' in intimate moments."

"You know that's not what I mean. 'Girlfriend' sounds like we're teenagers. Or golden oldies. 'Significant Other' is pompous. 'Lover' doesn't cut it on public occasions. 'Life Partner' seems like

an insurance ad. Nothing says it all so well, so suc-
cinctly, as 'My Wife.' "

"You mean, like 'My Car,' 'My Apartment' . . ."

" 'My Luscious Plump Aromatic Succulent
Little Submarine Sandwich.' " Dave shut me up
with another bite of the hoagie. "Let's eat. Or talk
about Ringo."

We didn't.

7

Surely I had better things than Ringo crowding my mind and clamoring for center stage. I'd far more enjoy delving into the mysteries of restaurant prices. I particularly wanted to find out how much it costs to reach for the sky—to run a rooftop restaurant. That meant Two Views.

Despite what I'd told Ringo, I'd already written my review of the restaurant and it was about to appear. While I'd voiced some serious criticisms, it was close enough to a rave that readers were probably going to complain that they couldn't get a reservation. Nevertheless, I wasn't sure the owners would still feel friendly after the review, much less that they'd trust me to probe their trade secrets. I'd find out in a couple of weeks.

But I was impatient. After the first week, I asked Brian about Two Views' reaction. He re-

ported that at first the owners had been angry
about my negative comments, but once they realized that their business had increased by 30 percent since my review, they reassessed their
reaction. They even took to heart the criticisms
and set changes in motion. They'd become more
careful about undercooking the starches—the
beans and potatoes—and they now offered diners
sharing the porterhouse the option of carving it
themselves rather than getting it already sliced.

The time seemed almost ripe to approach them
about letting me look at their purchase orders and
balance sheets.

"These guys are impulsive," Brian warned me.

We were both taking a break from the restaurant business, drinking *caipirinhas* in my loft,
early on a Sunday afternoon. The windows were
wide open to the summer that had led us to crave
these icy drinks of *cachaça*—Brazil's answer to
tequila—poured over lime wedges mashed with
sugar. Lily was clanking pots in the kitchen, creating an impromptu brunch inspired by the alcohol. Brazil had brought to mind *feijoada*, but she
didn't feel like eating meat. So she was concoct-
ing what sounded to me like a Brazilian salad
Niçoise: black beans topped with diced tomatoes, onions, red peppers, and hard-boiled eggs.
She was wondering whether the can of elegant
tuna someone had brought me from Spain would
perk up the concoction, but I urged her to think
Latin America rather than Europe. Olives and or-

ange wedges would be more seemly. It hardly mattered, though. I knew that after two caipirinhas, anything Lily served us would taste delicious.

I also anticipated that the drinks would inspire Brian to come up with just the right approach for me to convince his bosses they should let me study their costs and prices. So far the drinks hadn't worked, so I encouraged Brian to simply talk about Two Views' owners, hoping that among the three of us we'd forge a plan.

"Kirk—he's the older one—will probably like the idea right away. He's an outgoing guy and he likes to take risks, to push the envelope. He's the one who developed the idea of a big-meat and vegetarian restaurant under one roof, and he loves to talk about the place."

"You like him?" I knew you could tell a lot about a restaurateur's openness and honesty by what the employees thought of him.

"I think he's great. In fact, they're both great. They're young but they have a lot of experience in the business. And they're ready to listen to the people who work for them."

"They're brothers, aren't they?" Their press releases didn't note this, but I'd read it somewhere.

"Yes, but they don't like to emphasize that. They seem to think it will make people take them less seriously or something. I don't know. But I think it's amazing that two brothers can work together the way they do. They're really different, and they seem to appreciate that about each other."

"What's the other one like? Ben, right?"

"He's quieter. Slower to agree, maybe because he's more organized. He thinks things through before he makes up his mind."

"Are you saying I should approach Kirk, since he might be more receptive and enthusiastic about my idea?"

"No, you shouldn't jump to that conclusion. You or he would still have to convince Ben."

Lily brought in her creation and joined us at the coffee table. The platter of black beans looked like some exotic flag, with stripes and streaks of red, yellow, white, green, and orange blaring against the black background. We all admired it for a minute until Lily handed Brian two spoons and invited him to toss the ingredients. It became a muddy mass. Pretty unappealing, in fact.

Brian portioned some for each of us; I noted that his technique with serving spoons—both held in one hand—had grown so natural he might have been born to it. He looked a little skeptical as he took his first bite, mirroring the way I felt. But sometimes when it comes to food—or to people—what's ugly to the eye turns out to be, on further exploration, quite delicious.

We toasted Lily, accomplished composer of sonatas and brunches. Lime, alcohol, and black beans made an inspired match.

So did Lily and Brian, I observed as the conversation lulled and we concentrated on eating. He handled my picky and demanding daughter with the same smoothness he brought to manipulating two spoons in one hand. He made both tasks look effortless. And she'd been learning to relax in his presence without needing to test him or protect herself. She seemed to be growing sure and trusting in his company. I'd never found a relationship with a man that easy when I was that young.

They even thought along the same lines. I'd seen it happen before: one of them started a sentence, and the other finished it. It wasn't a matter of one stepping on the other's feet, it was two people acting as one.

"Kirk and Ben are really enjoying the limelight," Brian began. "They've never had that before. They're a little shy about it, though."

"And they've got this ingrained politeness," Lily continued. "That's why . . ." she paused as she looked at Brian to confirm that their thoughts were running in the same direction.

"You might do best to approach them in public. In the dining room, maybe at the height of the evening."

"And maybe try to get them both at once."

That wasn't the way I'd planned to ask, but Brian and Lily had a point. The quicker their response, the more likely it would be positive, especially if they were inexperienced enough that they wouldn't anticipate problems. And they probably would hesitate to say no to me in the company of others. Anyone who's raised kids knows that a parent is more likely to agree to a child's demands when they're made in a public place. Not that Kirk and Ben might fear I'd throw a tantrum in the dining room if I were refused, but they'd want to seem agreeable in public.

"When's your night off this week?" I asked Brian. "I don't want to risk your seeming involved with me, so it might be less awkward if I approach them when you're not there."

When Sherele heard I was returning to Two Views, she invited herself and Homer along. The only thing Homer loves as much as Sherele and his detective work is good food. And she'd claim that food is at the top of that list. Homer had been grumping ever since he'd read my Two Views column and realized what he'd missed when he'd had to turn down my invitation once before. Sherele had tried to cheer him up by offering to take him there as her treat, but Homer hates to let any woman pay—except me, of course, when I'm on expense account. Thus she figured that if she quietly paid me back for her and Homer's share, he wouldn't have to know he'd been treated from a woman's own pocket.

"It's not that he's cheap," Sherele defended Homer, "it's just that he hates to spend that money so soon after he could have dined for free with you."

"I'm glad to give him another chance, now that

I've got a good excuse for going back. It will be especially interesting to see what a restaurant is like after I've reviewed it. That alone will make it worth the trip. Besides, I'll need all the help I can get to convince the owners to let me do a story on Two Views' finances. If Homer's coming, I'll bet I can even persuade Dave to put up with an evening at a half-vegetarian rooftop restaurant."

Dave agreed and Homer accepted with gratitude, but the D.C. Homicide Department wasn't as cooperative. Dave was standing by my desk when Homer called to apologize. He had to work late once again.

"Maybe you dames should go on your own so you can have a chance to talk about subjects such as Homer and me," Dave suggested, all too obvious in his relief at the possibility of staying home with a beer and a pizza.

"We'd much rather talk with you than about you," Sherele swiftly stepped in. "And we can all three talk about Homer."

Dave was shaking his head.

I really wanted him to go, since he can be awfully persuasive with potential sources. But I didn't want him there scowling and wishing he were elsewhere. Surely there were some straws for me to grasp.

One straw arrived right on cue, though it wasn't one I'd have hoped for.

"Looks like a summit conference here. Am I interrupting? Dave, I was hoping I could lure you out to dinner with me tonight. Something I wanted to talk to you about. I've got a table at Two Views."

It was Ringo, with his usual uncanny timing.

Dave tried to play the gentleman. "Sorry, Ringo, but I've already got a date. At Two Views, in fact. I couldn't stand up such formidable women as these two." He smiled at Sherele and me, proud to be making a show of throwing his lot with us.

It was the wrong tactic, and I knew it. Ringo had no shame.

"I'll just join you, then."

Dave tried to backtrack. "You probably want a little more privacy for our talk, Ringo. I'm sure Chas and Sherele wouldn't mind if I met you for a drink first, before I had dinner with them."

"It's nothing they can't hear. I'll be glad to make it a foursome. Just let me know what time, and I'll cancel the reservation I have."

Ringo slithered away, leaving Dave looking guilty and miserable. He tried to make amends. "Give me a half hour to work it out. I'll go and make some excuse to Ringo for your having to cancel our dinner. I'll insist on taking him to some other place instead. Then you two can go alone to Two Views."

"It's not your fault, honey. Don't worry about it. We can take him along. I'll work it out." I sounded more optimistic than I felt.

"You're willing to risk that? I'm impressed."

Dave looked so pleased with me, I was glad I'd chosen the high road.

"I can handle it. I know he's in tight with the Two Views' owners, so maybe that would even help my case. Either I'll broach the subject before he comes or you can take him off to the bar for a cigar after dinner."

"I'll go iron my necktie." Dave's good cheer had been revived. Mine hadn't.

8

At least we got to the restaurant before Ringo this time. I didn't want to risk his sticking me with the bill for another expensive bottle of wine, and I intended to talk to the owners before he arrived, so I'd told Ringo our reservation was a half hour later than it really was. Sherele and I settled in with sauvignon blanc by the glass. Dave made himself as comfortable as possible with a beer.

Two Views' owners were apparently late, too—they weren't in the dining room. I worried that I'd picked an evening when my prey wasn't going to show up at all, but Dave found a way to ease my distress when the waiter brought our drinks.

"What's with Kirk and Ben?" he asked the waiter. "Are they out casing the competition or spending their first profits in the Bahamas?"

The waiter looked confused. "Bahamas? Where

did you hear that? Kirk and Ben wouldn't leave this place for so much as a trip to Baltimore. They never take a day off. Not even one at a time."

"I guess they must be in the kitchen, then." Dave searched the dining room carefully, a good act since he didn't know what either of them looked like.

"Actually, they're in the basement. The trout tanks. There was some problem with the temperature or something."

"Trout tanks? I didn't know you served live trout here. Why are they kept in the basement?" Now Dave was wearing his puzzled look, though I knew he couldn't care less about trout.

"It's an experiment. We've been getting a lot of requests for fish, from people who aren't meat eaters but not quite vegetarians. And the owners insist on nothing but the freshest—swimming 'til the moment they're ordered. They just put them in last week."

"You'd think they'd want the fish tanks out in the dining room where everyone could see them," Dave probed. "Or are they afraid to offend the real vegetarians by displaying creatures whose lives are going to be sacrificed for dinner?"

I could see he was angling for satirical material. He likes to occasionally poke fun at Washington ways for the Sunday Op-Ed section.

The waiter seemed horrified by Dave's interpretation. He hastened to correct it. "No, no, nothing like that. They're just playing it safe. They'd heard an alarming story about when Windows on the World opened years ago. It had a trout tank at first, but because the World Trade Center was so tall, every time the trout were delivered, they died on the way up in the elevator. Pressure or something. So even though we're in a far lower building, Kirk and Ben aren't taking any chances with prematurely expiring fish. Anyway, the bosses will be back any minute, and I'll send them over if you'd like."

The waiter seemed relieved to find an opportunity to retreat. He knew we were reporters, and he apparently feared that anything he said might come back to haunt him over tomorrow morning's muffin and latte. Thereafter he made a point of looking extremely busy whenever he attended our table.

I'm sure it didn't help that when he left, Sherele, Dave, and I escalated our trout jokes to such ridiculous extremes that our laughter made us choke on our drinks.

"One more example," Sherele said, "that dining is actually a branch of theater. You, Chas, are really a theater critic with a fork."

"The fork is the crucial part, my dear." I waved one at her to emphasize my point. "While a great meal is a drama, and even has several distinct acts plus a climax, the play's not the thing. Dining is a lot more than entertainment. It's fueling the body. It's science—of cooking and nutrition. It's a tool for sustaining life. It's stroking the senses. It's partaking of society."

"It's theater with calories."

Sherele held up her glass of wine to signal the waiter that she wanted another. We all nodded and held up our own glasses as soon as she caught his eye.

"May we offer you a toast?" A smiling, curly-haired young man appeared at our table with a bottle of champagne. Just behind him came another, his dark hair flopping over happy eyes, this one flourishing five champagne flutes. Kirk and Ben had risen from the building's depths and were about to offer us a glass of bubbly.

"Only if you let me put the champagne on my expense account," I said. "We'd love to drink to your restaurant, but my editor's feelings would be hurt if you didn't let him pay for it."

"If you must," Ben answered. They weren't going to make me uncomfortable by insisting I break my ethical code. I liked that.

"We'd be honored if you pulled up chairs and joined us." Dave knew how to set the scene for an interview.

What immediately impressed me most about Kirk and Ben was that they were more interested in discussing my criticisms of Two Views than my compliments, though they'd obviously been delighted by the latter. They weren't pushy about it, but they made it clear that they'd appreciate any guidance I was willing to offer.

"We have a lot to learn," said Ben. I'd rarely heard a restaurateur say that before.

"I do, too, and I could use some help on that," I told the two of them. "I want to do a story on what it costs to run a restaurant. I'm particularly interested in restaurants that have special challenges—like a rooftop location."

"And you want to do us," Kirk preempted me. The corners of his mouth kept turning up briefly like a sun peeking from clouds. He was excited about the publicity.

Ben's caution kept his mouth firmly in check. "How much would you need to know? I wouldn't want to see our private matters in print."

"I'd let you decide how much you're willing to tell me." I was ready with this answer. Any reporter knows that the major hurdle is getting permission to do the interview. Once a subject starts talking, if you take it slowly and carefully, most likely your problem will be having more information than you can use rather than too little. Some subjects are so experienced with the press that they remain cautious from the beginning of an interview to the end, but those are celebrities, politicians, and the like. First-timers only hold back information until they get caught up in telling their story. Then your problem is turning off the flow politely when you run out of time. It's a little like psychotherapy.

Kirk and Ben didn't need to exchange a word with one another; a glance did it. Theirs was a well-honed partnership.

"Let us think about it," Kirk said. They'd need some conversation, but in private.

"We'll tell you by the end of the evening," Ben added. They even had that figured out: Kirk gets the first word, Ben gets the last. I was impressed.

"You don't need to decide tonight," I suggested, not wanting the subject to be raised again while Ringo was there. "I'll call you tomorrow." Mission accomplished. I could lower my defenses and enjoy the rest of the evening.

As they left us, both of them were so preoccupied that they didn't notice Ringo heading toward our table. Ringo thought they'd spotted him, and held out his hand, expecting it to be shaken. Kirk and Ben walked right by, both looking inward and not absorbing their surroundings. Ringo's face froze in an instant's embarrassment, but he quickly recovered. He looked for someone else to save him, and was rewarded with the president of Marriott, sitting one table away and ready with a handshake to respond to Ringo's.

Once his hand was properly and publicly shaken, Ringo could settle for our company. "Sorry to be late," he said, even though he wasn't. "The president had something he needed to clarify for this piece I'm writing."

The president of *what*?

I wasn't going to fall for the bait, neither were Dave and Sherele. Dave just refilled his glass of champagne with the last of the bottle and offered it to Ringo, saying, "Journalism's a jealous mistress, my friend."

From that point on, the evening was far from predictable. For a start, Sherele ordered a steak, Ringo and Dave ordered vegetarian entrees. Dave must have been in his investigative mood; I'd never seen him order a vegetarian anything. Except maybe a white pizza, and then only after he'd finished a pepperoni one and was still hungry.

I, of course, ordered the trout.

"The first time I ordered a live fish, it was in China," Ringo told us after we'd all tasted my trout and declared it worth a trip to the basement for every order. "I think it was a goldfish."

"Carp, you mean," I corrected him, then felt ashamed of myself. I was still on edge with the guy and was letting it show.

"Carp. Of course. Thanks, Chas. I couldn't help thinking of that fish as something swimming around in a little kid's bowl, and I could hardly eat it even after it stopped flapping on the plate. I only tasted it to be polite, but maybe if I'd been able to think of it as carp, it would have seemed more like food."

For once Ringo wasn't bragging. He was even admitting to a touch of human weakness. I'd have expected him to profess not a moment's hesitation at eating a fish that was still breathing. Then he surprised me still more.

"I've never seen couscous with such big grains. How do you think they make it?" Ringo was not only confessing that there was something he didn't know, he was implying that I might know more about food than he did.

"It's called Israeli couscous. It comes that way, packaged. Couscous, after all, is like pasta, made from finely ground grain, and it can be rolled into pellets of any size."

"Here's to the expert," Ringo said as he raised his glass of chardonnay. "I also compliment you on your choice of wine. I haven't had the Argyle Reserve before."

"Thank you. It's amazing what you can find when you break away from California vineyards. I'm only beginning to learn about the wines of the Northwest myself."

Then Ringo turned his charm on Sherele.

"What do you think of the plans to renovate Arena Stage? After your last three reviews, they ought to be adding more seats. And dedicating them to you."

"You thought I was too easy on them?" Sherele, too, was a little wary of Ringo.

"Oh, no, certainly not. It's just that your descriptions were so eloquent, they would have made any reader call up and reserve a seat." He was laying it on a bit thick, but it was in good cause.

"You're too kind."

This little lovefest was beginning to give me heartburn. A Good Ringo wasn't really more attractive than an evil Ringo, I thought, feeling some guilt at my churlishness.

I called for more wine.

Kirk and Ben brought the next bottle personally. Each had cruised by the table a few times to check on our welfare, but this time they paused to stroke Ringo's ego.

"We hope you like the trout, Ms. Wheatley. And for you, Mr. Laurenge, we are planning to have a special treat next time you come. We've located a source for Santa Barbara prawns and are bringing in abalone from there as well, now that we have our fish tanks in order."

"Music to a California boy's ears. Now, if you could only fly in your produce from Chino Ranch, I'd never have to return to my hometown."

"If it can be done, we'll do it," they said, both of them. Then they backed off before Ringo could think of another impossible mission.

"You grew up in L.A.?" Dave asked as he refilled Ringo's glass, which Kirk and Ben had refilled just moments before. Talking about fish, Ringo was also drinking like one.

"Only the first few years. Anaheim after that." Nobody at the table seemed to take any special notice of that.

"I assume your parents were Beatles' fans?" Sherele asked, a question nobody in the newsroom had dared voice yet.

Ringo drained his glass of wine and looked as if he hadn't heard the question. Dave poured him another.

"I don't mean to—" Sherele backtracked.

"No, it's okay," Ringo said, "I was just thinking about how to explain."

"You don't have to—"

"I hate my name, and I know what everyone else thinks of it. I've been expecting somebody to ask me for a long time. Don't apologize. I guess it's easier to answer your question now and get it over with, so I might as well." He slurred the "s" in "somebody" and "so." I didn't think he'd have considered answering the question if he were sober.

"My father, he couldn't stand the Beatles."

"Then how'd you get the name?"

"It all started with my two older brothers. John and Paul."

"Beatles . . ." Dave pointed out the obvious.

"Not at all, at least not at first. You see, my father was a Catholic scholar, so they were named after popes."

"So then he became a Beatles' fan?"

Ringo poured himself another glass of wine before he continued. He examined the glass as if it were a crystal ball that told the past rather than the future. His voice took on a flat inflection; he sounded like someone reading unfamiliar material.

"My father detested the Beatles. Always did and always will, I suppose. That made my mother all the more a fanatic. One day she went to the courthouse and gave my brothers official middle names."

"Lennon and McCartney," Dave supplied.

"Of course." Ringo emptied the glass and poured again, but the bottle was empty.

Sherele slid her half-full glass over to him. "And you've got a brother named George?" Her voice was so filled with sympathy that tears sprang to Ringo's eyes. Mine, too.

"A sister. An older sister."

"A sister named George?"

"Yeah. Worse name for her than Ringo, except for one thing."

"What was that?"

"Mom hated Ringo Starr."

Dave had waved at the waiter, signaling for another bottle of wine, and there was a lull in the conversation while the waiter removed the metal capsule, wiped the lip of the bottle, struggled with the corkscrew, and poured a little for Dave to taste. I always feel as if someone's hit the "Pause" button when a waiter or busboy shows up at the table in the middle of a personal conversation. Everyone freezes.

When the waiter left, Ringo swallowed nearly half his glass and continued. "Mom figured George was kind of a pretty boy; that was her justification for giving his name to her daughter. With me, she was just resigned—to an unexpected fourth child and to using her least-favorite Beatle's name."

He drank again. Dave refilled his glass, while Sherele and I sat in stunned silence. Ringo had lost his harrumph. He looked like a sad overgrown boy as he continued, telling us more than we ever would have asked or even wanted to know.

"My father, of course, had no say in it. He wasn't even on the scene any longer. Mom had decamped with John, Paul, and George, and found herself pregnant with me."

"Did your father ever try to change your name or give you a nickname more to his liking?" Sherele's voice was so soft, it was almost like an unspoken thought.

"He never had the chance. I never saw him. I'm not even sure he knew I was born."

I might have thought Ringo was putting us on, but his face told otherwise. I even felt a lump in my throat; for a moment, my animosity toward Ringo was smothered in pity. The air at our table felt gray and heavy.

Lest the silence embarrass Ringo, we all scrambled for something to say. I couldn't find much. "What did your mother do when she left your father?" I didn't particularly want to know, but I couldn't bear to leave the air empty of sound.

"Well, she went to Anaheim. She figured that even without any experience, she could get a job there. Disneyland, you know. Always needs to hire people."

"It can't have been all bad, being a kid growing up in Disneyland." Dave, too, seemed to be lamely trying to fill up the conversational emptiness.

His instinct had been right. Ringo grinned, or if it wasn't quite a grin, at least his mouth widened and curved faintly upward. "It had its moments, in fact it was great living there when I was a small boy. For a while I really believed I was one of the Pirates of the Caribbean," he said. "And I've never gotten over learning that there was no Snow White. Compared to that, giving up on Santa was easy."

"And Peter Pan?" Sherele ventured.

"My hero. My alter ego. Me, my dream of me." Ringo had slowed to sipping his wine and began to sound playful rather than morose. "At least Peter Pan turned out to be true, after a fashion. I actually could fly away, which I did the first chance I got."

"When was that?" Dave sounded more relaxed, too.

"Sixteen. I skipped as many grades as my school would allow, so I could graduate as early as possible. I knew I'd need at least a high-school diploma for whatever I wanted to do."

"And what was that?"

"Anything but work for Disney."

"The others stayed?"

"Yeah, they loved it. George even got a Mickey tattoo on her thigh as a graduation present. But I loathed the place as soon as I began to grow up. I loathed them, too, the whole fucking Beatles' mania of Mom and my sibs, the Disney cuteness. By the time I managed to leave, I never wanted to see any of them again. We're one sick family, if you can still call us that. You won't be surprised to

hear that none of us is married. My brothers
wound up back in L.A., in Hollywood. But my
mother and George are still with Big Brother
Walt."

"What do they do there?"

"I couldn't care less." Ringo looked as if he
couldn't care more. His forehead was taut with
rigid furrows and his eyes held a liquid sheen that
threatened to spill over. Tonight was the first time
I'd seen any expression of insecurity take a stand
on his face.

Dave hates maudlin. His patience ran out. He
signaled the waiter for the check.

Ben and Kirk, making the rounds of the dining
room and saying goodbyes, stopped at our table.
They hoped our dinner had been all right; we assured them it had been wonderful. Then, to my
alarm, they got down to business.

"We'd be honored to help you with your story,
Chas."

I tried to interrupt to tell them we could talk
about it tomorrow, and Dave attempted to divert
Ringo's attention, but we both failed.

"There may be a few trade secrets we'd prefer
to keep to ourselves, but we don't think they'll
detract much from your research. If that's satis-
factory to you, we'll be glad to open our books to
you and schedule whatever face time you need
with us."

Ringo snapped back to his alert everyday
mode. "What story?" Taken by surprise, he hadn't

been able to hide his avid curiosity about our business.

I was finished with cowering. I might as well deal with Ringo head-on. "I'm using Two Views as a case study for my story on restaurant costs and pricing. You remember, we talked about that when I was looking for the most expensive restaurant in the country. Since you'd already planned to write about Ginza Sushiko, I've taken another tack."

"Good thing I agreed to join you tonight."

What did he mean, agreed to join us? What an outrageous statement. Didn't he mean it was a good thing he'd invited himself to dinner?

But Ringo wasn't finished stepping on my toes.

"I've already planned a feature on Two Views as a startup business. Bull's very excited about my idea. And I'm sure Kirk and Ben would rather be on the front page than back in your section."

Kirk and Ben looked puzzled, pleased, confused, then made a discreet retreat when I burst out, "Cut the crap, Ringo. You planned your story ten seconds ago, as soon as you heard what I was doing. This is my story, and you can't get to Bull first this time because I've already talked to him about it."

Whether recognizing defeat or being so drunk he couldn't maintain a coherent position, Ringo immediately switched gears. "Money. I'm sick of writing about money. Nobody even wants to read about money anymore. Dollars and cents. Numbers. Bottom lines. That's not what the public cares about, really cares about. Quality of life, that's what counts." He was slurring again, as if the drunken Ringo had just trampled the lucid one.

Sherele and Dave shared looks that combined boredom and disgust. They put their napkins on the table. Waving the white flag? Throwing down the gauntlet? Preparing to leave? A bit of each.

I remained mesmerized by the twists and turns of this egomaniacal mind.

Ringo blathered on. "Success isn't a matter of counting, it's a matter of feeling. How do we feel, how does it make us feel, what do we feel like having? Those are the questions people are asking." His voice ran down and the next sentence trailed off. Ringo was gone from our conversation and dreaming with his eyes open.

I made quick work of paying the bill and, out of Ringo's hearing, set an appointment with Kirk and Ben. Everyone got up from the table, Ringo staring into space, his eyes half-closed. We aimed him toward the door and he shuffled along, a few steps ahead of us, while we remained alert to catch him or keep him from straying.

"I guess we'd better pack Ringo into our taxi and drop him off," Dave said, unable to hide the reluctance in his voice.

"I'll give you a ride," Sherele offered.

"Thanks, but that's not necessary," I told Sherele. To Dave I suggested, "Let's just send him in his own taxi. I'd hoped to walk for a while." I hated ending the evening without a walk.

"Why don't I take Ringo home? Then you two can walk as much as you want," Sherele offered.

"I can't foist him off on you."

"Don't be silly. It's on my way. I'll just shove him in and shove him out. No problem at all."

"You wouldn't mind?"

"Not in the least, as long as you help me get him to the car. He told me his building has a doorman, so I'll find help at the other end."

Ringo stumbled, then muttered thanks and apologies as we half-carried him to the front door. It seemed simpler to bring the car to him than him to the car, so Dave walked Sherele to her parking space while I stood over the propped-up Ringo.

"You're the patron saint of the fledgling restaurateur," Ringo said, his eyes looking sharp once again. He seemed to shift in and out of drunkenness; I preferred him mush-brained.

"Are you feeling all right?" I certainly didn't want to get into an argument with him.

"You're the one who can make a restaurant a success, a big fucking success."

I started counting the marble panels in the lobby. I wished Sherele had used the valet parking, even though she hates having someone else park her car.

"I, however, am far better at making failures."

A confession of fallibility? From Ringo? I automatically made a polite protest. "You're far from a failure, Ringo."

"No, not being a failure. You don't listen as acutely as one would expect from someone in your position, Chas."

Was this guy really drunk? "Listen acutely?" That didn't sound like booze talking. I kept silent. I just wanted the evening to end quietly.

"I said I am better at making failures. Making others fail. Restaurants. Other journalists. You."

That wasn't booze, it was madness speaking. I moved a few inches farther from him. I didn't need to be in position to keep him on his feet; in fact, I'd be more than glad to see him fall on his face.

Sherele's car pulled up and the valet, who'd been smoking outside, rushed to help her out. Dave propped open the door and glanced at Ringo, who had slipped back into his semico-matose mode against the wall.

"Everything okay?" Dave stroked my hair and kissed me in that corner of my temple that waits for him to do just that. "Our colleague behaving?"

"No worse than ever." I just wanted to get this over with.

The doorman, finally having gotten the drift of what was happening, moved to help Dave support Ringo to the car. If I'd been in a better mood, I might have seen their clumsy ballet as comic.

They folded Ringo into the back seat, and Dave started to climb in next to him. I realized he'd changed his mind about letting Sherele take the drunk home alone, and I reluctantly admitted to myself that he was right. I opened the front passenger door.

"Not a chance," Sherele said. "I don't need you two to come along. I'm a big girl. I can drive him home myself."

"We'll walk after we drop Ringo off."

"You'll never find a taxi in his neighborhood, or in mine. And I'm not so generous as to offer to double back to your house after we dump Ringo."

After a few more protests, we saw that Sherele was adamant. She not only insisted on freeing us from the burden, but refused to allow us to feel guilty about it. She drove off with her cargo of dozing Ringo.

The air was sweet with relief as Dave and I strolled east along M Street. His arm was across my shoulders, mine was hugging his waist. As we walked, he planted occasional kisses in my hair. We stopped every block or two for a more serious and mutual kiss.

At first we didn't talk, then started gradually, with a few words, phrases and, finally, a conversation. Ringo was on our minds. Not Ringo himself, but the effect he had on us.

"You don't really see him as a problem, do you?" That had long been puzzling me about Dave.

"I see him as a guy with problems. But no, he's not a problem for me." Dave paused, thinking over my question to answer it more fully. "He's one of those men who tend to suck up all the air around them. That makes some of his colleagues panic, of course, and feel jealous, even desperate. But someone who's good, really good at something . . ."

"And arrogant," I added.

"And arrogant," Dave agreed, "makes enemies. People are naturally generous when a guy's at the bottom of the ladder. He'll find plenty of helping hands to boost him up. But once he's climbed, especially if he's climbed higher than most, those hands are far more ready to pull him down."

"To sum it up, you think that what's important is that he's really good at his job, not how he does the job or whom he tramples in order to do it."

"That's a pretty harsh way of stating it, but yes, Ringo is good for the paper, and that makes him good for all of us who work there. I recognize that there's some cost involved, but for me the cost is justified. I'm impressed, not threatened."

"And I'm acting threatened?" I sounded defensive. I was defensive.

"Don't take that as a criticism. Your view is naturally different from mine. In a way, I suppose, he is more threatening to you. He's competition. He's a restaurant groupie. He wants to write some of the same stories you want to write. But you don't need to feel as bothered by that as you do. You're the best in your field. Everyone knows that. He can't take any of your success away from you, he can only cause you to give up a possible assignment here and there. But there are more than enough to go around."

"I don't totally agree, but I admit you're mostly right. I'm more bothered by him than I should be. It's as if he has a homing device that probes those insecurities I don't even admit to myself. He's amazingly efficient at getting to me, with hardly a wasted word. By now I cringe when I see him coming. My adrenaline goes on the alert when I hear his name."

"You shouldn't allow him that power over you. You take him too seriously."

"Here's one thing I worry about. I'm afraid this is my pattern. Maybe I just like having an enemy. It gives me a diversion, a hobby."

"Crossword puzzles would do you more good."

We were in front of the White House, walking down the middle of the street that was closed off from cars when the area was transformed into a fortress. As we did on every other block, we stopped and turned to each other. This kiss was longer, three-acts with a buildup, a few surprises, and a sensational finale. I hoped the president was watching.

"Let me think up an even better diversion for you," Dave murmured.

We hurried to the corner and hailed a taxi. We were too impatient to walk the rest of the way home.

9

Of all Washington's secrets, the one it would do the world the most good to know is that the fall days are sensational. Pity the countless tourists who slog through hot summer air so thick you could spoon it. In spring, even at cherry-blossom time, the weather is cruelly thoughtless, alternating a sparkling cool day with a stiflingly hot one, and dumping torrential rains whenever you least expect them. Fall days in Washington tend to be a perfectly permissive temperature that allows you to wear your shorts and sandals into October if you wish, but tolerates long sleeves and even a jacket if office formality suggests it. The air is clear, the humidity is low, and for a month or two everyone feels comfortable.

This year we had a preview of fall in August and the glorious weather brought a new batch of picketers to the *Examiner*. They were a low-key bunch, not even bothering to keep their posters in full view as they leaned against walls and lampposts. They shared doughnuts and sections of the *Washington Post*—as effective a campaign against the *Examiner* as their signs would be anyway. They looked too contented to protest. One man who was conscientiously walking with signboard held high was whistling a Sousa march. As I hummed it on my way up in the elevator I realized it was the sweetest and subtlest protest of all. It was *The Washington Post March.*

My mood turned sour when I saw Sherele's desk occupied. By Ringo. I tried to keep in mind Dave's admonitions. I might not like Ringo, but I didn't have to feel threatened by him. He didn't have to spoil my day.

Even more, as I approached my desk, which is next to Sherele's, I tried to feel sorry for him. The boy with no father and an unloved name.

"Where's your sidekick?" Ringo swiveled his chair to face me before I sat down.

"She's hardly a sidekick, Ringo. She's one of the top five theater critics in the country by any measure. I can't imagine whom she could be a sidekick to."

"Damned good looker, too."

There I went, my adrenaline storming through my blood vessels, washing away the calm I'd forced on them. The creep should keep his demeaning observations to himself.

I decided to at least act unaffected by whatever Ringo said.

"Sherele doesn't come in this early. Would you like me to pass on a message to her? I assume you've come to thank her for getting you home safe last night."

"Safe and sound. Very sound."

Was there a leer in that voice? Determined to ignore it, I put down my purse and briefcase and started organizing my desk for the day's work.

That accomplished something. Not what I'd hoped—Ringo didn't go away. But he changed the subject. He even found something interesting to say.

"I'm curious about something that must be one of the greatest frustrations of your job."

That got my attention. He was addressing the feelings of someone besides himself. In fact, he sounded sympathetic. And he wanted to hear my views. The Good Ringo was awake this morning.

"I assume you're referring to something besides hangovers."

"That, too," he said, wincing. "But what I really had in mind was that it's so much easier for a good restaurant to degenerate into a bad one than it is for a bad restaurant to improve."

"Isn't that true with any kind of human endeavor? Excellence is harder to achieve than mediocrity."

"Of course. But I was pondering the role of the critic. Perhaps criticism can influence a restaurant for the better, point out faults that the restaurateur can correct."

"I hope so."

"Most often, though, the critic serves as a directional guide: go to this restaurant, don't go to that restaurant."

"That's an oversimplification, but yes, probably that's what we do."

"Thus there's the question of the critic's power. As we've discussed before, a critic can make or break a restaurant."

"Restaurateurs think we can, but I think the truth is far more intricate. If a critic praises a restaurant, presumably it is a restaurant worthy of praise. Thus it has what a restaurant needs to be successful. And when a critic pans a restaurant, the critic doesn't make it bad, just reveals that it's bad. Logically, the restaurant fails because it is bad, not because the critic has publicized its faults."

"Reason tells us that's true, but you're not giving your profession quite enough credit. Don't you think you could close a good restaurant?"

"Of course not. I can't even close a bad restaurant."

"You're being too modest. If you tried, really tried, you could close the best restaurant in town. If the power of the press can bring down a president, closing a restaurant is child's play. Even I could close a restaurant."

"Not a good one, or a successful one."

"Wanna bet?"

Ringo leaned over and touched his finger to my lips. It was so intimate a gesture from him that I was astonished. And mute.

He walked away without another word from either of us.

I'd vowed not to waste time being angry with Ringo. Now I added that I wasn't going to expend any energy trying to figure him out, either. Our conversation left me puzzled, but at least it left me.

After a half hour of sorting e-mail and snail mail, trashing the junk and filing the rest, I was fully occupied with work. I started a list of questions for my Two Views story and searched the Internet for material on restaurant finances.

No wonder I'd been floundering about where to start my research. The National Restaurant Association—always good for pithy facts and figures—calculated that by the end of the century the country had 815,000 restaurants. Once I realized that, I admitted to myself that choosing the single most expensive restaurant or the one with the most interesting problems was impossible. Not only are there unmanageable numbers of restaurants, but within them there are too many variables: wine prices, appetizer or side dish prices, lunch vs. dinner, highest vs. average dishes, urban or rural, large or small. I'd been right to simply plunge in and make a choice. Two Views would do as well as any of the other 814,999.

More to the point, I needed some benchmarks

that would suggest how Two Views fit the norm. Not so difficult, as I discovered.

The perceived wisdom in restaurants is that food cost should be no more than one-third of revenues. Less, of course, is better. That means that the thirty-dollar steak should not cost the restaurant more than around ten dollars. The most profitable restaurants manage to keep their food costs as low as 18 percent; on the other hand, the food costs at Washington's pricey Lespinasse, in its first year or two, climbed to over 70 percent. Needless to say, the restaurant revamped and brought in a new chef.

The formula doesn't work item by item. Meat is expensive. Because a restaurant requires consistency in availability, quality, and portion size, meat often costs the restaurant more than it would cost the diner to buy it at a local supermarket—especially since supermarkets hold sales. Filet mignon might cost a restaurant fourteen dollars a pound. Offbeat menu items cost even more. Take buffalo: a trimmed steak can easily cost the restaurant fifteen dollars a pound, and since buffalo is considered he-man stuff, a pound isn't an unusual portion size.

That doesn't mean a restaurant loses money on everything it sells, of course. What it spends excessively on meat or seafood, it makes up on pasta or lettuce. From nothing more than a few cents' worth of flour and mere pennies' worth of egg, plus a diced tomato, basil, and olive oil, a fresh-tomato fettuccine can be marked up a dozen times its food cost. A green salad, even with fancy baby greens, is in the same profit league. So, that one-third food cost is meant to be calculated over the entire menu, not item by item.

Wages and benefits are usually figured at 25 to 32 percent of gross. At high-end restaurants, though, they climb above 40 percent, and with top chefs and managers now demanding six-figure salaries, that gross has to be substantial to keep a first-class restaurant alive. Rent is typically figured at 5 to 7 percent. That leaves less than one-third of the restaurant's income for utilities, repairs, linens, advertising, cleaning, repayment of debt, not to mention the flowers and all those charitable contributions restaurateurs are expected to make.

Where's the profit? Often nowhere. An optimistic restaurateur hopes for 10 percent pretax profit, feels relieved if it's at least four percent, and often sees none for years. The best that can be said for half of the restaurant businesses is that at least the owner won't starve.

I was so absorbed in figures that I didn't hear Sherele arrive. I jumped when I looked up and saw her there, in the same chair Ringo had vacated, staring at her unlit computer screen.

"You're awfully quiet today. No hello?"

"Hi."

Sherele's greeting could be barely heard, but its chill made me shiver. I looked closer. She looked drained, her face chalky and her eyes flat. She held her body as if it were stiff and achy.

"You okay? You look terrible. Hangover?"

Sherele nodded, slightly.

On second thought, she didn't look just hungover, she looked sick or angry. I couldn't tell which. I belatedly noted that she was dressed for winter, in a long-sleeved turtleneck and flannel skirt. I reached over to feel her forehead. No fever. Did she flinch because she was startled, or was she shaking me off?

"Are you sick? If you feel half as bad as you look, you shouldn't have come in this morning. How about if I take you home?"

"I'll be all right. I've got to finish my column. For Sunday." Sherele was dragging the words from cold storage. They had no music to them, sounded slow and dry.

I took Sherele's hand; it was as limp as an empty glove. "Look, my friend, I know what a driven, ambitious chick you are. But even you can miss a deadline once in your life. Helen can find something to fill your space. The *Examiner* will soldier on."

"I'm almost done. No big deal." Sherele's eyes were on the screen. Or on something behind the screen. "Just let me be." A hint of steel under that flabby tone.

I felt a spark of defensiveness. Was she angry with me? Did she resent our letting her shoulder the burden of Ringo last night? No, on second thought, I realized I was reacting with my habitual paranoia, or at least the residue from what I'd been patiently chipping away at over the decades. This wasn't about me. Sherele simply had no energy for responding to anything. Probably a virus.

"Let me know if I can help," I said, and reluctantly turned back to my work.

I didn't get much done, not with Sherele silent and grim beside me. I strained to keep myself from looking at her. At the best of times hovering irritates Sherele, and today she seemed excruciatingly sensitive. I wanted to probe what was wrong with her, but I didn't dare.

It was so uncomfortable for me to sit there unable to help, much less talk to Sherele, that I considered leaving. I rejected the idea, though, because at least if I stayed I could keep a watch over her.

I started to call Kirk and Ben to tell them what I'd need for our first meeting, but my phone rang just as I was reaching for it. Out of the corner of my eye, I caught Sherele jump at the sound of the phone.

It was Lily telling me she'd meet me at my office rather than at the restaurant tonight.

Sherele managed to start her computer rolling, and appeared to get some writing done. Who knows, though? Maybe she was typing nonsense, as I was. But she was concentrating intently, her fingers flying. After a while she got up and went into Helen's office, probably to report to our boss that her Sunday column was ready. Sherele's such a pro, she would finish her column while she waited to be rescued from a flash flood. She returned to her desk and gathered her things.

"I'm going home. Maybe get some sleep."

That was it. No explanation, no telling me how she felt. Not even a goodbye. I started to stand up, ready to insist I take her home. She held up her hand to fend me off and shook her head. Wordlessly, she made it clear that my help wasn't welcome. Sherele the stoic: she was comfortable in the role. I definitely was not.

"Call me if you need anything. Chicken soup. Vitamin C. Anything."

I couldn't tell whether Sherele had heard. She gave no sign. She just walked toward the elevator as if she were climbing Sugarloaf Mountain.

10

"What's for dinner?"

Lily was dressed like a grown-up with a job to-day, so it took me a moment to spot her as I got off the elevator in the lobby. She was still experimenting with images, this time varying her gauzy, flowing earth-child layerings and go-go-girl exposures with the new twist of a simple dark suit.

"I like it, Ms. Boucheron." I gave her a kiss, then twirled her around to view the back. Nice suit.

"You may call me Lily—if you're going to feed me something delicious and soon. I'm starving." Lily kissed me back. "Do you really like this? Is it me?"

"It's one of the many yous. And it's definitely one I like."

I took her arm and we made our way to the

door, though our progress was slow because several colleagues stopped Lily to say hello and give her a hug.

"Hey, Lily, how's it going?"

"Nice threads, sister."

"Hello there, young 'un. Got a day job yet?" That was Vince, business always on his mind.

"Would I be dressed in a suit if I didn't have a day job?" Lily loved Vince's cantankerousness. I think she harbors a hope that I'll eventually turn into one of those fascinating, cynical, speak-my-mind-and-everyone-be-damned old ladies (except, of course, in regard to her). She wants me to take lessons from Vince.

We were finally alone together, heading west, arm in arm.

"Where are we going?"

"I thought we'd try Hometown. You in the mood for matzo ball soup and pot roast?"

Lily grimaced. "Pot roast? Me? You're taking this suit too seriously, Mamma."

"Only kidding. They have a parsnip gratin and fried sweet potatoes. I know you'll love them."

"You've got my number. One hungry belly at your service."

As we walked, we talked about Lily's day: two school concerts and an after-school break with Brian between his lunch and dinner service. No wonder she looked so happy.

I told her about last night's dinner and my

restaurant-finances research. Then I got to what was really on my mind: Sherele.

"She's probably coming down with the flu," Lily said. "You know how mad it makes Sherele to feel vulnerable."

"You're probably right," I said as we approached Hometown.

It had a line out the door. The restaurant doesn't take reservations. Lily looked dismayed. When she's hungry, she's hungry. She's never been patient about waiting for food.

I didn't want to ruin our companionable mood. But I couldn't think of a nearby restaurant on my reviewing list. I felt frantic for a moment, then had an idea.

"I've already eaten here twice. I've soaked up enough of the atmosphere, so I just need to taste more dishes. Let's do carryout."

"Wonderful idea. What a clever mamma I have." Lily gave my arm a squeeze. "Are you sure you'll be able to tell enough from carryout?"

Lily doesn't usually concern herself with the needs of my job, so she was acknowledging the generosity of my suggestion.

"No problem. I know exactly what I've got to try, and none of it will be hurt by waiting a while before it's eaten. That's the beauty of old-fashioned home cooking. It was devised to wait in the oven or at the back of the stove for the menfolk to come back from the fields."

"Even sweet-potato fries?"

"Maybe not sweet-potato fries. They're a new invention anyway. But I've already tried them, so I'll just get you a small order you can eat right away, to keep you alive until we get home."

"Excellent. I've got an even better idea, though. Let's take the food to Sherele's and feed her, too. If she's not up for company, then we can go to your place."

"Great. I'll go call her while you wait in line."

"Wrong. You know Sherele; she hates admitting she's needy or vulnerable. If you call her, she'll say no. If we just show up, she'll really be glad, and since turning us away would be rude, she won't feel she has to make a show of not needing any help."

A half hour later we were at Sherele's door, our fingers greasy from sweet-potato fries and our arms full of bags whose aromas were driving us wild. Three kinds of soup, chicken potpie, cheese grits, Brunswick stew, collard greens with country ham, eggplant casserole, parsnip gratin and, for dessert, a bread pudding, apple pandowdy, and Virginia peanut pie. If Sherele wasn't home, we might be driven to sit down and eat it all on the front steps.

She took awhile to answer the doorbell.

"Sherele, it's Lily. Mamma and I are here with matzo-ball soup, cheese grits, and bread pudding." Lily knew the power of starches. "We're so hungry we'll eat them right here on your front stoop if you don't let us in, and then Mamma will eat your portion and get fat. It'll be all your fault. And you'll probably get evicted for having such messy friends."

She did it. I could hear Sherele guffaw at the other end.

"Can't let your mamma get fat," Sherele said, then buzzed us in.

Sherele looked a lot better than she had when she'd left the office. She still showed strain around the eyes and a glint that said "don't mess with me," but even that softened when Lily wrapped her in a warm hug.

Sherele hugged Lily back. With me, she accepted affection but only minimally returned it. I concluded that she really was angry that I'd foisted Ringo on her last night. I wished I'd done differently.

And I didn't know the half of it.

Lily took charge. First she looked Sherele over from head to toe, as if deciding what to prescribe. She seated Sherele at one end of the sofa and brought her a quilt.

"You and Mamma talk. I'm going to set out this stuff. You want tea or something stronger?" Again Lily took a minute to appraise Sherele.

"Bourbon." Sherele wasn't any less taciturn then she'd been at the office, but her mouth wasn't as taut and her shoulders were no longer hunched. She didn't look her usual glowing self, but if she'd been battling a virus or a cold, she clearly had it on the run.

"How are you feeling?" I cautiously asked Sherele as I sat at the other end of the sofa. If I'd been asking myself, my answer would have been, "Awkward."

Lily handed each of us a bourbon. Straight. I sipped, Sherele chugged. Lily took her glass to refill it.

"I'm not sorry to see the two of you, Chas, but I don't feel much like talking."

That was a start.

"That's okay. How about some music?"

Sherele nodded. I got up to pore through her CDs. I felt less awkward with something to do. Smoky, soft Cole Porter songs seemed right.

"I'm sorry, Sherele, that I dumped Ringo on you. Will you forgive me?"

"Not your fault. It was my own damned fault."

We sat silently while I worked up to another sentence.

Lily brought a tray with three mugs of soup and a basket of Parker House rolls and set it on the coffee table. "We've got matzo ball, goulash, and corn chowder. Sherele, which do you want to start with?"

"Corn." I wondered whether she'd chosen that because it required the fewest words.

Sherele warmed her hands with the mug, then took a sip. She obviously wasn't going to offer much conversation, and I felt tongue-tied. Lily once more took the lead.

"Mamma was afraid you were sick, but that's

not the problem, is it, Sherele?" Her eyes were intent on Sherele's face.

Sherele shook her head. "No, sweetie, I'm not sick."

Lily got up and knelt in front of Sherele's end of the sofa. "I think I know." Very gently, she reached to Sherele's turtleneck sweater and pulled it away from her neck. It was streaked with an angry red welt.

"Bite?"

Sherele nodded and burst into a string of curses. At least she was talking.

I was stunned.

"Ringo? You and Ringo?"

"Not me and Ringo. Just Ringo." Sherele's voice sounded like a glass with a crack in it.

"He raped you?" Lily asked very gently, but the words made me feel as if I'd been punched in the stomach.

"No, he didn't get that far. He's too out of shape to beat me down. But he surprised me with this." Sherele touched the welt and flinched.

I was staggered. I didn't know where to start with my questions, or even whether I dared ask questions. Lily seemed to have no such qualms.

"Did he hurt you anywhere else?"

"Not really. Not physically, anyway. I just vomited all night thinking of him and the things he said."

"It might help if you talked about it."

"There's not much to say. I was stupid. Naïve. Me! Naïve!" Sherele curled up tighter on the sofa and fell silent.

"You're the wrong generation, Sherele. It took one more generation before we began to admit the existence of routine, everyday aggressions of men against women, to talk about them, to learn to protect ourselves."

"I never would have expected a colleague, such an uptight and pompous colleague . . ."

"Every man. That's what women of my generation have come to accept. We have learned to protect ourselves by memorizing one sentence: Every man is a potential rapist."

"And racist."

That knocked Lily, too, into silence. I might be more awkward than she in discussing sexual attacks, but neither of us could talk confidently with an African-American about racism.

Sherele filled the void. "Every woman cringes at the thought of being called a cunt. But it's special hell to face being called a black cunt by a white man."

I couldn't say anything, I could only reach over and pull Sherele toward me and wrap her arms in my arms.

She felt taut, didn't seem to welcome my touch. I pulled away and waited for her to talk.

"I hated his smell as I drove him home. The wine mixed with the sweat of his embarrassment and jealousy. He kept muttering about you horning in on his territory at Two Views. I couldn't wait to drop him at his door."

She stopped for a moment. Lily offered her a mug of soup—matzo ball this time—and she sipped a bit before she handed it back and continued.

"It turned out, the schmuck had no doorman. There was nobody around. And he was still too drunk to walk straight. At least that's what I thought." She took another sip and set down the mug. "Much as he nauseated me, I didn't have the heart to just dump him in a heap at the door. As I should have done." This time she just stared into space, shaking her head at Lily's offer of more soup. "I asked him for his keys. He tried to get them from his pocket but couldn't seem to manage it. I was tired of waiting and wanted to get home, so I reached into his pocket for them. Like a fool."

"He had a hard-on?" Lily is far bolder about such things than I am.

"I should have just left him to fend for himself. I should have realized he'd manipulated me to touch him. Most important, I should have thought it odd that a guy so drunk could still get it up. What an idiot I was."

"Not an idiot. Compassionate. You're just too compassionate for the scumbags of the world," I said. I couldn't imagine Sherele leaving anyone helpless at the doorstep. She'd behaved totally in character. Dave and I should have protected her. We shouldn't have abandoned her.

"What I can't get over is what a good actor he was. I didn't have the slightest doubt he was falling-down drunk. I only saw him as a disgusting and childish young man, and a colleague who'd probably be embarrassed to face me in the office the next day.

"At first I found the situation just an irritating responsibility and a few minutes' hard work, guiding him up the stairs and keeping from knocking us both down."

"No elevator?"

"Not even an elevator. And he'd told us he had a doorman. Anyway, I got him into his apartment and he slammed the door behind me. I reached to open it again, and suddenly he wasn't drunk at all. He grabbed my hand and put it in his pocket." Sherele stopped to shudder. "No, not his pocket. He'd somehow unzipped himself."

Lily pretended to gag. I didn't need to pretend.

"When I pulled away, he grabbed me and held tight. I guess I was more surprised than scared. Disgusted, too. But he acted as if we were having fun, that this was love play. He kept talking about the taste of chocolate skin and how he'd always wanted to get at the melted chocolate inside me."

She stopped again. Lily held out the soup, but Sherele waved it away and shoved off her blanket. She unfolded herself and stood up, stood tall, in fact. She was no longer limp, but inflamed, beginning to pace as she talked.

"I kept telling him to stop. I tried every tone of

voice I thought might work. I tried cajoling him, offering him motherly advice, pulling rank, scaring him. I tried anger. I tried being weak and pitiful. He just took it all as a game. And every time I wiggled free, he'd capture me again. We were more evenly matched than I'd have expected.

"Finally he decided that what I was doing was asking him to play rough. He kept talking about black women and how he'd always heard they liked it spicy. Oh, it was so disgusting. Then he said he just couldn't resist taking a big bite of me, and he sunk his teeth into my neck.

"That snapped me. I guess I roared or something, and I startled him just enough that he loosened his hold. I ran."

"I wish you had come to me, or called me." I felt so guilty I could barely squeak out those few words.

"I didn't want to talk to anyone. I just wanted to come here and try to forget it happened. I didn't want to see anyone." Sherele, standing by the window, looked deflated all over again.

Lily was the one fired up this time. "You're going to call the police, aren't you?"

Sherele gave her a long, slow, dark look. "This is not police business, it's my business."

"What did Homer say?" Lily isn't easily deterred from pursuing a point.

"Homer doesn't know. And neither of you is going to tell him." Sherele's voice was fierce.

"He'll know as soon as he sees you."

"He's not going to see me. I'm going to tell him I'm sick and contagious, and refuse to see him until this is gone." She fingered her neck. "I've got some stuff that will make it heal fast. If I need more time, I'll tell him I've got to go visit my mother. He won't want to come along if he doesn't have to. And Chas, I expect you to back me up on this with Homer, even with Dave."

"Don't worry, sweetie. You handle this whatever way feels right to you." I was throwing in my lot with sisterhood.

"I want you both to swear that you'll tell no one about this. Not a word. Not to anyone. Ever."

Lily sent me a withering glance and kept up the pressure. "Sherele, you can't let that rapist get away with this. Think about other women"

"No, Lily, I won't think about other women. There are no other women in this. There's just me, a middle-aged black woman he thought he could get easy. The way he saw it, he'd be doing me a favor by letting me sample his young white cock. This wasn't rape, it was an insult. It was the deepest, most abusive kind of disrespect to a colleague, a show of power. But I'm not a Victorian woman taking to her fainting couch. I refuse to act like a victim. It's not a police matter, it's a score to settle between me and him."

"If women don't report rapes—"

"What do I have to show the police? A love bite? They'd laugh me out of the station house. There's no semen, I have no bruises. And for

God's sake, I was in the man's apartment. Where's my legal case?"

"You've got to try—"

"Try what? Putting up with public humiliation? Making sure everyone knows about this? Lily, you know what kind of treatment women get when they cry rape, even when they've got broken ribs and airtight witnesses. That's the difference between your generation and mine. You expect the legal system to protect you. My generation knows that you've got to make your own justice."

While I was in sympathy with what Sherele was saying, I had some reservations. I thought she should tell Homer, and I said so.

"You're talking about Dave, not Homer. Dave's a different kind of guy. A liberal white man, an investigative reporter who's used to getting all riled up about things and working them out by writing about them—in a cool, objective way. Homer's a policeman. His way is to track 'em down, lock 'em away, sometimes even beat them up. And he's a black man whose woman has been humiliated by a white man. You think he would leave that alone?"

"Come on, Sherele, you're making Homer out to be a street tough. He's a detective. A professional." I felt embarrassed for Sherele to be comparing Homer unfavorably to Dave.

"But how do you think he got there? He's still a street cop under it all."

Lily didn't buy Sherele's explanation either.

"What are you really afraid of? Not vigilante justice from Homer."

"Well, if he doesn't want to go after Ringo on his own, he'll insist that I report him. I'm just not taking any chances."

I was confused. Sherele was arguing both sides. Lily figured it out before I did.

"It sounds to me as if it's not Homer's reaction to Ringo that worries you, but his reaction to you. You're not taking any chances on Homer knowing what kind of a situation you got yourself into. Are you afraid he'll be jealous?"

That hit home. "We've said enough on this subject," Sherele snapped. "It's my business how I handle it. Just remember that you've both been sworn to secrecy."

She started gathering the dishes and silverware, signaling that the evening was at an end. Lily and I helped her, and we all wound up uncomfortably close in the kitchen. There we realized we'd forgotten to eat the rest of the food.

"You take it," Sherele insisted, stuffing it back into the bags and trying to hand it to Lily, then me.

I'd caved in on everything else. I felt like a turtle cowering in its shell. So I grasped for a place to take a stand. "Lily doesn't need it, and neither do I. You've got to keep the food."

There. I held firm. Now I'd have to go back to Hometown again.

Sherele hugged us when we left, but there was a tinny undertone to our warm goodbyes. We cut them short and hurried out the door because the phone started ringing. Lily and I stood in the hall for a moment and heard Sherele's answering machine click on.

"Sherele, where are you? I've been trying to find you all day. Is everything all right, honey? Maybe I forgot you had some out-of-town interview. Call me back soon, babe, or I'm going to start to worry." It was Homer's voice.

11

I've always believed there are two kinds of people-in-love. Some are dreamy and distracted, the others are expansive. They spread around their excitement, they treat all the world to their joy.

So it is, I learned, with people-in-hate. Sherele came to work the next day in body only. Her mind was off in another world. She only answered me—if she did at all—after long, uncomfortable moments of silence. She let her calls switch over to voice mail. She was a portrait of sullenness.

Ringo, on the other hand, seemed energized. He radiated venom. While it was obvious to me that he had made Sherele a particular enemy, he seemed to be treating the entire newsroom to his vicious mood.

He wouldn't leave Sherele alone. He passed by

her desk a dozen times a day, often with some snide or leering remark.

"Skirt shrunk in the wash?"

"Shove it." Those were the first words I'd heard from Sherele since lunch.

Another time: "Scooped by the *Post* once again."

"Up yours."

But Ringo was too ambitious and too twisted to limit himself to such relatively harmless word-play. He launched a campaign to unnerve and humiliate Sherele professionally.

Suddenly Ringo became a theater buff. We should have seen it coming: the business of theater became Ringo's new obsession.

One day Sherele came back from a press conference at the Kennedy Center fuming and tossing papers into the trash. That was sign enough to alarm me; Sherele never clears off her desk or, when she does, it's a slow and laborious process.

"What's wrong?"

"What makes you think something's wrong?"

"You're trashing your desk." I reached over to retrieve a notebook from the floor, where her papers had scattered. "Surely you don't mean to throw out your notes from yesterday's interview."

"It hardly matters," she said, but she grabbed the notebook anyway.

"You're quitting?" Sherele always quits the *Examiner* when she's angry. But she never goes so far as to tell Bull.

"They don't need me here. They've got Ringo."

"What did twitchface do this time?"

"He horned in on my press conference. When I got there, he was already stuffing his face with cookies and monopolizing the board chairman. He had the nerve to paste a look of surprise on his face and ask me, in front of everyone, 'You're covering this press conference, too?' As if *I* were the interloper!"

"Okay, he's a greedy SOB. But he's just playing silly games. That doesn't make him the theater critic. He can't invade your beat."

How wrong I was. But I didn't know that until the next day.

Ringo had ambushed Sherele. He'd found a clever angle on the Kennedy Center's news, and his story ran on the front page, while Sherele's had been reduced to a sidebar on the jump.

Sherele didn't come to work the following day. When I called her at home, I found myself talking repeatedly to her answering machine.

Sherele got over that particular humiliation quickly, though, certainly more quickly than I would have. As I'd learned over the years from Sherele herself, any black woman who had achieved her level of professional success had to have been mighty resilient. In this case, she seemed to have hit bottom, then dug in her heels and bounced back. She returned to her desk the next day a changed person. "It's time to have some fun," she told me. "I've turned the corner. I've buried Ringo. I'm my own woman again."

In the days following, her behavior lived up to her word, even if—as I suspected—her heart didn't quite keep pace.

Ringo, the man smitten by hate, wasn't able to get a rise out of Sherele anymore. She treated him as if he were a mere thirty-two-year-old upstart with a tendency to make a fool of himself.

Thus he had to shine his evil light elsewhere. He stepped up his subtle and blatant assaults throughout the newsroom. He was generous with his snide comments on people's appearance, sometimes making them directly and other times indirectly. He showed an awe-inspiring mastery of gossip as a form of sabotage. His innuendoes set waves of suspicion lapping through the newsroom. I'd never seen so many of our reporters and editors snapping at each other or refusing to talk altogether.

Ringo's pattern was to try out his tricks on Sherele, then when she ignored them, go on tour of the newsroom with variations. He called one of her best sources and tried to wheedle an exclusive on a story, promising he could get better play for it than Sherele could. The source reported the call to Sherele, who used it to taunt Ringo deftly. A stranger to shame, Ringo went on to his next victim. He scoured the newspaper for mistakes—his plan was to go over reporters' and editors' heads to mention them to their bosses—but when he caught one of Sherele's, she showed that Ringo was the one in error.

His attacks became more intimate, more personal. Even ridiculous. Ringo kept a hawkeye for food on people's desks and helped himself to candy, chips, even picked up people's sandwiches and took a bite. I've never seen desks so free of snacks as they were after people became prey to his scavenging.

Hatred of Ringo spread like a contagious disease through the newsroom. You could feel it. And it brought Sherele back to life. She and I talked of nothing else, but at least we were talking. We bitched, we ranted, and we schemed. Most important, we laughed.

While Ringo hadn't invaded my territory this time around, his relentless misbehavior and the general malaise of the newsroom were making me depressed. Sherele and I separately complained to Bull, but he dismissed us as oversensitive and suggested that we were jealous. He gave no hint that anyone else was complaining to him.

Dave had by now seen Ringo for what he was and finally joined our efforts to overthrow him. He closeted himself with Bull to persuade him that the newsroom needed to be saved from Ringo. Not that he was any more successful than we were. Bull accused Dave of being co-opted by me.

The problem, Dave reminded us, was that we had no proof of anything significant, only suspicions. Without substantiation of any real infractions, our charges were reduced to Ringo's hurting our feelings. Our gripes sounded like whining. I wished I could tell Dave about Ringo's attack on Sherele. I also wished that she would report it to Bull, but she was adamant about keeping it her secret.

Thus we were driven to that most ineffectual of responses, as are frustrated whistleblowers everywhere. We kept lists. We documented every deed we could attribute to Ringo. Of course, that fed our obsession.

Sometimes I wondered whether Bull had a point. Sherele and I saw Ringo's sadism everywhere. We began to suspect that Ringo turned up the volume on colleagues' speaker phones so that when they played their messages, the entire newsroom could hear, at least until the victim figured out where the volume control was or hit the stop button. When we heard people grumble about crank voice mails and e-mails, we attributed them to Ringo, even if we weren't sure.

The storm clouds in the newsroom were so thick that I hated being in the office. I spent as much time away from it as I could. That meant I was getting a lot of research done at Two Views.

The more I saw of Kirk and Ben, the more I respected what they were doing. Here were two young men who not only showed good instincts for the restaurant business, they'd retained the humility to recognize that they had a lot to learn. They sought the wisdom of more experienced restaurateurs, but didn't simply try to milk them for information. They were generous in return.

They went to exhaustive lengths to seek the best ingredients, then they shared their sources with their competitors—who soon became their friends. When another restaurateur needed a crate of chanterelles in a hurry, he knew that Kirk and Ben would unhesitatingly share what they had. When someone else's dishwasher didn't show up, Two Views would somehow find a fill-in. And if a chef's nephew arrived from Palermo with no money and no job, Kirk and Ben would find him work somewhere, through their growing list of friends among farmers, wholesalers, importers, and restaurant owners.

At the same time that the *Examiner's* newsroom was becoming ever more dispirited, the local restaurant scene was growing more vigorous, and the chefs and owners were forming a stronger community. The contrast was stark to me, and the lesson powerful. In each case, the mood had been created by one or two people. Ringo was spreading misery; Kirk and Ben were the source of widespread good feeling.

I started spending mornings in Two Views' offices. We developed a routine that was so pleasant I wished I could stretch out my project for the entire winter.

I'd arrive before the chef, but the kitchen was in full swing. The pastry chef would have been working for hours already; I could tell when I walked through the door and took one deep breath. Fall was in the air, with pumpkin-pecan crisps and pear bread puddings. France's custardy clafoutis were being reinterpreted with cranberries replacing the cherries. Cranberries added color and a sharp fruit tang to bitter-chocolate tartlets, too. Sue, the pastry chef, would press a small napkin-covered basket into my hand when I greeted her.

"I hope you haven't eaten breakfast," she'd say.

After the first day, I certainly hadn't eaten breakfast.

Every morning Sue invented new varieties of rolls. Lemon multigrain braids, rosemary Parker House, walnut brioche—I never knew what flavors I'd discover when I lifted the cloth. As I settled at whichever desk was free, one of the staff would bring me an espresso and a tiny hand-thrown crock filled with sweet butter.

Sue's repertoire was impressive. "You must have had a guru," I said, wondering how such a talent had been nurtured.

"LeNôtre," she answered.

I wasn't surprised that one of France's top pastry chefs had inspired her. "When were you in France?"

"I wasn't. I worked with him when he opened the Chefs de France restaurant at Disney World. A long time ago. Before I discovered how proud we could be of America's own pastry."

Sue's wasn't the only talent I sampled regularly. As the morning wore on, someone would show up with a small plate of mushroom-eggplant pâté. "The chef asked if you wouldn't mind tasting this for him," he'd say as he'd leave without waiting for an answer.

Or a trio of colorful pinwheels, one green, one orange, and one red, would be placed at the corner of the desk. "The chef apologizes for the inconvenience but would be grateful for any comment."

The only comments I could think of were, "Luscious, luscious, and luscious," as I sampled the spinach-gorgonzola, butternut squash, and beet-horseradish soufflé rolls.

I felt a little guilty letting Two Views feed me for free, but the staff made it hard to refuse. I decided I'd show up with a treat for the staff on my last day.

I'd try to make that moment as far off as possible.

In between these lovely vegetarian interludes, I worked. Really.

I varied my approaches to try to get a wide perspective on how the restaurant's finances worked. One day I'd talk to Ben, another to Kirk. I organized my questions differently each day, once by monthly expenditures, another time by costing each dish, then by capital expenditures, debt, profit, and loss. Eventually it all began to make sense to me.

Looking at income, I learned that a restaurant of this caliber depends on alcohol for about a third of its sales. And those sales are far more profitable than the food sales. No wonder the staff is more eager to sell you another martini or bottle of wine than an extra order of mashed potatoes.

The proportions are far different when you look lower down on the food chain. The cheaper the restaurant, the more its profit comes from food. No three-digit bottles of wine. On the other hand, labor costs and overhead are lower. No expensive crystal or china to break, no floral arrangements.

When I stepped back and looked at the restaurant industry overall—with the help of Kirk and Ben's computer files—I saw why so many investors chase after this particular rainbow. In the Washington area, more than half of every dollar spent on food is spent in a restaurant. That adds up to five billion dollars a year. The way I saw it, even if they were a mere 4 percent, a two-hundred-million-dollar profit is a pot well worth pursuing.

What's a boon to restaurants today is that everybody's ordering fish. Tuna and swordfish are fairly pricey (which makes a swordfish boycott a convenient political stand), but salmon, now that it's farm-raised, is far more glamorous than its price warrants. A two- to four-dollar portion of salmon can be marked up to twenty-four dollars or more in a fancy restaurant. Even with the wraparound—the garnishes and vegetables—it's profitable.

"Not as profitable as sushi, though," Ben said, when I asked him about the markups.

"Sushi is a luxury. Top-quality fish . . ."

"Just consider the size of the portion," Ben interrupted, he was so fired up by the subject. "And look at what restaurants are charging nowadays. What once was priced at $3.50 or $4.50 now brings almost twice as much at those really fashionable sushi places. And all you're getting is an ounce or two of fish and a little rice. Oh, yes, wasabi and soy sauce. Must cost all of a dollar."

Ben seemed to keep every price in his head.

"What's your most expensive ingredient?" I asked him one day. "Certainly not foie gras?"

"A mere $56 a pound," he said, waving his hand as if to chase away a puff of smoke. "Though if you figure the price per portion, it's right up there. A three-ounce appetizer we sell for $20 will be a big loser for us once you add non-food costs."

"Caviar?"

"Around three hundred dollars a pound, but it stretches far. An ounce might cost us about twenty dollars, and we can sell it for $50. Hardly worth a second thought, as luxuries go."

"I'd guess truffles." I knew that the price of white truffles, especially, had flown so sky-high that a pocketful could buy an Italian sports car.

"I'd agree with that. At $350 for black, they're merely in the caviar range. But the last time I checked, white truffles were more than $1,200 a pound. I'm relieved that truffles are in season for only a few months each year. In this case, it's very convenient that we refuse to use any frozen products except ice cream."

"Then what's your most expensive year-round ingredient?"

"That's easy. Saffron. It's $700 a pound."

"How long does it take you to use up a pound?"

"We haven't been open that long."

I was getting a sense of the outgo. Next I tried to understand the income.

"What do you need to become profitable?"

Ben had an immediate answer. "A full house would be nice. Some wise restaurateur said that the biggest expense to a restaurant is an empty seat. Next down the line is the customer who by-passes the beverage menu in favor of tap water. One of the problems, though, is that people expect Washington restaurants to be cheaper than New York's, yet most of our costs are the same. Our rents, our labor costs are right up there. What would really help our bottom line would be if more of our customers were vegetarians."

"Less-expensive ingredients, right?"

"Exactly. No matter how high the cost of mesclun and baby eggplants, it can't compare with the wholesale price of steak. Sometimes I wish we'd opened an Italian restaurant. A chic Italian vegetarian restaurant—that would be easy street. You wouldn't believe how rich I could get selling pizzas. They are the single most profitable item on a menu. I could make a whole pizza for fifty cents and sell it for twelve dollars. Throw on another fifty cents' worth of seafood scraps and I could price it even higher."

"So you yearn to open a white-tablecloth pizza parlor?"

"I'd call it Spago if that name weren't already taken," Kirk said with a dreamy smile, the kind you see when men are talking idly about Michelle Pfeiffer or Demi Moore.

"Italian vegetarians. Those would be the ideal customers. Especially if they were big boozers," Ben added as I dug for another notebook. My first one was full. "Honest vegetarians would also be nice; you'd be amazed how much it costs a restaurant to replace stolen menu covers and to make up for bad checks and credit cards. At least since we're on the roof we don't have any flower boxes for people to rip off. They do walk out with the flowers from the restrooms, even the guest towels and toilet paper."

"Customer theft can't compare with staff theft, though," Kirk added.

"I'm told that even the most careful restaurateur has to allow at least 5 percent for that."

My other notebook was full, too. I turned it over and started labeling the back cover; I'd just have to fill up the reverse pages. To buy time, I asked one of those throwaway questions a reporter keeps ready—a question to which I more or less knew the answer. "Even if you're not profitable yet, a restaurateur's expense account supports a nice lifestyle, doesn't it?"

Kirk jumped in on this one. "We haven't had time to take advantage of it yet, but yes, traditionally a restaurant's income is in part used to enhance its owner's life. As in many businesses, it pays for our cars, our dinners at other restaurants, our trips to conventions. And we all know that food conventions are a lot more entertaining than, say, pipe-fitters' conventions. Should we ever find time to take a vacation, we can probably expense it. And many restaurateurs' businesses support beach houses and boats, which, they insist, are necessary for entertaining."

"I'd be overjoyed to have the chance to put a movie ticket on my expense account," said Ben. "Or even have time to see a movie and pay for it out of my private funds."

Kirk liked talking about the big picture.

"Do you know which is the highest-grossing independent restaurant in the country?" he asked me one day.

"It's got to be Disney World."

Kirk responded with a smirk, then qualified his question. "Outside of theme parks."

"I'm sure it would be in New York, but I couldn't choose between Tavern on the Green and Windows on the World. Funny how similar their names are."

He honored me with a slight bow. "And their gross sales. Tavern's just over thirty-four million a year, and Windows is just under thirty-two million."

"Once you get into those double-digit millions, it hardly matters."

"It turns out that four of the five top-grossing restaurants are in Manhattan. What's more interesting is that number four is in Wheeling, Illinois. Bob Chinn's Crab House grossed nearly twenty-five million in 1998. With only 650 seats compared to Tavern's one thousand. And its average dinner check was less than half of the big guy's. That meant it needed to serve nearly a million people that year."

"Do you have any idea which is the biggest restaurant?" I asked.

"Free-standing? I'd say Venus de Milo, in Swansea, Massachusetts. It has 2,500 seats. On the other hand, the Varsity in Atlanta serves two million customers a year. But since its dinner-check average is only five dollars, it grosses a mere nine million. The same goes for the Rascal House in Miami Beach: 1.3 million customers, just over nine million gross."

"No wonder. It's still the best deli in the country. What about in Washington? Who's your biggest competitor?"

"The Old Ebbitt Grill, up around twelve million. And its owner, the Clyde's Restaurant Group, has two other restaurants that earn more than seven million each. I'm not looking for that kind of volume. Our model is more like the Inn at Little Washington. Two seatings a night at most. I'm looking to be viable, not wildly profitable. And even that will take a couple of years."

He was thinking small and I was thinking big. I

remained intrigued by gigantic restaurants and how they worked. I put that story possibility in the back of my mind to let it ferment, not yet realizing it would eventually serve as a perfect cover for my hidden agenda.

12

When the information flows for a reporter, work feels like sap rising, spring in the air, a ticket to a hit show. That's how it went at Two Views that week. I spent my mornings experiencing the thrill of the hunt, then taking a notebook full of juicy data back to the office to mull over. My focus was sharp and my heart was light. I was as buoyant as if I'd just fallen in love.

Two Views had been an ideal choice for my research. Not only were Kirk and Ben generous in sharing information, I grew more enchanted with them and their restaurant as I saw how passionately and sensibly they ran their business, and how humbly they accepted their success. So I was glad I'd already reviewed the place. I would hate to have to try being objective about their food and service now that I'd grown so fond of them. It's easier to criticize strangers.

I was also having trouble maintaining my professionalism when it came to Ringo. I had to keep my feelings to myself, and I've never been good at that. Kirk and Ben admired the man. Why not? He did write riveting stories and turned out more copy than anyone else in the newsroom. His name came up at Two Views every day, not just because he had a story in the paper each morning, but because he hung out at the restaurant several times a week. The staff was flattered to have the patronage of such an illustrious journalist.

As for Ringo, he was drawn to my desk as a moth to light, though I actually thought it was Sherele's adjacent desk that was the perverse attraction. Now he either elaborately ignored her, bumping into her as if she were invisible, or greeted her with some snide comment on her clothes or what she'd written that day. At first Sherele got up and left whenever he approached, but after a while she stayed put.

"I don't want to give him that much control over me," she told me afterward. "I intend to make it clear that he doesn't faze me and he can't budge me from my desk." She sat tall and cool when Ringo came by, and honed her venomous retorts. She was getting good at ridiculing Ringo.

I was trying to learn.

"Working on something interesting?" Ringo

had a way of looking at my computer rather than me when he talked, so, as usual, I switched to my screen saver when I saw him coming.

"No, I leave all the interesting stories to you." What I really hated was that I grew witless in his presence. He made me so angry I was tongue-tied. I came up with such lame responses I felt like a surly adolescent.

"Whatever happened to your Two Views story?"

"Not much."

"You'll never get any real substance out of them. I know the types. They come off as all innocence and graciousness, but they're a cagey couple. They won't tell you anything you don't already know. Waste of time."

"You might be right."

"Besides, it doesn't look good for a restaurant critic to get so cozy with the principals in a restaurant she reviews. You need to protect your image more carefully. People are beginning to talk."

"I think I can take care of my image, Ringo." He was escalating. He was overplaying his hand. I smelled victory.

"Let me know if I can help you. Some of these restaurateurs I've come to know would be glad for the publicity and eager to open all their books to you. I can give you a list."

"Mmmm."

"Gotta go see Bull. Stop by my desk if I forget to send that list to you."

"Mmmm." I was trying hard to keep my mouth

shut. I knew if I opened it for one word, a torrent would follow. At screaming pitch.

Finally I grew so tense having to hold my tongue that I, unlike Sherele, caved in and went to lengths to escape Ringo's visits. Any time I saw him heading in my direction, I'd hit the "Close" command on my screen and take off for the women's room or the water fountain.

Once, though, I knocked the stapler off my desk, then forgot to hit the "Close" command.

I returned to find Ringo still at my desk. He was scrolling through my Two Views notes, which I'd left visible on my computer.

"Get your paws off my keyboard, Ringo," I said.

He was so startled, he tripped over my chair in his retreat. I followed him across the newsroom, yelling at him, calling him a spy, a snake, a petty thief. Heads snapped up. Looks of horror were replaced by half-hidden smiles. A few outright guffaws.

Ringo barreled into the men's room. I was tempted to follow, but managed to restrain myself. I strode back across the room to my desk, my face warm and flushed, first with embarrassment but then with victory as I took note of my fellow reporters along the path. They were giving me thumbs-ups, doffing imaginary hats in tribute, clapping in silent applause. One bowed, another thumped me on the shoulder. Nobody said a word, but it was a gauntlet of silent tributes.

The next day I discovered the first step in

Ringo's revenge. Helen, my editor, stopped by my desk and asked me to come to see her when I had a moment. If Helen wanted to talk to me in her office rather than at my desk, it was something private, something important. I quickly found a moment. I hit the button to store my notes—I'd learned that lesson since Ringo had arrived—and accompanied her to her office.

"Chas, why have you changed your mind about the Two Views story? I thought it was going so well." Helen had closed the door but not even waited until she sat down at her desk before she got down to business. For such a patient person as Helen, this rush was an indication of considerable agitation.

"I haven't changed my mind. I'm getting great material. What made you think I'd dropped it?"

Helen settled into her chair and reached across her desk to pat my hand. Her calm was restored. But mine was about to be blown away.

"Don't worry about it. I'm sure it was just a bit of confusion."

"What confusion? Who said I was dropping my story?"

"I'm sorry I brought it up. It's nothing. We're all looking forward to your story."

I adore Helen. I admire her. She's the most human presence in the *Examiner's* management. But still, she is management. And when she turns secretive and patronizing, I want to explode. I feel betrayed.

"Helen, you can't start something like this and not finish it. You're better than that. It's not like you to treat people this way." I knew how to shame her out of her managerial autocracy.

"I just didn't want to upset you. I know how you feel about Ringo—that was quite a performance yesterday when you chased him across the newsroom—and there's no point in adding fuel to the fire. I'll take care of everything."

"Take care of what? I should have guessed Ringo had a hand in whatever this is. Look, Helen, we've always trusted each other. Don't start playing games now."

Helen took her time to answer. She's like that. She thinks about what you've said and doesn't respond until she's turned it over and examined all sides of it. "You're right. Not that I like stirring you up more. But I guess I should let you be the one to worry about that." Helen rubbed her temples and sat back in her chair. She looked ready to take a beating, or to take more of a beating than she'd already endured. "Bull mentioned in this morning's meeting that Ringo was doing a story on Two Views as part of a series on the new, young professionals. I protested that since you were already using Two Views as the focus for your story on restaurant finances, we'd be showering far too much attention on that one restaurant."

"Damned straight, we would. Ringo knew I was doing Two Views. That's exactly why he chose it. It would make no sense to feature the restaurant twice, and his story would undoubtedly come in first." I had leaped out of my chair and was yelling by now.

"Calm down, Chas. Bull knows very well we can't do the same restaurant twice, and that you started your story first."

"Then why did he approve Ringo's?" I was hovering over Helen's chair. She stood up suddenly, forcing me to take a step back.

"Let's both sit down to talk about this, shall we?" It worked. By the time I crossed her desk and took a chair, I was calmer. For an instant.

Helen continued in a voice soft enough that I had to lean forward and concentrate to hear her. It's another effective trick she uses to quiet the room and thereby cool overheated reporters. "That's where the confusion came in. Ringo told Bull he thought you had dropped Two Views from your story. He'd heard you were going to switch to another restaurant."

"Bullshit!" I shot out of my chair and started marching around the room again. "Ringo knew very well I hadn't dropped it. How could he lie so baldly? And how could Bull believe him? All he had to do was ask me."

"I'm sure Bull assumed that Ringo wouldn't dare to make up a tale so easy to disprove."

"Ringo would dare anything. Anything his fiendish mind could dream up. That man doesn't deserve to live and breathe our air." I stormed out, leaving Helen to resume rubbing her temples and recover from the battering she'd anticipated.

As I said, though, that was only the first part of Ringo's attack, a mere warning bell signaling me that he now knew what I was doing. He couldn't bear my horning in on his privileged position at Two Views, which he had grown to consider his personal hangout. My intimacy with Kirk and Ben, even though it was solely in pursuit of a story, had sparked his jealousy. Of course, I didn't expect at first that he was going to punish everyone concerned.

Next he showed me that he also knew about my looking into his past. The message was that the two-bit games were over, and he was playing higher stakes.

After my confrontation with Helen, I went home with a headache, and by the time I got there, my throat was scratchy. I remembered Ringo accosting me last week with a damp handshake, then complaining that he had a cold as he withdrew his hand and produced a soggy handkerchief to wipe his nose. I was ready to blame anything on Ringo, even an impending cold.

At home I poured myself a Bloody Mary—as good a cold remedy as I know—then quickly moved on to two aspirin. I was out of zinc lozenges and echinacea, but I had plenty of my old reliable defensive medicine, vitamin C. I shook five of my thousand-milligram tablets into my hand and was about to wash one down with the Bloody Mary when I realized that their color was right, but their size was wrong. These white pills were not vitamin C.

My hand shook as I imagined being as dead as E. G. Lansing.

But Ringo hadn't been in my apartment, I reminded myself.

Yes, he had. I'd let him in once, when he'd brought me flowers from the farmers' market. Was that when I'd lost my house keys? I was beginning to connect the dots.

I was in a rage. I roared and cursed Ringo and swept those five pills into the sink. I nearly vomited at the thought of what he might have done to me. I hurled the bottle at the wall, then thought better of it. Grateful that pill containers are plastic nowadays, I scuttled around my bathroom gathering up every tablet.

They were evidence.

Homer answered on the first ring.

I didn't take time to say hello. "Could you get something tested for me? Some pills? In a hurry?"

"Chas? What's the matter? I could try."

"This would be unofficial. But I'd want you to keep a record in case it became official later on."

"Are you all right? What's wrong?"

"I'm fine." I forced myself to slow my breathing and smooth my voice. "Getting a cold maybe. But I have a hunch I need to follow up in a hurry.

Can you help without getting yourself into any trouble?"

"For you, babe, I'd risk the gallows. You need some pills tested, eh? I'll see what I can do. How quickly?"

"Yesterday?"

"Why not? Miracles are my specialty. Where are you?"

"At home."

"Perfect. I've got to be in your neighborhood in an hour anyway. I'll stop by on my way."

Homer had frown lines between his brows when I opened the door a half hour later.

"I'm fine, really I am," I reassured him. "And I've just mixed a batch of Bloody Marys with enough lime to cure all colds present and future."

Homer coughed.

Once he had a Bloody Mary in his hand, I told him about my encounter with the vitamin C, though for his sake and mine I stuck to the observable facts and didn't share my suspicions of Ringo. Homer handled the bottle with a handkerchief, though we both realized there'd be no useful third-party fingerprints on it. He was following rules.

He shook a pill into his hand and bounced it a bit, as if weighing it and assessing its texture. He brought it close to his face and peered at it. He smelled it. He nudged it over, looking closely at the other side. Then he did something so shocking that I yelped.

He licked it.

"Be careful!"

Homer gave me a somber look, then dissolved into a slow smile, which built into a laugh. "It won't kill you," he explained. "Then again, it won't cure you of anything."

"What is it?"

"Altoids."

While Homer enjoyed a warm chuckle, my blood ran cold.

Altoids might have been a harmless—if frightening—warning, but Ringo's attack on Kirk and Ben was far more serious than the petulant maneuvers he'd attempted on me. It was an affirmation that Ringo's jealousy was building to forest-fire proportions and threatening to consume lives and livelihoods.

The first hint came when Kirk called me and asked me not to come that day. He and Ben had a meeting that was going to last all morning.

"I won't need you with me at this stage, so why don't I come anyway and just go over my stack of papers?" I suggested. He had already pulled out plenty of material for me to go through on my own.

"I'm sorry, but the meeting is going to be in our office."

Lame excuse. I could use another office, or the banquet room. Something more was going on.

"Is everything all right?"

"Fine," said Kirk. "Sure, fine." I wondered if I heard a crack in his voice.

"What's—"

Kirk cut me off. "I've got to . . . I'll call—" In fact, he cut himself off, hanging up the phone abruptly.

Had the chef quit? The IRS subpoenaed the files? The trout mounted an attack on the elevators? I felt puzzled. It was unlike Kirk to be abrupt. But I felt relieved to have some time alone to think about Ringo and a chance to pull myself together.

By noon, I'd forgotten all about Kirk's strange behavior. I was about to meet Lily for lunch because it was a school holiday and she wasn't working. That always brightened my day.

Georgetown restaurants can't depend on lunchtime for their business. They're not in much of an office neighborhood, and they're too far from downtown or Capitol Hill to routinely draw lawyers, lobbyists, and politicians, the big spenders. What's more, these restaurants suffer from the community's shortsightedness nearly three decades ago when Georgetowners campaigned against having a subway stop in their precious neighborhood. They didn't want to risk "bad elements" having easy access to their valuable property. It apparently never occurred to the business owners that the "good elements"—and their credit cards—would also be deterred from frequenting Georgetown if there were no subway access. Nor did anyone calculate the pressure on M Street, Wisconsin Avenue, and the few parking lots from the ever-increasing urban traffic that couldn't be diverted to public transportation.

So Georgetown is a mess. Rush hours and weekends, the streets look like long, narrow parking lots. The carriage-trade business has languished in favor of bargain-offering raucous youth-culture commerce, which makes its way to Georgetown despite (or because of) the inconvenience. That, in turn, further deters older, richer, and more sedate spenders. A fine restaurant has hardly any chance unless, like the rooftop Two Views, it has some spectacular and unique asset.

The other expense-account restaurant that thrives in Georgetown despite the traffic and image problems is Citronelle. Its unique asset is Michel Richard, the owner/chef who brought his national reputation from Los Angeles and has attracted a steady stream of the dining-obsessed wealthy from everywhere. Its location at the eastern end of Georgetown, closer to downtown, gives it some advantage. A parking garage underneath the restaurant helps, too, though that's the whipped cream, not the cake.

Thus, Citronelle is singular as a Georgetown restaurant that can draw a lunch crowd. Once it was established as a top-class kitchen, its off-the-beaten-track location also began to attract politicians when, in rare moments, they didn't want to be "seen." While the restaurant can't count on it, some days Citronelle's lunch hour is as busy as the Senate dining room's.

Today was one of those days. I was glad I'd been overcautious and made a reservation.

Lily was back to her layered look. She unwrapped herself from cape, scarf, and sweater, leaving a vest that reached to her knees over a skirt flowing to her ankles. She piled her debris on the chair opposite me and sat in the one beside me after she greeted me with an enthusiastic kiss and hug.

"It feels like playing hooky, having a fancy lunch on a weekday. This was a great idea, Mamma." Lily loves Citronelle, not only for the wicked sweetness of Michel Richard's flirting, but for the beauty and whimsy of its vegetarian dishes. Her favorite is a large glass bowl of what at first look like colored bubbles but on closer inspection are vegetables in every seasonal hue, carved into balls and tossed in a brothy pesto. Basil and garlic envelop the table when it arrives. Lily says she feels as if she's eating savory candy or a vegetable circus. I know what she means— that's Michel Richard's gift, the ability to turn seriously exacting food into a playful experience.

Michel, though, didn't seem playful. He was fretting.

That's what restaurateurs do. They moan and groan when their dining rooms are full. It's too much, they complain. They wish they could cook for just a few diners so that they could serve them perfectly.

Sure. I believe that as much as I believe those who vow that their new restaurant is going to be modestly priced so that people can come for a casual everyday meal. Restaurateurs like to see themselves as dreamers. Yet they can't close their eyes to the clink of money.

Today, though, Michel's success was indeed causing him trouble. His dining room was full and his phone was ringing constantly. The rich, the famous, the pushy, and the entitled were demanding tables. Tables he didn't have.

"I don't know what is happening," he moaned, though his eyes were sparkling at Lily. "Suddenly I have twice the customers I had last week." He left us in order to suffer at another table. He was making the rounds.

"That's odd," Lily said as she watched Michel go from table to table. "Two Views told Brian not to come in tonight. Not enough business. He was told they might not need him all week."

"It's hard to believe they wouldn't need him," I said, watching Michel schmooze with the next table. "When I was there yesterday morning, they were talking about what a busy week it was going to be. Are you sure something isn't going on between Brian and the maître d'?" Brian had occasionally complained about his boss; maybe he'd been indiscreet with his criticisms. He'd run into that problem before.

"No, he and Brian have been getting along very well lately. The owners were very apologetic about laying him off and told him they'd make it up to him."

"But these days Two Views has been more popular than Citronelle. And look at this dining room. It's packed."

"Maybe Brian should look for a job here." Lily looked forlorn.

"Are you and Brian doing all right? The criticism thing again?"

"No, it's not that." Lily was stabbing the vegetables left in her bowl. I hoped they weren't a stand-in for Brian. "It's just that he gets moody. Frustrated."

"Impatient with his life?"

Lily looked at me the way mothers always hope their daughters will look at them, a warm mingling of pride, gratitude, and admiration. I love it when she makes me feel wise.

"You always know, Mamma. That's exactly the problem. How do you do that?" Her fork was transformed from weapon to tool once again. She finished the bowl in a few swift bites.

"Advanced training in mothering skills. That, plus knowing how little respect waiters get in this world of ours. We've turned chefs into gods and waiters into lackeys. Especially in this country, waiting tables is seen as something you fall back on when you're desperate between acting jobs or for summer vacations. In Europe, it's an honorable profession."

"But the money can be good."

"True, but it's erratic. And the payment is more personal than professional. Diners feel they are doing a waiter a favor when they tip him, rather than seeing a tip as his fair wages. So it's a vicious cycle; the pool of waiters gradually fulfills the low expectations of diners."

"Usually Brian loves his job. He enjoys making people happy, and he's proud of being such a good waiter. He knows how to do it right and he has an instinct for dealing with people. But still, he sees all the credit go to the kitchen and the maître d'. Nobody notices the waiter unless he's inept, and only rarely do diners know the waiter's name except at those silly restaurants where the waiter says, 'Hi, my name's Charlie and I'll be your server tonight.' Most diners don't even think the waiter has a name."

"The real problem for Brian is that there's such a narrow possibility for advancement in dining-room service. In this country, people are used to moving up the ladder quickly. At least that's the myth. But a restaurant has only one maître d' along with its many waiters and captains. So most waiters feel stuck, ignored, unappreciated, and mistreated. Not to mention, their feet always hurt. And that's enough to ruin anyone's mood."

We fell silent for a moment as we looked over the dessert menu, and that was when I overheard the next table.

"It was nearly impossible to get a reservation

here by the time I called. I had to pretend it was for the secretary and go through the kitchen."

That might sound humble—secretaries and kitchens—but in the language of Washington and of restaurants, it means the secretary of state or defense or some such cabinet-level position, and going through the kitchen implies that the diner prevailed on the chef himself for a table when he couldn't get one through normal channels. The next part was even more interesting.

"I thought it was nice of me to call and let them know, and I expected the restaurant to be grateful, but the reservations clerk was so hostile I wished I hadn't bothered. I guess a lot of us were canceling. At least that's the way it sounded."

By now I had dropped all pretense of reading the dessert menu and was just listening in. Lily started to say something, but I signaled her to wait a minute. She looked puzzled, so I discreetly pointed to the next table. Then she got it. She, too, began eavesdropping.

"I love the place. But I'm not going to risk it. Not with my sensitive stomach."

What place? What risk?

"They say he almost died."

Lily's eyebrows shot up. She was leaning to her left to hear better. Who almost died? How?

"It's a shame for the restaurant, but it's their own fault. You've got to be so careful these days. With that *E. coli* and salmonella and all that stuff."

Food poisoning.

"It's got to be the end for that restaurant. Nobody will go there now, even if they clean up their act. It was a short life."

"Short and sweet."

Food poisoning at a restaurant. That would be big news. Especially if someone almost died.

"I don't feel like dessert. What about you?" I asked Lily. Suddenly I couldn't wait to get back to the office to start working the phones.

I suppose I could have asked Michel at Citronelle if he'd heard about a food poisoning, but I didn't want to draw attention to the fact that I'd been eavesdropping. And if he knew about it, he probably would have told me. This is the kind of gossip nobody in the business can resist. In any case, I was sure I could pin it down with a call or two.

By the time I got back to my desk, I didn't even need to make a call. My e-mail list was endless and my voice mail was full. Everyone who wasn't asking me about the food poisoning was telling me about it. Or some version of it.

After I'd read and listened to them all—which took a while, since more kept coming—I was pretty sure the incident had occurred at Two Views, though a few of the messages attributed it to another restaurant.

Some said an entire table of people had gone to the hospital. Others reported that the victims were felled right in the dining room, but that sounded unlikely since most foodborne illnesses take several hours to develop.

I heard it was the mayonnaise, the oysters, undercooked beef. One creative thinker left me a message that a terrorist group had contaminated the imported olives with a virus that was highly contagious as well as lethal.

I called Two Views, but the phone was busy. I kept hitting the redial button until I got through, but all I got was a recording. After holding for five minutes I gave up. I called Kirk and Ben's private lines, but they were busy, too. I tried every number I had for the restaurant, with no success. I went back to reading messages and started answering my phone rather than leaving the calls for voice mail.

The most prevalent story was that a group of senators and journalists had dined at Two Views the night before last, and one of the wives felt queasy. She passed out—some said—and another wife helped her to the restroom, where she proceeded to barf up her dinner. After she returned to the table, the other wife dashed for the restroom and followed suit. By then, several others were feeling queasy as well. The unaffected ones wanted to call an ambulance or at least take their ill friends to the hospital, but the two women who'd been most sick insisted on staying. The idea of going to the hospital was dropped (the merely queasy couldn't very well consider a hos-

pital necessary if the violently sick ones didn't).
So everyone eventually wound up going home.

That was only the beginning. By the next day,
nearly everyone in the group claimed to have
been sick all night, and someone who had tallied
up who ate what concluded that the mayonnaise
was the culprit.

Two Views makes a specialty of its mayonnaise.
It gets its eggs from a farm that certifies them free
of salmonella, and it uses a variety of olive and
nut oils, citrus fruits and vinegars, herbs and
spices to make a colorful array of sauces that have
become its signature. On this particular evening,
the chef had concocted a grapefruit-jalapeño mayonnaise requested by the group, and to start the
meal, the meat-eaters spooned it over their steak
salad while the vegetarians dolloped it on their
roasted artichokes. They'd used it all up and
called for more before the first person got sick.

Restaurants are constantly fielding complaints
that someone was made sick by their food, but
most of them are false alarms. Stomach upsets
have countless causes, from viruses to overindul-
gence. Sometimes allergies are the culprit. Very
few times is spoilage the cause. But try telling
that to someone who's upchucked an expensive
dinner.

Since no cause is likely to be proved, and the ill-
ness is generally gone within a day, these mum-
blings about food poisoning generally disappear
without a trace. This case was different.

Not only was this a group of public figures with familiar names and talkative ways, the timing couldn't have been worse for Two Views. The night after the unfortunate dinner party was an annual fund-raiser, the kind that nobody ever wants to go to but everyone attends anyway. Everyone, that is, except two of the senators and their wives.

Their absence was noticed. And it was explained endlessly. None of the explanation appeared in print, or even on television, but it was hinted at so obviously that anyone who wanted to speculate on the reason for their absence could fill in the blanks, especially after a few minutes on the Internet. The news spread so far and so quickly that I wondered why we need newspapers and TV at all.

Of course, since I work at a newspaper, I can usually catch the hot gossip without stepping beyond my four walls. And I did. As in the civilian world, the stories conflicted. Somebody died, nobody died. It was the mayonnaise, it was tainted beef. The owners were denying it, the owners had been hauled off to jail, charged with criminal neglect. The only thing everyone agreed on was that Ringo was writing the story for tomorrow's paper, and he was nowhere to be found.

It wasn't until late afternoon that I got through to Kirk.

He hung up on me. "I have nothing to say to the

press," he announced when he heard my name.
Clunk.

I called back and got a busy signal.

Eventually I got through again, and this time I
encountered Ben.

"Don't hang up, Ben. I'm not calling as the
press. I'm calling as me, Chas, and I feel terrible
about what I've been hearing. Is there some way I
can help?"

"Kirk told me he'd hung up on you. You have
to excuse him. He's a wreck. I am, too, almost. But
I can't just sit here and watch it all come tumbling
down without doing something. We've got to do
something. I just don't know what."

With each sentence, his voice trailed off, then
abruptly started up again. He sounded erratic.
Definitely a wreck. It was painful to listen.

"Look, Ben, I know what a great job you've
done. You and Kirk are pros, have become pros
younger and quicker than any I've seen. This is a
blow, but there are things you can do to overcome
it. The faster the better. You've been a big help to
me. I'd like to help you if I can."

I'd like to save my restaurant-finances story, too.

"I don't know how you can help. Or how anyone can help. We're closing tonight; we had all big
parties, and they canceled. I don't know whether
we'll have enough reservations to make it worth
opening tomorrow, or the next day."

"What I can do is invite you out to dinner. Then
we can talk from there."

"Kirk won't talk to the press. And I think he's probably right."

"This will be off the record. Absolutely. Trust me."

I hate when people say, "Trust me." It makes me worry that I shouldn't. But in my desperation to help Two Views, it slipped out. Fortunately, Ben is of the "trust me" generation.

"I don't know if I can eat, but I definitely can drink. I'll meet you. And if I can persuade Kirk, he'll be there, too."

13

I suggested a bar in Adams Morgan called Millie
& Al's. It had gone through a flurry of popularity
with yuppies in the 80s, but that was short-lived,
and by the early 90s it had been allowed to drift
back into its position as the least gentrified
English-speaking drinking place in the neighborhood. We wouldn't run into anybody we knew.

As usual, especially in the hours between late-
afternoon pick-me-ups and late-evening calm-
me-downs, Millie & Al's was nearly empty. At the
bar were two mountainous men, one with a long
gray ponytail and the other with no hair at all.
They hunched over their beers in a companionable silence that gave the impression it hadn't
been broken in five years. The only other table occupied this early in the evening was the domain of
a tense shambles of a man who sat with a loaf of

sliced white bread stacked vertically on a plate, and an empty plate beside that. Between gulps of beer he lifted each slice from the top of the pile—using knife and fork—and transferred it to the other plate, then cut it into pieces and ate it as if it were a steak dinner. He wiped his mouth with a napkin after each bite.

I was mesmerized. I didn't even see Kirk and Ben come in, so I was startled when they pulled out chairs at my table. They sat down in unison, neither saying a word. I pointed to my beer. Ben nodded. Kirk shook his head and said, "Scotch. On the rocks. Double." I would have pegged him as a martini man.

"I'm glad you're here," I ventured as I stood up to get their drinks from the bar. They didn't look as if they could bear the dry interval until the waiter might get around to us.

Millie & Al's knows how to pour a drink in a hurry.

Ben sucked down almost half his beer as soon as it hit the table. "If our restaurant weren't already dead, I'd worry that Ringo's going to kill us in print," Ben said by way of breaking the silence.

Kirk's scotch clearly wasn't his first of the afternoon. He took it slower. Then he added his first words. "Not if we get him first."

"Shut up, Kirk. I've heard enough of that." Ben glowered at his brother and finished his beer.

By that time, the waiter had showed up. "Another?" he asked Ben.

"All around," Kirk answered, and to emphasize the point he took a long swallow of his double scotch.

I nodded to the waiter, and finished off the beer I'd been nursing. That gave me another moment before I had to join the conversation. I'd been holding back as I observed the brothers, hoping for a clue as to what would be my best approach.

I went for optimistic. "I heard that Ringo's writing something for the *Examiner*, but I think that will most likely help. I don't know yet what really happened, but it can't be as bad as half the rumors, so a factual explanation will put this back in perspective. It's not as if anybody died," I finished lamely.

Kirk muttered something that sounded like, "Not yet." Ben was talking at the same time, so I couldn't be sure.

"Kirk's had a head start on us," Ben said very quietly to me as he gestured to our glasses. He wasn't telling me anything I didn't know, but his hinting that Kirk was half drunk was positioning us as coconspirators, making us allies.

I took the opportunity to try to get at what the real story was.

"Ringo's a good reporter, the best. He'll get it straight. But having the eyes and ears of two reporters is better than one. Why don't you tell me exactly what happened, and I'll try to make sure I get to look over anything that's going into the paper."

Kirk and Ben each seemed to be waiting for the other to speak first. They'd look at their drinks, then steal a sidelong glance at each other. This kind of anticompetition wasn't going to get us anywhere. I'd have to prod them.

"Let's start with the basic facts. How many tables got sick?"

"None." Ben barely managed to eke out the word.

"You mean only the table with those two senators?"

"None." This time it was Kirk, and he was forceful about it.

"Are you saying none of the rumors is true? That nothing at all happened?" Now it was I who felt queasy. Such rumors don't start without any kind of inciting incident. Something happened. And if Kirk and Ben were going to lie about this, how could I trust anything they'd been telling me about their restaurant?

The sidelong exchange of glances continued. Neither was ready to speak. I'd have to try a new tack.

"There were two senators at dinner the other night?"

They nodded.

"And someone at the table called later to report that they'd become sick?"

They shook their heads.

"So this food-poisoning rumor just grew out of nowhere."

Ben shook his head. Kirk drew on his scotch and found his voice.

"It was one of those crowd-hysteria things."

"Go on. I'm listening."

"You know, the way one person on a crowded street looks up to the sky and pretty soon everyone else does, too. And eventually someone insists there was something to look at. Like a flying saucer."

I knew what he meant, but I didn't want to let him off that easily. I was looking for him to explain the connection to the food-poisoning rumor.

Ben stepped in. "What he means is that nobody got sick from our food. But people thought they did."

"Let's start from the beginning."

"It was a table of ten. And they'd been drinking already by the time they arrived." As if to illustrate his story, Ben chugged the rest of his beer. He turned to signal the waiter for another round. Playing his part in the well-honed team they always seemed to be, Kirk picked up the story.

"They were having a great time. Joking, noisy, turning to talk to people at the next table. Your usual Capitol Hill drunks."

Ben interrupted, obviously not liking the direction Kirk was taking this. "They took a long time to order. Then, as sometimes happens, they didn't want to deal with the menu, so they all ordered the same thing. More or less. The men ordered meat and the women went vegetarian."

"So if people actually did get sick from your food, it could only have been the men or the women, not both." I was trying to define the case detail by detail.

"Not exactly," Ben continued. "The mayonnaise went on the beef salad and the artichoke salad."

"And that's what was seen to be the culprit when people got sick later?"

"Nobody got sick later." Ben was adamant.

"You've lost me. Let's get back to the sequence of events."

"A few bites into the first course, one of the women . . ."

"A senator's wife." Kirk's tone was mocking.

"Whoever. She passed out for an instant. She revived instantly, but she looked really pale. She got up and looked around frantically, and I immediately went to help her. She asked where the restrooms were."

"She also said she'd had too much to drink," Kirk interjected.

"She didn't say that right there and then, she said it to me as I accompanied her and her friend to the women's room."

"Where she barfed her guts out. On the floor." Kirk was providing the embellishments.

"She looked much better when she got back to the table. Her friend was the one who looked queasy by then."

"Wouldn't you, if you'd spent five minutes in a

closed room where your friend had just spewed all over the floor?"

Kirk didn't have to persuade me. My stomach lurched merely from hearing about it. "That was it? That wasn't food poisoning. Not even spoiled mayonnaise would act on somebody that quickly."

"That was only the beginning," Ben continued.

"Then came the hysteria," Kirk said. "By the end of the evening, several of the group had been persuaded that they felt sick. At least slightly nauseated."

Little of this fit what I'd been told. "I heard they went to the hospital. If they did, the tests would prove whether or not your food had been involved."

"Now I wish they had," Ben said, sounded achingly sad.

Kirk looked more angry. "I think there was a ringleader. He turned a small, unfortunate, and not-so-unusual situation into a major crisis. He tried to persuade the two women to go to the hospital, and he started talking about feeling sick himself and kept asking everyone else, 'Don't you feel sick? You're looking pale.' "

The story was tumbling out now, first from Kirk, then from Ben.

"He talked it up so much that everyone began to believe him. And feel sick."

"So why didn't anyone go to the hospital?" I wasn't quite following.

Kirk explained it. "The first woman, the one

who really got sick, was feeling better after she threw up. She wanted to eat her dinner; she didn't want to miss the rest of her big night out. So she refused to go to the hospital. And if she wouldn't go, the rest, who didn't have anything like the serious symptoms she'd had, would feel pretty foolish going."

That made sense to me. "So they all stayed?"

"Yeah. And they all finished their dinner, right down to the chocolate truffles."

"Then how did the rumors get out of hand?"

"On the telephone the next day. The way I heard it, someone called every one of the guests, told them he was sick as a dog, and asked in a very leading way if they had been okay after the dinner. He also suggested that almost everyone else had been sick."

"And that wasn't true?"

"Nobody reported it to us. Nobody went to a doctor, as far as we could discover."

"Then how did the rumor get around so fast?"

"That's easy. There was that big fund-raiser the next night, you know the kind. Everyone hates to go but feels obligated. The two senators saw their chance, so they used upset stomachs as an excuse to stay home, and the ringleader, who went, even though he'd supposedly been deathly ill, told his embellished story to everyone he saw. Two Views became the poster child for food poisoning. The cancellations started coming in last night, probably from cell phones in the ballroom."

"Most people don't bother to cancel a restaurant reservation," I said.

"These were groups. We had their credit card numbers," Ben explained.

"By morning, people were calling to complain that they'd been sick after their lunch last week or dinner a month ago." Kirk was beginning to slur his words.

I felt a large lump weighing down my stomach. I knew what a death knell this could be for a restaurant. Entire food manufacturing companies had been felled by a single charge of food poisoning, and restaurants are more vulnerable to the whims of a fickle public.

The outline—and the injustice—of the disaster were obvious to me by now. I'd need time to think how I might help avert it. I hoped that the details might give me some inspiration.

"Let's talk about the mayonnaise. It was the only ingredient common to the men's and women's meals, right?"

"Right," they said in unison.

"Was that connection made later or during the meal?"

"That damned ringleader started talking it up right away. As soon as the first woman got sick," Kirk said remarkably distinctly. He sounded as if adrenaline were clearing his head. "Right away, he began to lecture everyone on the dangers of mayonnaise. Salmonella in the eggs, spoilage from sitting out of the refrigerator."

"He even threw in *E. coli*, which has nothing to do with mayonnaise." Ben's adrenaline had raised his decibel level. His voice rang through the near-empty room. He stopped short, looking abashed.

Kirk took up the complaint. "It was pretty obvious to me that he was trying to make them sick."

This was a new wrinkle. We were straying too far from the facts, and I didn't want the conversation to deteriorate into wild charges. "Why do you say that? Sounds far-fetched to me."

"Kirk's not exaggerating, Chas. As soon as the first woman fell ill, we kept a careful watch on the table. He was working at making the rest feel queasy with his food scares and discussion of the symptoms. And he pushed the booze. Kept filling people's glasses and offering little toasts and challenges to drink up. You'd have thought he was getting a kickback for every bottle of wine."

"That's not the kind of kickback senators get," I said, hoping to tone down Ben's charges and get back to real details.

"I'm not talking about the senators. You still don't get it, do you?" Ben shook his head slowly back and forth, looking at me as if I'd just flunked the first word in a spelling bee.

"Get what? You're right. I'm missing something here."

"Mr. Ringleader. Mister Ringo Laurenge Ringleader."

"Ringo was there?"

"Come off it, Chas. You know he was there—he is your colleague, isn't he? Why else would we be so sure your paper's going to bury us? He was the one who invented this fictitious food poisoning. Dreamed it up, persuaded everyone at the table to believe it."

"Then he made sure everyone kept believing it the next morning, and he told the world at the party the next night."

"The guy is a master. He didn't miss a trick; not a single opportunity slipped past his grasp."

"I couldn't believe it. I'm still left wondering what he has against us, why he wants to kill our restaurant, after he's practically lived there since it opened."

"Maybe it wasn't personal. Maybe he just wanted to see if he could do it." Ben might be calmer than Kirk, but now he sounded the more cynical of the two, at least until Kirk finished his thought:

"Put the most popular new restaurant in town out of business, single-handedly, in the space of barely more than twenty-four hours."

For long, painful minutes I couldn't say a word. I had no words to say. Kirk and Ben sounded absolutely on target.

I finally found my tongue. "I'll have a double scotch on the rocks, too."

14

The first step in stopping the flow of lifeblood from Two Views would be to gag Ringo. No reporter with a vendetta could be allowed to vent in the pages of a newspaper. Even if it couldn't be proved that Ringo had a vendetta, his story would be tainted by his having played a role in spreading the rumors. If Bull knew, he'd certainly call Ringo off the story.

Dinner could wait. Until tomorrow if necessary. I had a more important job to do.

I didn't want to face Ringo, so I took the coward's route and retreated to my apartment to mount my campaign by phone. I curled up in my red velvet rocker with a quilt and the *Examiner*'s telephone directory, and set to work to rescue Two Views.

Bull wasn't at the office. He wasn't at home. He

didn't answer his cell phone. I left messages, but knew that they'd probably be retrieved too late. I even tried Bull's secretary at home, but she, too, was stumped. He always keeps his cell phone turned on, she insisted. I wondered whether he'd encountered a restaurant that asks customers to check their cell phones, or confiscates them after the first ring.

To get Ringo's story tabled, I'd have to find another path through the *Examiner's* labyrinth of power. I talked to Ringo's editor, but he was so offended at my stepping out of line and questioning his judgment that he couldn't seem to hear the substance of what I was saying. One more enemy I could add to my tally at the *Examiner*.

The story was going in tomorrow's paper, and the deadline was looming. Every minute counted. My next step was to call Dave to enlist him in heading off the disaster.

That was a miscalculation. The conversation didn't go well. Dave reminded me that editors have enough intelligence to spot an unsubstantiated charge and require evidence to back it up. He dismissed my concern that Ringo was genius enough to carry off a hoax. By the end I bitterly accepted that Dave was too much a part of the system to question it, and I was wasting precious minutes arguing with him.

I tried Helen. Ringo's story wasn't in her chain of command, but she'd know how to get it quashed. She didn't answer, so I left an urgent message. I knew, though, that whenever she called back, it would probably be too late.

As I dozed in my chair I tried to convince myself that Dave was right. The system has built-in checks and balances. Editors are trained to be skeptical. The *Examiner* has lawyers who make reporters jump through hoops before they'll approve any story that might be the subject of a libel suit. If Ringo's story wasn't airtight, it wouldn't run.

Even if Ringo's editor didn't believe my charges, the fact that I'd raised questions would make a difference, Dave had reminded me. An editor would have to take that into consideration when he edited the piece; he wouldn't risk leaving himself vulnerable to repercussions if the story went sour. No editor in Washington ever forgot Janet Cook or Stephen Glass, whose highly acclaimed stories turned out to have been fabricated. Cook's had even won a Pulitzer before it was discovered that the reporters who'd raised concerns in vain to the editors had been right and that the heroin-addicted child Cook had featured was an invention. Those scandals had left disfiguring scars on the relationship between journalism and its reading public.

When I woke early the next morning, stiff and aching from having spent the night curled in my chair, at first I thought it was still evening and there was time to head off Ringo's story. Then I realized that light was seeping from under my window shades. I looked at my watch and felt my stomach lurch.

It was too late. Nobody had called. The *Examiner* was spreading Ringo's venom throughout the entire metropolitan area, on doorsteps and in vending machines, stacked on newsstands, piled on hotel counters, stuffed into mailboxes and flying through the ether to websites. Hundreds of thousands of people were going to read about Two Views' food making people sick. At least that many more were going to hear about it at work and on Metro, at coffee breaks and smoking breaks, in meetings and at lunchrooms. Still more would catch it on the network news; it certainly would make the local newscasts, and national networks would probably pick up on it since it was a Washington scandal and involved members of the Senate.

I was wrong. Oh, the story ran, and it did indeed promise to be devastating to Two Views. But I was wrong about it being libelous and full of false assertions.

I was right, though, about Ringo's genius.

The story was keyed on the front page and ran as a lead in the Lifestyles section. Very clever. It was presented as a feature rather than news, and it was highly visible without looking overplayed.

The genius was that Ringo hadn't simply run a gossipy feature story—which would have required him to quote multiple sources and present more than one point of view—he'd written it first-person, as the diary of a stomachache. It wasn't merely gory, it was hilarious. He'd balanced it on the narrow edge between spoof and reality. There was nothing in it that charged Two Views with food poisoning, but after reading it nobody would want to dine there.

Ringo stuck to the facts he'd observed firsthand and he named names. He described the sick senator's wife and her queasy friend, the pleas that they get themselves checked out at the hospital, and the epidemic of perceived stomach upsets that followed. Ringo reported conversations that rang alarms but didn't speculate as to their veracity. He told of his spasmodic bowels and sleepless night—who could prove him wrong? And he described his image of poisons running rampant through his digestive tract. He couched it in fantasy but it was as effective in planting ideas in readers' minds as any medical findings would have been. More so, since it was so god-awful funny. Instead of being a direct accusation, it was an essay on a man's battle with his stomach.

There were anchors in fact. Ringo reported who didn't show up at the benefit the next night. And playing the even-handed reporter, he noted who did. He made a point of trying to track down Kirk and Ben for comment, even documenting the six specific phone calls he made to their office. All of them were during our drinking bout at Millie & Al's. Ringo hadn't allowed much leeway for getting a response on such a critical story. Yet the public would see the upshot as the owners having avoided calling Ringo back, since his calls ran through dinner hour, when a restaurateur would be presumed to be on the premises.

Vomiting, diarrhea: the words are death to a restaurant. And the fact that the *Examiner* had considered the incident worthy of reporting would be seen by the public as verification of Two Views' being responsible. But the story was so ghoulishly entertaining that even insiders who recognized that no specific charges were made—that it was actually a no-news story—would agree that its placement as an entertaining feature was valid. Possibly nobody had ever written a more witty and memorable picture of gastric misery.

The newsroom bubbled like New Year's Eve, while I felt like a New Year's Day hangover. As I threaded my way to my desk, I heard reporters repeating Ringo's lines to each other. I saw them clutching their stomachs, pretending to stick a finger down their throats. The child in us, fascinated by bodily functions gone awry, lies close to the surface. And all over Washington today, it was breaking free.

Everybody was laughing, and nobody was considering at whose expense.

I couldn't face Kirk and Ben, though I knew they'd need every smidgen of support offered to them. I felt responsible. I should have found a way to head off Ringo, since I was the only one outside of Two Views who knew the whole story. And I was afraid that I had set off Ringo's wrath against Two Views in the first place.

If I couldn't muster the courage to call Kirk and Ben, at least I could confront Bull and rant about what a slimy story he'd run. I didn't think it would accomplish anything. In fact, I had no idea what could be accomplished at this point even if Bull could be persuaded to take action. But I needed to act, if only to placate my roiling conscience.

Bull wasn't willing to even see me, much less let me shower him with abuse.

"No time this morning, Wheatley. Make an appointment." He barely looked up from the newspaper he was reading when I barged past the secretary into his office.

"I'll summarize the newspaper for you and save you five minutes," I protested, and sat down anyway.

"I said I had no time." He voice bellowed from his massive chest. Its volume would have been enough to blow me in the direction of the door if I hadn't been seated. Bull seldom lets loose like this. I figured that meant he knew why I was there.

"I know it's too late to do much about it, but at least you should hear the whole story about Ringo's phony food poisoning. And you probably want to know about the lawsuit." I knew that would get his attention.

"What lawsuit?" He didn't look up, but I could tell that he'd stopped reading.

"The lawsuit over Ringo's food-poisoning story, of course."

"That's crap. There's nothing to sue over. They're bluffing."

"So was Ringo. No, there's no lawsuit, at least not yet. But nor was there a food poisoning. Ringo made it all up."

"Wheatley, just what do you expect to get out of all this? You've developed a thing about Ringo. I know that. Everybody in the newsroom knows that. What's more, I don't have time for your whining today. Make an appointment if you're here to whine."

"Look, Bull, just because Ringo was clever enough to skirt libel in today's story doesn't mean it's worthy of the *Examiner.* He's putting a good restaurant out of business for no reason other than to show that he has the power to do it. And you're abetting him. I find it humiliating to work for a paper that would allow this. I've had it. If you tell me to get out without listening to what I have to say, I'll get out for good."

"Crap."

I got up to leave.

"Sit down, Wheatley. You don't think you're going to leave my office without telling me what's going on, do you? You haven't resigned yet, so I'm still the boss. And it's high time you told me what's happening around here."

That's Bull, always turning a defeat into a victory. If somebody murdered him, he'd certainly find a way to make everyone believe it was suicide. He just had to be in control.

I knew that. I didn't always remember it at the right moments, though. If I did, I'd have saved myself a lot of trouble over the years.

I sat down again, pretending I was being forced to give Bull what he wanted rather than accomplishing exactly what I'd wanted. I didn't need to win, I needed only to make my case.

"That was a compelling story Ringo wrote. Too bad it wasn't true." Now I was the one turning my reactions inside out. I hadn't meant to suggest I'd prefer the story were true.

I'd made my point, though. Bull leaned back in his chair and started acting like an editor.

"Give me some facts here. What do you mean it wasn't true? How do you know? You're going to tell me the man didn't have the runs all night? You weren't there."

He paused while I pulled my thoughts together, then he leaned forward so hard his chair thumped. "Or were you?"

"Ugh, for pity's sake, Bull, that's not what I meant. No, I'm not hanging around Ringo's bedroom in the middle of the night."

He looked relieved.

I had his full attention now, so I quickly outlined to him what Kirk and Ben had told me. I explained to him what I knew about the time

sequence of food poisoning and how ludicrous it
was to think that a drop of mayonnaise could immediately make somebody sick. I described how
Ringo had planted suggestions and dwelled on
nauseating details to encourage his fellow diners'
queasiness. I repeated Kirk and Ben's assertions
that Ringo had further sparked rumors among the
group the next morning and built upon the im-
pressions he'd planted, spreading them widely at
the benefit that night.

I knew I was constructing a fairly flimsy struc-
ture, having talked only to the interested parties
from Two Views and not followed up by interviewing the other diners. But that could be done
today if Bull were willing to press on to investigate this. The weak link would be Ringo. Nobody
could prove or disprove his gastric disorders. And
he knew that; that's why his story was based on
his personal experience, especially that which
went on in the privacy of his home.

Bull's reaction was going to boil down to one
question: Did he trust Ringo?

He did.

"Okay now, Chas, I've listened. And maybe if
you checked with both senators, their wives, and
whoever else was there that night, you'd find that
they weren't quite as sick as they said. Or that
they weren't sick at all. And if you want to call
them, you can do it on my say-so. But it's going to
be nothing more than a waste of your time. Because you're not going to prove that Ringo didn't

have the runs all night, and that's what the story was about."

He was right.

"And it was a damned good story," Bull concluded. "Just the kind of story this newspaper needs. A great read. Something everybody's gonna talk about for the rest of the day. And tonight Ringo and the *Examiner* are going to be on the six o'clock news. All the networks."

As so often happens when I go to see Bull these days, I left feeling even worse than when I went in. I hadn't convinced him; rather, he had convinced me of the futility of my efforts. Even so, I didn't want him to see my defeat.

"The *Post* would never have run such a sleazy piece of junk," I shot back at him from the safety of the door.

I couldn't take my frustration to Dave. He might agree with Bull. I didn't want to talk to Sherele about it because her anger with Ringo was already eroding her more than it should. And after Bull's charge that everyone in the newsroom sees me as out to get Ringo, I didn't feel comfortable pouring out my story to anyone else at work.

15

Sometimes when I'm looking for comfort, I find it by giving comfort. I went to see Samir.

Samir Said is one of the loves of my life, one that's outlasted a tiny spark of a romance I had with his son, Robert. Samir is old-world Lebanese, a crumpled yet vital man living in a bravely cheerful institutional-looking retirement home as if it were a Middle Eastern palace. The guy, even in his wheelchair-bound and mentally shaky old age, knows how to live grandly. He also has a well-credentialed sense of the devious, honed by decades in some secret service or other. He can spot subterfuge, he can unravel it, and he can devise elegant counterattacks for it. No sooner had I met him than he constructed for me the most delicious method of trapping a murderer, and thereby transformed me into a hero.

I got all the credit, so I keep trying to pay him back by bringing the newest delicacies I find in my forays around the city. And when I can't transport the foods themselves to his tiny bed-sitting room, I bring him his favorite material for reading aloud: menus.

I stopped at home to gather the packet of treats I'd been collecting for him.

"Ah, cherie, I see a gold tassel peeking from your bag. Something French today?"

"No, Continental."

His face fell. "Not one of those menus listing such abominations as surf and turf or beef Wellington? I thought Washington had banned them."

Samir is an unabashed snob. That's part of his charm. His habitual delight combined with his enthusiastic disdain for anything but the best makes his approval feel like a bath of truffle butter. If he likes you, it means he's examined you and pronounced you first-class. You're certified to participate in his re-creation of the Arabian nights.

I couldn't leave Samir disappointed for longer than a moment, so I pulled out the menu from my bag. "You should know I wouldn't really bring you anything so crass as a Continental menu." I handed him the blue velvet card with gold lettering matching the tassel that bound it. "It's a program. From that big charity benefit the other night."

"No wonder your Senate behaves in such an irresponsible and bad-tempered manner," he said as he read the menu printed on the inside. "All that meat and no vegetables. Just meat and shell-fish. A menu to show off its expense rather than to speak to the appetite and the soul."

"And from what I hear, the caviar was lump-fish." I knew that would give him great perverse satisfaction.

"You didn't actually go, did you?"

"Not a chance. I only put on my ball gown for authentic beluga."

"Have you ever had golden beluga?"

"Not often, but yes, I've tasted it. I thought it was fabulous, at least until I found this." I pulled out a small round tin from the bottom of my bag and handed it to Samir. I knew he could read the Russian label.

"Oh, my dear, my dear Chas." Samir had tears in his eyes. I was afraid he'd be embarrassed for me to notice, so I turned my attention to the shelf of photos across from his bed.

He reached out and took my hand, then kissed it, then he also kissed the tin.

"It has been many, many years since I've tasted golden osetra caviar. I don't know how you found it, and maybe I should not ask. But for me, it is the ultimate. The wild tang of the osetra and the ex-quisite delicacy of the golden. The perfection born of opposition."

Samir's appreciation put my gift to shame. Whatever I did for him or gave him always paled in comparison to his gratitude. He made such ceremony of accepting gifts.

He twirled his wheelchair and scooted the few feet to his stash of tableware, quickly unearthing two scallop-edged matte black plates the size of a demitasse saucer, and two tiny spoons carved of mother-of-pearl. He glided toward his inlaid-wood end table and set it as if for a dollhouse tea party. From a shelf underneath he pulled two lace napkins. And a bottle of vodka.

"The glasses are behind you, my dear. I apologize that this is not iced," he said as he uncorked the vodka. I'd never seen a bottle like this, shimmering like seawater and obviously handblown.

"I have crackers, if you like," Samir offered as he spooned an elongated mound of the golden sturgeon eggs onto each plate, both a generous tablespoonful. "But if I might suggest, eating something this rare and precious should be interrupted by no other taste or texture. Except for the alcohol, of course."

He poured vodka to the top of each thimble-size glass and held his up for a toast. I held mine alongside his and clinked with him as he said, "To your future. May it, too, be golden and a little wild."

The caviar was every bit as glorious as Samir had described it. I hadn't tasted golden osetra before, and didn't plan to lavish such extravagance on myself, so I'd been hoping Samir would insist on sharing it with me. More than hoping: I knew he would. We silently savored it, egg by egg at first, then rolled our eyes and licked our spoons and ventured to taste two, then three, then a whole tiny spoonful. We dragged out the eating as long as was humanly possible. And at the end, pleasure mingled with a tinge of sadness that the mound was gone.

"We must have some more," Samir said as he opened the tin once again. Our miniature servings had accounted for a third of the contents.

"No, I couldn't," I protested, not wanting to see Samir's treat disappear all at once. "You must keep some for later."

"I insist."

"Absolutely not." I took the tin from his hand and closed it. "I'm too full. Couldn't eat another bite. But I will take it to the kitchen for you and ask them to keep it for your midnight snack."

Samir swiveled his chair to reach into a drawer and pulled out a battered metal box. It was labeled "Anchovies."

"First we must hide it in this. I have determined that everyone in the kitchen hates anchovies."

I set the anchovy box with the secret caviar next to my purse so I'd remember to take it to the kitchen when I left. Then I settled in with my glass of vodka, ready for a good talk with Samir.

"You have a problem," he said, his eyes sparkling with anticipation. Samir loves solving my problems, at least the big, sticky political or legal problems I am inclined to bring him. Ethics isn't his strong suit, but he's amazing at figuring out how to investigate secrets or to exact retribution. If it's shady, it's Samir's meat.

Ringo, I knew, would fascinate him. No book, no crossword puzzle or computer game could give him more pleasure than would figuring out how to bring a character like Ringo to his knees. And he'd certainly want to save a fine restaurant like Two Views.

He asked dozens of questions. After a while, I wondered whether he was asking questions merely to stretch out the visit. Especially when he had me recount every dish I've tasted at Two Views.

Then he drove me away. At least for a few minutes.

"Go, my dear, and see what is happening elsewhere in this golden-age vipers' pit. I need time to think."

I took the anchovy box down the hall, quiet except for the thump-thump of metal walkers with their rubber tips beating a gentle tattoo. I smiled at the octogenarians doggedly pacing the length of the hall, but they were too intent on their slomo version of jogging to return my greeting. The kitchen staff, though, had all the time in the world. Their frozen lasagnas were thawing, their canned green beans were simmering, their instant mashed potatoes were waiting patiently for that quick moment of reconstitution. The cooks all turned busy the moment they caught sight of me, but that involved a lot of grunting as they heaved from their chairs and dropped their magazines.

"How ya' doing, Chas, you got something good for us today?"

I was a regular in this kitchen by now, usually including a treat for those who feed my friend Samir, when I brought a delicacy to be stored for him. I hadn't brought one this time, assuming that Samir would polish off the caviar in one sitting and I wouldn't be encountering the kitchen staff.

"Sorry, but I was in too much of a hurry this time. All I've got are some anchovies for Samir."

Just as he'd anticipated, they all scrunched up their faces in disdain.

"Nasty stuff," said one.

"Don't put it near my sticky buns," warned another.

I squeezed the box into a corner, making sure the anchovy label showed, and thanked them as I left quickly. The smell of the green beans was about to do me in.

On the way back, a woman in the walker parade looked up and smiled as if she'd just finished the marathon. "Two more laps than yesterday," she boasted, beaming.

"Sounds worth an extra scoop of ice cream, to me," I said, smiling back.

"Oh, no, my dear. Got to watch my girlish figure. And, of course, my cholesterol."

At what age can people stop worrying about the long-term health implications of everything they do?

Samir had clearly thought. And thought clearly.

When I returned to his room, he was sitting back in his chair with his hands folded over his belly, looking like a cross between Buddha and the Cheshire Cat.

"Nothing like a little caviar to sharpen the mind," he said by way of greeting.

"Or anchovies, as the case may be. You look as if you've come up with some solutions for me."

"Not answers, my dear, but questions. Paths for you to travel. This is a problem you will ultimately solve on your own, and it will take some time. The way I can be useful is to assist you in getting started."

"I'm listening." I pulled out my reporter's notebook. That's how I listen best.

"First, let us speak of matters of the heart, so we can clear the mind for action." Samir is an old softie; I should have expected this.

"My heart or yours?"

"I have no heart any longer, you know that. I wore it out long ago."

I gave him a wry smile. He likes to think of himself as all hardened steel, or at least he likes others to think of him that way. Except when it's useful for him to be viewed as a befuddled old teddy bear. Or when he wants some younger woman to believe she has the key for opening the steel doors to his sweetly melting core. Complicated man, that's Samir, at least in his well-aged state.

He went on to lecture me about Dave. "You must not expect a woman and a man to see the world through the same lens, no matter how much they love each other. Every self has different interests, and we must be true to our own self-interests if we are to maintain our separate integrities."

"That makes sense. Up to a point."

"Dave would not hurt you, nor would he let you be hurt, at least not any more than you can handle yourself."

"True."

"And this Ringo, you are strong enough to handle him yourself. You don't need Dave to protect you, nor to agree with you."

"But how can Dave be so often accepting, even supportive of such an evil man?"

"That's not the point. The point is that Dave is what you call an investigative reporter. Thus he must be supportive of the role of investigative reporters, the bad ones as well as the good ones. He must allow them to fail as well as achieve. He must be unswervingly in favor of their freedom to act in their jobs. Just as a spy might not like another spy's methods or even loathe another spy personally. But he must always support his opponent's role as a spy."

Now we were getting into Samir's home territory. He must have felt very strongly about getting this message across to me if he invoked the world of spies to capture my attention. I was touched that he would raise his vulnerability, dig into the realm of his secrets in order to convince me.

"You must not take Dave's inconsistent reaction to Ringo personally. It is not a matter of Dave versus you. It is Dave taking the side of the job of reporting, even when it is muddied and tarnished. At some point he may be able to separate his interests from this other reporter's, but he must come to that on his own, not because you demanded it of him. We all must seek our own cures for problems that entangle our emotions; we cannot have them forced upon us. It does not work for very long to borrow somebody else's feelings."

"I'll work on that." I wasn't sure I could buy what Samir was selling, but I intended to give it a try.

"And now I will stop talking of matters about which I know nothing—the workings of the human heart—and will address the problems with which you flattered me by asking for my assistance."

"I consider you an expert on everything."

Samir actually blushed and uttered a small "hmmph" as he settled in for a strategy session.

"The usual weapons of war won't do you any good in this case. Guns, knives, poisons—you're not in that kind of battle. But make no mistake, this man is waging war, and you need to be armed. What you need is the most subtle and powerful ammunition: information. You must get to know this Mr. Laurenge better than he wants anyone to know him. Know his secrets, his vulnerabilities, the details that could be dangerous to him. Leverage, that's your weapon. And you're a journalist; you're trained for this kind of campaign."

I wasn't writing down what Samir was telling me, I was furiously jotting down the ideas that he was sparking: previous colleagues, former landlord, family, school friends, ex-girlfriends, rivals. Possible sources were ricocheting around my head as if Samir had lit a Roman candle.

"I think I know where to start," I blurted, as pieces of widely spaced conversations clicked into place. "I can't be obvious about this, at least not yet. So I'm going to begin in Florida."

"That sounds like an appropriate place to look for secrets, especially if this autumn continues to be chilly. As for the more immediate problem, quenching the fire he has started to incinerate your friends' restaurant—"

"Not exactly my friends—" I'm sensitive about being seen as the promoter of restaurants I admire.

"I understand. Forgive my clumsy manner of expressing myself. English is not my first language, as you know, and sometimes I slip a little."

"Oh, no, I apologize. Please. I'm afraid I get defensive about being seen as too cozy with restaurateurs."

"We are both apologizers. I like that in you, it is a graceful and effective tool. I only wish I could have met you when we were both much younger and I could have taken part in your early training. My dear, what I could have taught you!"

I'm not sure I would have wanted to learn all of

what Samir could have taught me. I adore him now, when his iron core is slightly rusted and his edges have dulled, when his weapons are only intellectual ones.

"Samir, I am happy to know you now, in your golden age. Even in these two short years, I've learned more from you than from any teacher I've ever had."

"You flatter me, my dear. I love to be flattered." His puffy cheeks dimpled for a moment, then clenched again into their serious mode. "But we must return to business. This restaurant that you feel has been mistreated by your newspaper because of Mr. Laurenge, it, too, must fight with a campaign of information."

This time I took notes. Samir dictated a series of issues for Kirk and Ben to address and suggested how they address them. Some of it I'd already figured out, and I'm sure they had, too. But Samir has a way of organizing a battle plan that is both elegant and simple, covers all bases, and illuminates the underlying logic. He recites strategies like poetry.

"There is one more thing you must do," Samir concluded.

"Bring champagne for us to celebrate the eventual victory?"

"I will provide the champagne. No, my sweet, there is one more victim of this troublesome colleague, for whom you must develop a plan."

"Sherele."

"Yes, Sherele. She is a strong woman, but powerful winds have been testing her resilience. First the theater and now this Ringo."

I'd told Samir only about Ringo's professional attacks on Sherele, not the sexual one, but he seemed to guess there was more.

He was adamant. "It is imperative that you break the spell with which he is poisoning her, and do it before she musters the desperate strength to destroy him or herself."

"I've been struggling with that."

"Remove her from the scene. R and R, I believe, armies in your country call it. Create some distance between her and her nemesis and give her an opportunity to heal in peace."

"It had crossed my mind." I closed my notebook and sat back, watching Samir, who in a mere hour or so had swept all my problems into one tidy pile and wrapped them in a neat disposable package. Just watching his mind click away helped me to organize my thoughts and strengthen my resolve. "I'm going to take her to Florida with me."

"It's not the Mediterranean," he said, his dimples returning and his eyes softening in memory of Lebanese beaches, "but I hear it is an agreeable vacationland in its own way."

I left Samir daydreaming of bathing beauties circa 1950.

16

My first project was to persuade Bull that he wanted me to go to Disney World. As I expected, it wasn't hard. I started with the most salient facts: how little it would cost. Airfares were down, and while the theme park was an expensive vacation for the average family, I anticipated that Bull would cue the travel department to discreetly accept any special reductions and free tickets offered to journalists. Once Bull was convinced the trip wouldn't cost him a lot, I figured he'd be ready to see Disney World as just the kind of Joe six-pack story that he believed sold papers.

"I'll think about it, Wheatley."

That meant yes, but he didn't want to appear to cave in to a mere reporter.

"I'll think about it, too," I said on my way out. If

I acted as if I wanted this trip too much, Bull would be wary.

My friends were harder to convince.

"I can't imagine why you'd want to go to Disney World," Sherele said.

Dave nodded in agreement. "I know, everyone says the food is bad and overpriced."

"I'm told it's a good idea to take your own lunch," Sherele added.

"Probably so," I agreed. "No matter. I'm not going because I think the food will be good, but because it is the most American of eating places. I want to look at it as one enormous restaurant that serves everything Americans think of as food. Every kind of white-tablecloth food, every fast food, every family-dining sort of food, a world of cuisines Americanized for the tourist—I have the feeling that if I look at it closely and carefully, I'll learn something new about how we Americans think about our food." I'd been working hard on that speech, and I hoped it didn't sound canned.

"I'm not sure—"

"I'm not sure either, and that's the point. I want to approach it with a fresh mind, to see beyond the clichés. To see what it says about us and the way we live."

"Biting off a big chunk, aren't you?"

"Yes, but I don't have much to lose. I can always just fall back on the usual making fun of the Big Bad Walt. After all, since I made Bull think it was his idea, I don't have to prove it worthwhile. I just have to churn out some copy."

Dave hates to hear me aim for anything that's merely ordinary. He's the most demanding colleague I know, as demanding of himself as of me. So I expected him to weigh in at this moment, and he did.

"Chas, even if Bull is ordering you to go— which he's not—there's no point wasting your time if you're only going to write one more cynical piece on the Disney organization. You shouldn't even entertain the possibility that you might settle for that."

Sherele echoed him in her own, gentle way. "I have no doubt that if you go without preconceptions, you'll find a perspective on Disney food that nobody's written up before. It is, after all, an entertainment that speaks to every age group, every kind of vacationer. It probably feeds more people, and more kinds of people than any other single enterprise. I'd be curious to see how they do it. And I'd sure love to try the Tower of Terror."

This was a new Sherele. She'd never been a roller-coaster or amusement-park fan, as long as I'd known her. Once, when we went to Kings Dominion, she'd worn spike heels and a dress that made her the day's main attraction. I don't think she went on a single ride.

"The Tower of Terror? Aren't you the gal who quakes in her high heels at the idea of a Ferris wheel?" Dave had teased her mercilessly after our amusement-park day, and was ready to do so again.

"Ferris wheels are just boring. And I don't like all that jerking around on roller coasters. But the Tower of Terror is the ultimate drama. You've seen its precursor in countless movies: the drop from a cliff or in an elevator shaft. That was even used on *L.A. Law* as a lame way to get rid of an irritating character. But just think: at last, an opportunity to really feel what it would be like to drop thirteen stories. The body's greatest drama in the space of a few seconds."

"It sounds like you should go along with Chas and do a companion piece on theme parks as theater," Dave said, stealing my lines.

This was easier than I'd expected.

"Bull would never pay for it," Sherele said.

"Why not?" Dave expanded his idea, maybe to head off my hoping he'd go along. "It will hardly cost him anything. The airfare's dirt-cheap this time of year, you'd share Chas's hotel room for not a penny more. Even the food would be free, since she'll have to taste far more than she could eat anyway. The biggest expense would be admission to the park, and knowing Bull, I'd bet he's getting that comped anyway."

Sherele had grown more enthusiastic as Dave talked. "I do have a ton of time accumulated. I'll bet he'd be thrilled if I offered to give up some of that in exchange for this trip."

"You've got me convinced." It was as if I'd written Sherele's part. "I'll make the pitch to Bull, as soon as the time looks right."

And I'd tell her about my other agenda, too, as soon as that time was right. Some time when Dave wasn't around to try to dissuade me.

With the first part of my program in place, I turned my attention to Two Views. I didn't feel it was suitable to give Ben and Kirk advice; that's not a journalist's role. Still, I felt the *Examiner* should be undoing the damage it caused. So I fudged. I "interviewed" the two brothers about their response to rumors of food poisoning and asked questions in such a way as to give these clever young businessmen ideas about how they could retrieve their good reputation.

Maybe they didn't need me. They launched a campaign that was thoroughgoing and dazzling, and certainly it got the food world talking. First, they issued press releases that were not merely defenses of themselves, but explanations by the country's most respected doctors and the Centers for Disease Control on patterns of foodborne illnesses. They outlined the possible toxins, their sources, and the incubation periods. They discussed prevention for restaurateurs and diners. They devised a chart that made this complicated subject relatively easy to understand. And they sent it to newspapers nationwide. An epidemic of articles appeared as a result, since the press release offered predigested research to harried reporters, and the brothers had cleverly keyed it to

Thanksgiving, Christmas, and New Year's. Two
Views was garnering publicity as the guru of safe
dining.

Of course the restaurant removed mayonnaise
from the menu, but it didn't make much of that
publicly. Kirk and Ben obviously didn't want to
draw attention to their particular food-poisoning
charge.

"We're eventually going to put it back on the
menu," Kirk told me. "And when we do that,
we're going to give it a lot of hoopla. We're planning to have a saucièr roaming the dining room
and making the mayonnaise to order. Can't get
much fresher—or safer—than that."

"We can't afford to do it yet," warned Ben, his
voice never rising above a gloomy monotone during our interview. "We don't have enough customers to warrant it."

"We've got some other ideas, but we're still discussing them," Kirk chimed in. He sounded more
upbeat, though a little forced. "We're thinking of
announcing that we keep a full-time inspector in
the kitchen, and promoting Two Views as having
the cleanest kitchen in the country."

I had my doubts. So did Ben. "We're afraid it
sounds too defensive, that it could backfire."

"It might not be what you'd most want to be
known for," I agreed.

"We've tried a few discounts and special offers," Kirk said, his voice rising to a question mark
at the end, obviously asking for my opinion.

"That's tricky," I offered. "You don't want to look as if you're having a fire sale. Coming across as defensive can chase away customers. Nobody wants to eat at a hungry restaurant."

"That's what I thought," Ben backed me up, spreading his blanket of gloom ever wider.

"I don't think we're ever going to be the same," Kirk said, sinking into the mire with him. "I am beginning to admit to myself that we probably can't recover." His voice broke.

I couldn't ask any more questions. I feared my voice would break, too. So much for objective journalism.

While Kirk and Ben tried to woo back their public, I brooded over the third problem Samir and I had discussed. I looked to mend my relationship with Dave. He didn't even know it was broken, because on the surface we seemed fine. But I was simmering inside, feeling Dave was downplaying Ringo's destructiveness at the expense of being sympathetic to me and our colleagues. He trusted the process of journalism to set itself right, and didn't take seriously enough the newspaper's disservice to Two Views. The more exercised I was, the more he tuned me out. This was a side to Dave that made me uncomfortable, though I was trying to pretend to myself that it was only a minor problem and that one of us would get over it.

We couldn't discuss it directly yet. Whenever I brought up the subject of Ringo, Dave and I were snarling at each other within minutes. I realized I couldn't expect Dave to hate Ringo just because I asked him to; as Samir had reminded me, he would have to draw his own conclusions about this viper. I couldn't resist, though, constantly bringing up new evidence to hurry along Dave's conversion. I overplayed my hand. Dave flinched every time I mentioned Ringo's name.

At my age, I'd learned that not all problems have to be solved immediately, so I decided to let this one slide awhile. Dave might need time to re-think his position, a chance to change his mind on his own without my driving him to it. I'd have to let him have an opportunity to save face. What I wanted, of course, was for him to hate Ringo. I not only needed company in my loathing, I couldn't bear to think of Dave as insensitive.

I was losing my credibility elsewhere, too, as Ringo became my obsession. Even Helen headed the other way when she saw me coming. I didn't blame her. I was rabid on the subject, and un-doubtedly a raging bore.

Every time I walked into Bull's office, he held up his hand as if to stop me.

"What is it this time, Wheatley?"

That wasn't a very encouraging greeting from a boss, but I was used to him by now. And I knew he was telling me that he didn't want to hear another word about Ringo. Not when sales were up, ads were pouring in, and Ringo had kept the *Examiner* on the tip of everyone's tongue. Ringo was the most successful investment Bull had ever made, and he didn't want me to tell him to sell.

"I've come to inform you that I'm ready to do your bidding."

"You're finally going to review Burger King?"

"No, worse. I'm primed to go to Disney World, as you've wanted me to do."

"As I've wanted you to do? Hah! But I agree that at last you've shown some taste. I'll let you go, as long as you don't expect to hit me up for another trip before the end of the fiscal year."

"I've got one condition, though."

"Somehow, Wheatley, I thought I was the boss, and I was the one to make the conditions."

"I need the practice, just in case I ever get to be a boss. Besides, I think this is a condition you would have made if you'd thought of it first."

"Go ahead. I'm always curious when people purport to know how I think."

"I want to take Sherele along."

He didn't explode or throw me out of the office or even laugh at the idea. In fact, he listened patiently while I explained how Sherele and I could collaborate on an essay about food and theater. I explained that it would cost him very little, since we'd share a room and the food I'd already need to try.

He asked a few questions, but neither of us mentioned the real reason for my taking Sherele: the possibility that a change of scene might rein-

vigorate her. Worried that he needed more con-
vincing, I started to introduce the subject of
Sherele's pressures, but he cut me off.

"Are you trying to talk me into this or out of it?
Don't waste my time with therapeutic mumbo
jumbo. Just get going, Wheatley, and book you
and Sherele on a plane before I change my
mind."

"Thanks, Bull. I appreciate—"

"Make sure you get a cheap flight, or the
deal's off."

By the day of our trip, Sherele had regained
more of her old vitality than I'd seen since Ringo
had attacked her. She showed up at my loft in a
tropical flouncy pantsuit under her cashmere
cape, and she was wearing more makeup than I'd
seen on her in weeks, which meant just enough to
remind one how beautiful she was.

I, on the other hand, was in my bathrobe, my
bags only half packed. I'd been hunkered down in
front of the television, watching reports of Hurricane Floyd heading for Cape Kennedy—and Disney World.

"I tried to call you, but you'd already left," I
told Sherele when she started chewing me out for
not being ready. "They've canceled our flight. Disney World's closed."

Sherele's apathy was last week's diagnosis. This
week she had rejoined the world, and now she
was furious that it wasn't ready to welcome her.

"They can't do that. Disney World doesn't

close. What kind of fucking cowards are they, hiding out in the face of a little storm a hundred miles offshore? The whole world's gone soft."

I let her rant for a while, glad to see some reaction from Sherele, even if it was negative.

When she ran out of steam, I was ready with the good news. "It's not as if we had to be there at a particular time. The airline will make good on our reservation as soon as the planes fly again, and I've already talked to the Disney press office. They'll reschedule our reservations at a moment's notice. As for us, I think we should consider this an enforced vacation and take the day off. Let's go to lunch."

"That's no vacation for you. I have a better idea. Let's go shopping."

That's not usually my idea of recreation, but since Sherele is the world's best personal shopper, it sounded good to me. She knew exactly what was on sale at Nordstrom's, and ushered me to the Metro heading toward Pentagon City.

By the end of the afternoon, I had a flouncy tropical pantsuit, too, and a pair of sunglasses that made the pantsuit seem a bargain. We stopped for a late-afternoon drink at the Ritz-Carlton, so we could slip off our shoes and regain some strength before tackling the return Metro at rush hour.

It's impossible to be seated in a bar with Sherele and spend five minutes uninterrupted. Men from miles away, it seems, immediately come buzzing around her. The first two brought garment bags with them.

"We couldn't leave without paying our respects to the prettiest women north of Dade County," said the sandy-haired one, politely including me in the compliment, though his eyes were solely on Sherele.

"Compliment registered," Sherele said, turning her back on him.

I was intrigued, though. "You're leaving for Florida?"

The rejected man turned to me, ready to accept second-best. "Taking off in two hours. Want to come along? You've got time to pack." He tried to leer, but wasn't very practiced at it.

"I was just surprised that you've got a flight. Aren't Florida airports closed?"

He looked nicer when he reverted to normal conversation. "They were earlier today. In fact, we were supposed to leave this morning. But Floyd was a dud. Didn't ruffle a hair on South Beach. All systems are go, again."

His friend joined in once the talk went beyond pickup lines. "Fortunately we called as soon as the airports reopened. Got the last seats to Florida today."

Sherele and I looked at each other and stood up in unison. She slapped some bills on the table for our drinks, and we wished our informants a good trip as we fled the bar.

Five minutes later we had seats on a flight for Orlando early tomorrow morning, though not without a few ominous threats about calling vice presidents and general counsels.

Sherele went home, eager for a shower and a quiet evening when nobody knew she was in town. Ordinarily I'd have craved the same, but I have a perverse mind: now that I had no restaurant I needed to visit, and both Dave and Lily were otherwise occupied, I didn't feel like being alone. I decided to hang out at the office, spending a little time organizing for the frantic week when I returned from Orlando.

By the time I dropped off my purchases and repacked, I was hungry and I had no food in the house. I took a detour through Chinatown and picked up a grilled lemongrass chicken from a Vietnamese carryout on Sixth Street to eat at my desk. By then, it was eight o'clock, and the newsroom would be nearly empty, so I could eat it without everyone coming to check what the restaurant critic eats on her night off.

Even Helen had left. I'd belatedly thought to report to her that our departure had been postponed. In her absence, I figured I should inform Bull, especially now that it was too late for him to expect any work from us this day.

Bull's secretary was gone, so I just walked right in. The first thing I saw were shoes. Bull was behind his desk, talking to a pair of shoes. When the scene fell into place, I realized Bull was deep in conversation with Ringo. And Ringo had dared to prop his feet up on Bull's desk.

Bull's jaw dropped when he saw me. It's a big jaw, hard to miss. It appeared to me that he was throwing Ringo a warning glance, but Ringo was so focused on himself that he missed such subtlety. He went on speaking, not realizing someone was approaching from behind.

"First I'll do the Kennedy Center, then Arena Stage. I'll save the Broadway theaters for December, when Washingtonians are likely to be traveling to New York."

"Chas, what are you doing here? How come you're not in Orlando?"

I decided to ask questions before I answered any. "What's this about the Kennedy Center and Broadway? Is Ringo now writing about the theater as well as restaurants? Maybe it would be more cost-effective to ship off the rest of us to the mailroom and classified advertising, and keep a reporting staff of one."

Ringo swung his feet off Bull's desk and turned in his chair to face me. "You're letting your insecurities show, Chas," he said. I could see two smudges on Bull's polished mahogany desk from Ringo's heels. "You don't have to do it all, just do it better."

Bull decided to ignore the whole exchange and return to his original question. "What happened with Orlando?"

"Hurricane Floyd. We're going tomorrow. That is, unless Sherele needs to stay behind to protect her desk from Ringo's muddy shoes."

That didn't faze Ringo. He just reached over to stuff his mouth with one of Bull's madeleines. Bull had turned madeleines into a passion lately, baking them himself and inventing new flavors such as marzipan and tangerine. The plate was only half full. Ringo must have been there awhile.

"Chas, this is a big enough newsroom for everyone. Ringo's approach to the theater is going to be very different from Sherele's, just as what he's done on restaurants is from a perspective other than yours. As talented as you and Sherele are, neither of you has to worry about competition."

For Bull, that was an extraordinarily generous admission. He generally considered compliments dangerous, and kept them safely locked away. Much as I worried that Ringo was going to chew wormholes into Sherele's job—and mine—I had to recognize that Bull was throwing support our way, and doing it in front of Ringo. It wasn't as good as if he'd squelch Ringo, but it was a first step.

I was still furious, of course. And hungry. So I decided to give in to the latter and feed Bull's ego a bit. I reached for the madeleines.

"They're anise," Bull said.

I hate anise. The hell with encouraging Bull the Gourmet.

I walked away from the plate, saying, "I'm about to have dinner, so I shouldn't spoil my appetite any more than Ringo's already done." I pulled a tissue from my pocket and made an elaborate show of wiping away the scuff marks Ringo had left on Bull's desk before I strode out the door.

I no longer felt like working, so I decided to have dinner with Dave. Over the phone. I opened my Styrofoam box of chicken and rice noodles, and dialed Dave's cell phone.

"Chas, where are you? Did you catch any of the hurricane?"

Knowing Dave, he'd be disappointed not to get a chance to face down 150-mph winds. To him, an earthquake or a tornado was an adventure. He probably dreamed of tidal waves.

"The closest I got to high winds was a couple of guys cruising for chicks at the Pentagon City Ritz-Carlton. Our plane was canceled, so Sherele and I went shopping. I hear the hurricane was a dud, though." I twirled my fork in the rice noodles, angling to spear a piece of chicken and some bits of fried shallots as well.

"Too bad. But I guess Disney World will be fun even with all the rides and towers intact. I heard they actually closed the park. First time ever. Sounds like a good story there."

My first bite awoke a ferocious appetite, so I forked in another mouthful and talked around it. "Looks like Sherele and I are going to need every good story we can get."

"What's got your dander up?"

I told him about encountering Ringo planning a

series on theaters and Bull letting him do it without so much as a warning to Sherele. I punctuated my angry report with bites of the lemon-grass-perfumed chicken and noodles.

"I wouldn't tell Sherele just yet," Dave said. "It would be a shame to ruin her trip."

The force of my hunger had subsided, but that wasn't all that made me feel better. Dave was acknowledging that Ringo was once again doing damage, that at least Sherele needed to be protected from him. I reveled in having him on my side.

"I feel awful about it," I said, more in sorrow than in anger. "She's so vulnerable these days."

"It's time Bull trimmed Ringo's sails. The guy has enough territory that he doesn't need to poach on Sherele's. Somebody's got to talk some sense into our stubborn-headed editor."

At last Dave was firing up and preaching what I'd been trying to tell him. For a wicked instant I was tempted to gloat, or at least goad. But the better part of me realized I should play it cool and let him take the lead. "You know newsroom politics better than I."

"I'm going to talk to Bull about it when I get back."

"You're the one reporter he listens to."

"Other than Ringo."

Was even Dave beginning to feel threatened?

17

✕

The only damage I could see in Disney World was the damage to the bottom line. The winds—and the park's unprecedented closing—had chased away enough visitors that attendance was at an all-time low. Epcot, the Magic Kingdom, MGM, the new Animal Kingdom, they were merely busy, not jam-packed. We found hardly a line at the Tower of Terror. We could walk right into Epcot's Test Track. As for the Magic Kingdom's afternoon parade, we could stroll alongside Cinderella and watch the dwarves cavort from inches away. Breakfast with Snow White was going begging; instead of having to reserve sixty days ahead, visitors found themselves being nagged to buy last-minute tickets.

The whole fantasy world sparkled. The air was fresh and warm rather than hot and muggy. It smelled green. I felt like a ten-year-old on a school holiday.

Sherele and I spent the first afternoon getting the lay of the land, finding our way around, noting the written and unwritten rules. Just as I'd expected, the crowd was a full sampling of Middle America.

"You can see it in the hats," Sherele observed. Baseball caps, facing front and back. Golf caps. Straw boaters. Hats for farmers, for sailors, for little girls on their way to a tea party. Sweat bands and sunshades. Families of five, all wearing identical headgear as well as matching shirts and shorts. And, of course, the hats that were nothing but Mickey Mouse ears.

Sherele was into the costumes—of visitors as well as staff—not to mention the stage sets and the music. Everywhere and always there was music.

She began to keep tabs on the props. The rolling props—strollers and wheelchairs. The theme props—the magic wands and stuffed animals. And the recording-for-posterity props—cameras, both still and video, enough to supply every Hollywood studio for years to come. Walking in a theme park, we discovered, is accompanied by constant danger: being run over by a stroller, being poked by a wand, being barricaded from the path by a wife whose husband is in the middle of filming the kids.

While the theatrical elements were even more lush than we'd anticipated, food was strangely underplayed. There were plenty of restaurants, and snack stands galore. More than five hundred altogether. But we saw hardly anybody eating. In fact, I'd never seen so many Americans in a public place without food in their hands.

I ate, of course. I started with popcorn; it was hot and crisp, too salty, but that was probably intentional, to encourage people to buy drinks. I went on to celebrate being in Florida with an orange; I considered it refreshing to find fruit stands in such a manufactured setting. For old times' sake I tried a Rice Krispies square, though I passed up, with regret, marshmallows dipped in chocolate and covered with colored sprinkles. The smoked turkey legs, a kind of Fred Flintstone snack, looked tempting, but they were large enough to feed a family, and Sherele was unwilling to commit herself to anything more than bottled water before the indulgent dinner she knew we'd be having.

With my very first snack, the popcorn, I solved the mystery of why almost nobody else was eating. As I carried my box to the entrance of "Honey, I Shrunk the Audience," I heard the litany I'd hear over and over until it tattooed itself on my brain: "No smoking, no eating, no drinking, and no flash photography."

Americans may be the world's most voracious snackers, but when it comes to a choice of eating or getting the most value from a $45-ticket to adventures, rides, and 3-D films, nobody's going to waste time on a cheeseburger. In their limited thrill-seeking hours at Disney World, people eat only when they have to, usually scarfing something down quickly, lest they reduce their chances for experiencing every attraction. For once, in this snack-crazed country, food comes second.

Not that Disney World visitors don't eat. After all, the place serves fifty thousand breakfasts alone, every day.

"We're the largest on-site food operation in the world," the press officer told us, thereby justifying my visit. In Disneyese, that means eighty billion "food encounters" a year. It also means fifty-five thousand employees—in corporate lingo, "cast members."

I hadn't anticipated that. I began to worry whether the plan I'd hatched with Samir was going to work, and wished I hadn't been so adamant about the element of surprise.

"How would you go about finding a particular cast member?" I asked the press officer. "Is it possible with just the first name and hometown?" Every cast member wears a small oval badge with that information on it, and that much I had.

"You need a last name," the Disney flack said.

"Try Laurenge. L-A-U-R-E-N-G-E. At the Chefs de France."

I'd checked that no woman like George had ever worked for Paul Bocuse in France, and when I put together Ringo's boasting of her working for Bocuse with his later telling us that she and his mother had stayed with Disney, I figured George had to be at the Chefs de France restaurant, which Bocuse ran with Roger Vergé and Gastôn LeNôtre.

"Nope, nobody by that name," the press officer looked up from his computer screen.

"Maybe she's moved to another restaurant. Could you check the whole theme park?"

"I already did. No Laurenge."

"The first name's George and it's a woman," I pushed further. "There can't be more than one woman named George."

"Doesn't give gender," he answered tersely, stroking his computer as if it were a pet I'd just insulted.

While the press officer answered his phone, Sherele conferred with me.

"She could be married."

"No, when Ringo poured out his life story, he told us that none of his siblings had married," I answered, thinking hard about a possible next step. Then, feeling that somehow Samir had prompted me, I had an idea. "Maybe she goes by her mother's maiden name. If they left the father or he dropped out of their lives, that would be pretty likely."

"Not that we know her maiden name."

Sherele was right. I'd been too cocky; I should have done more homework. I'd have to do it now.

When the press officer turned back to us, I thanked him profusely for the help and asked, "You don't mind if we come back once we have more information, do you?" I was suddenly so eager to leave that I stood up and dropped my notebook from my lap.

"Y'all come back any time. Have a good day," he said as we departed in a rush of retrieving our paraphernalia.

I was off like a Test-Track car. Sherele had to jog to keep pace.

"Where are we heading?"

"I want to find out Ringo's mother's maiden name, obviously. Before the press office closes."

"How?"

"I'm not sure yet."

"Aren't you going to ask Dave? He knows how to go about such things. Probably in Ringo's personnel file."

"Dave won't do that."

"For you?"

"Okay, I don't mean that he won't do that. But he won't think it's a good idea."

"And you're sure you do?"

That slowed me down. I took a much-needed deep breath, then I answered her. "Actually, I do think it's a good idea. What's not a good idea is to ask Dave to help us. He worries that we think too much about Ringo. He'll give us too many reasons why we should drop the subject."

"Who, then?"

"Homer."

"Not on your life."

We were stumped. And sweaty. The cool, fresh

after-storm air had been replaced by the more everyday Florida steam bath.

"I think better on orange juice."

Fortunately, a bench and a refreshment stand were nearby. Of course, everywhere you look in Disney World, there's a bench and a refreshment stand nearby. The fortunate part was that today there were empty benches.

Sherele left me holding the space and rounded up the snacks, the highlight of which were Mickey Mouse ice cream bars. She was really getting with the program.

Two ears into my ice cream, I had an inspiration.

"Vince. He has no scruples when it comes to Ringo."

"You're right!" Sherele eats faster than I do, and she was already licking the last of the chocolate from her fingers. "He enjoys snooping, and he's good at it."

"Besides, he's proud of being one of the first at the *Examiner* to hate Ringo. He loves to remind me, and this will give him one more chance."

We called Vince from a pay phone and stood by as he got back to us within an hour, bragging about his success. Sherele and I were sharing a tray of sushi—the biggest threat to the hamburger since Americans discovered pizza. Our sample wasn't bad for Central Florida sushi, and there's no more refreshing protein source.

"This is valuable information," Vince warned us before he spilled it.

"We know, and we thank you."

"No, I mean it. It's like a password. Next to a Social Security number, the mother's maiden name
is the most common identifier for accessing private information. Bank balances, credit card trans-
actions, all the personal financial matters. You've
got to be cautious about keeping this secure."

"So how did you get it?"

"There are no secrets in the financial world, not
if you really know your way around."

"You mean you looked in his personnel file,
right?"

"Naw, that's not my modus operandi. Takes too
much energy. I got one of the personnel gals to
look in his file. Told her I had a bet."

"Mr. Superspy."

"Why bother to pick a lock when you can just
turn the handle?"

"Wertzky," I reported to Sherele.

"Wertzky? That's worse than Laurenge."
Sherele looked discouraged. "Nobody's going to
change her name from Laurenge to Wertzky, even
if she hates her father."

"When a girl's first name is George, how can
any last name look bad? We might as well try it.
We're no worse off than before. At least there
aren't going to be a lot of other Wertzkys to throw
us off track."

We got back to the press office just under the
wire.

"Just about to close up here," the press guy

murmured after welcoming us with his regulation Disney smile.

"I'm sure this won't take long," I said as I walked over to his computer and stood firm. "Would you mind seeing if you have a George Wertzky among your cast?"

He tapped a few keys, peered closely at his screen, then tapped a few more.

"Nope."

Sherele and I looked at each other, drooping in unison.

"Are you sure?" Sherele prompted. "W-E-R-T-Z-K-Y."

"Oh, I know how to spell it," he said, turning to us and shrugging. "I just don't have a George."

"You mean you have a Wertzky?"

"Yep, but not the one you want. A Lucinda."

Sherele had an inspiration. "Where's she from?"

"Anaheim."

There couldn't be two women named Wertzky from Anaheim. Maybe George changed her first name, after all.

"We'll take her."

Lucinda Wertzky, the woman I'd been seeking as George Laurenge, was indeed working at a restaurant, albeit American rather than French.

We managed to get to MGM's Hollywood Brown Derby before the evening rush, and found Lucinda from Anaheim behind a potted palm, folding napkins.

"How y'all?" she asked with a big smile on her glossy lips. Fire and Ice, I guessed, that piercingly red Revlon favorite from the 50s. "What can I do for you?"

"I'm Chas, and this is my friend Sherele." This is a first-name kind of place, I'd learned by now.

"Sherele? Mighty pretty name you have. But I don't believe I've ever come across a Chas before."

"Charlotte Sue, when I want to be formal. It's a nickname my daddy gave me." I, too, was picking up the Disney drawl.

"Sorta cute."

"Some people think it's a man's name." I hadn't yet worked out how to broach my question. This might give me an opener.

"I guess you could say that."

"But I figure plenty of women have men's names, and they get through life all right." I was babbling, and Sherele was treating me to a look that questioned my sanity.

Sherele was too impatient to listen to me wander around looking for an opening. She jumped right in.

"In fact, we're looking for a woman with a man's name, and we were hoping you'd know her. We think her last name is the same as yours. Wertzky. George Wertzky."

"Nope."

Sherele and I deflated. Her shoulders slumped, my smile froze.

Lucinda peered at us both for a moment, pursing her vivid dewy mouth. "Her name's not Wertzky, it's Sand. She got married. For a little while, anyway. I think she picked him for his name. She's a literary type."

"George Sand! That's great!" Sherele practically quivered with delight.

I was still concentrating on the practicalities. "You mean she used to be Wertzky? Related to you?"

"Not Wertzky. That's my maiden name. George got my married name. Laurenge. Didn't have much of a ring to it, did it?"

"So she is related."

"About as related as anybody could be."

"You're Ringo's mother, aren't you?"

That name stopped Lucinda short. Her blush-pink cheeks turned nearly as red as her lipstick. She opened her mouth, then closed it again. Her eyes turned wary as she shifted them from Sherele to me and back again.

"Used to be." She stopped again, and when we, too, kept silent, she shook her head. "Lord, I haven't heard that name in a long time." Another pause. "You know my Ringo?"

"We work with him. In Washington."

"And he told you where to find me here? I thought that boy didn't even know where I was and couldn't care less." Her eyes were glistening. She looked around to see if anyone from the Brown Derby cast was watching, and slipped into a banquette. Sherele and I realized she was worried about getting in trouble, so we stood shielding her from view.

I didn't want to disappoint her by admitting that Ringo hadn't steered us to her, so I skirted the subject. "We were down here for work, so we thought it would be nice to look up you and George. She works here, too, right?"

"Oh, yes, George has been here even longer than I have. She got bored with restaurants, and now she's over there at the new Animal Kingdom. Always loved animals. Drives one of those Jeep things at the Kilimanjaro Safari. She got me this job here."

The tables were beginning to fill up, and white-jacketed waiters were roaming the dining room. Lucinda was fidgeting, looking increasingly nervous.

"We don't want to take up more of your time while you're working," I said, "but we'd love to get together with you and George after work, if we could."

"I'll have to call her and see what her schedule is. How do we get in touch with you?"

"For the time being, you could get in touch with us right here. I've been wanting to try one of the Brown Derby's Cobb salads."

I could see why starstruck Lucinda Wertzky Laurenge would like working at the Brown Derby. It's a dip into 1930s Hollywood, with its curved booths and caricatures of filmdom's famous on the mahogany and teak walls. The derby-shaped lamps are a little hokey, but who's going to complain about hokey at Disney World? And the food here is a safe bet if you stick with the classics. What could be bad about an immense plate of salad striped with diced turkey, bacon, chopped egg, tomato, blue cheese, and avocado? Toss it all together with the greens and the vinaigrette, and you'll understand what's kept this combination popular for seventy years. Of course, Disney, which can't leave well enough alone, offers a shrimp variation, but anybody who'd choose watery frozen baby shrimp over turkey deserves what he gets.

By the time we'd finished our grapefruit cake—another Brown Derby signature—Lucinda stopped by our table, bringing a fresh napkin as if she'd been bidden to provide a replacement, and invited us to come by her house for a drink after the park closed. She slipped us a map, meticulously labeled with every street we'd pass on the way, and enclosed her phone number in a slightly lopsided heart.

Investigating files and paperwork is a lot easier than probing people face to face, I had to admit, as several hours later our taxi raced along the long shopping strip that's Orlando. I'd been growing nervous about our subterfuge as our encounter with Lucinda and George grew closer.

"Remind me why we're doing this?"

Sherele didn't answer. Finding Ringo's family had, after all, been my idea.

"It's probably pretty sick that I'm still so obsessed with Ringo." I pressed the one-way conversation, reluctant to let her silence continue. "It's natural to be curious, of course. But do you think we're taking this too far? To badger that nice, innocent woman and her daughter?"

A grunt. Progress.

"Actually, now I'm more curious about his mother than about Ringo," I burbled further. "She's so frozen in the fifties. She's almost a time machine. And I am sort of fascinated by the world behind Disney World." That was a stretch.

"Hmmm." Sherele made her first contribution.

I grabbed it, hoping to draw it out. "Weak as they may be, there are some slight reasons I'm wasting a Disney World evening on this little project. Slight, definitely slight. We'll probably get something for our story, don't you think?"

That got a reply.

"Nope. Maybe something better, though."

Our taxi pulled up to the house before I had a chance to draw Sherele out further. I could at best take comfort in the fact that she'd begun to join the conversation.

At first glance, you might have taken George for the mother and Lucinda for the daughter. George's hair had begun to show gray, mostly in tendrils escaping from the tightly pulled-back ponytail twisted into a knot. And she had no trace of makeup. She looked well-worn.

The initial impression of Lucinda, on the other

hand, was that she looked shiny and new. It was only after a moment's examination that her fine web of wrinkles and the loosening skin on hands and arms became visible. Time's imprint was carefully wrapped in Lucinda's makeup and hair dye.

Inside their flat, unadorned box of a tract house, time had stopped around 1969. As I looked about, I wondered whether they knew what a gold mine of collectibles they'd preserved. Lucinda was carrying a bowl of Fritos and another of potato chips when she met us at the screen door, George lagging behind. The chips bowl had a smaller one clipped to the edge, filled with a beige cream, its sweet-sharp smell unmistakable. Lipton's Onion Soup dip.

"Excuse the mess. You know what it's like, being working girls. We just never get around to vacuuming during the week," Lucinda chattered as she ushered us to a sofa constructed of a long foam pad and two wedge-shaped bolsters. She placed the refreshments on a kidney-shaped wood-grain Formica table. A fat red-leatherette photo album took up the rest of the table.

George, in the meantime, said little beyond a perfunctory greeting, and edged backward. She leaned against the kitchen door as she looked us over. It was the farthest she could be from us without actually leaving the room.

"George, honey, why don't you get these gals something to drink?"

"Sure, Mom." George roused herself to stand

up straight. "What can I get you? Coffee? Tea? Orange juice?"

"Oh, Georgie, you know I'd planned something special."

George's eyes shifted away in a quick guilty squint, then returned to us. "I'm sorry. I wasn't thinking. How about a piña colada? My mom's are the best in Florida."

I hadn't had a piña colada since about 1970, and not because they weren't readily available. I caught Sherele's eye. It clearly wasn't one of her favorite drinks either.

We answered in unison. "I'd love one. I haven't had one in years."

George nodded and turned to the kitchen.

"The mix is already in the blender, sweetie," her mother directed. "Just add the pitcher of ice and keep the motor on for a full minute."

Lucinda hiked up her aqua pedal pushers and settled herself in the canvas butterfly chair next to the sofa, where Sherele and I were perched with our backs straight and our knees together as if we were job applicants. Lucinda passed us the bowl of chips, even though we could easily reach them on the table. We each took one and dipped it into the sour-cream mixture. All three of us nodded and smiled to one another. With the blender going, we couldn't talk.

When the whirring stopped, the evening really began. We thawed, at least a little.

"I have so many questions, I just don't know

where to start," Lucinda stammered. "I brought out the family album, so you could see Ringo as he used to be."

I'd need a couple of piña coladas before I'd be ready to face that.

George appeared at the kitchen door with a tray carrying four tall frosted glasses, each with a straw, a maraschino cherry, and a paper parasol. After she doled out the frothy drinks, George pulled a second butterfly chair to the other end of the sofa, so that we'd have to choose whether to look at her or her mother. Since her mother was the master of ceremonies, this assured George a minimum of observation.

"Is he married?"

Lucinda's question threw me off guard.

"Who?"

"My son."

Sherele and I looked at each other in dismay. Ringo's mother didn't even know whether he was married or not. Suddenly I wanted to offer our generous hostess some reward for her trouble.

"No, he's not married, not yet. But a good-looking guy like Ringo isn't likely to stay unattached too long."

Sherele's eyebrows shot up a good half-inch. Her eyes were telling me she thought I was possessed. Lucinda raised the glossy red corners of her mouth in a proud half-smile. I didn't turn to see George's reaction.

"You said he works with you in Washington,

D.C. A newspaper, isn't it? Just like he did in California. Is he doing a good job?"

"He's one of the most popular writers we have. Does a lot of TV, too." I thought that would please her, given that a quarter of the living room was taken up by a massive ancient console television set. Probably worth all these other mid-twentieth-century prizes combined.

"We don't get to watch TV much. It would be interesting to see him. Maybe you could send us a postcard sometime if you know he's going to be on it."

"Sure. How long's it been since you've heard from Ringo?"

Lucinda and I were carrying the conversation, stilted as it was. I realized Sherele and George were eyeing each other steadily.

"Ringo's never been much of a telephone-talker."

Lucinda couldn't have meant the same Ringo I knew.

"And he doesn't like to travel much." The Ringo in Lucinda's mind, I realized, fit her experience of him at somewhere around age fifteen.

"What my mother means," George chimed in for the first time, echoing my thoughts, "is that she hasn't heard from him since he left home. Almost a couple of decades ago."

"Now, George."

"Now, George, what?"

"I expect he's been busy," Lucinda said in a

whispery fading voice, a kind of mouse squeak that caught in a tiny sob at the end.

George's expression changed to reflect her mother's, the skin around her eyes suddenly puffing as if damming an onslaught of tears. She took a deep breath and changed the subject.

"What do you do on the paper?"

"I'm the restaurant critic, and Sherele's the theater critic."

"Those are important jobs."

"It doesn't surprise me that Ringo would have such important friends. And would send them to see us." Lucinda wasn't going to let the subject get changed.

George tried again to divert her. She picked up the photo album and leafed through it to a page in the middle. "Mom has some pictures of old Hollywood theaters in here. They're movie theaters, but you might find them interesting."

Sherele reached for the album, and the page was lost in the exchange. She flipped through in search of the theaters, but stopped and stared. There was a tiny Ringo, probably about seven years old but simply a miniature version of the grown-up man, holding a kitten high off the ground—by its tail.

Once again, Sherele and I were exchanging messages with our eyes. What kind of a kid tortured a cat so proudly? And what kind of a mother photographed such a moment and featured it in the family album?

George intercepted our glances. "That's our Ringo," she said, every word etched in acid.

"He had a lot of pets," Lucinda said, oblivious to George's tone and the photo's horror.

George was on a roll. "Oh, indeed, he had a lot of pets. None of them lasted very long. There was the puppy that drowned in the bathtub, and the parakeet with its neck broken, and the dog that somehow got garroted by the garden's wire fence."

"He did have a run of bad luck, that boy," Lucinda commented lamely.

"It was hard to attribute it to bad luck, once we got those two tabby cats."

Sherele was leaning forward, her body language urging George on. "What happened to the cats?"

"By then he was in his Josef Mengele stage. Openly conducting medical experiments. Observing death with the eye of a junior scientist."

"George, you were always hard on your brother."

George didn't pause. Sherele had made it clear she was an eager audience.

"It was also his early cooking phase, so he conducted his experiments in the kitchen. He tried mixing chili peppers in their food. He starved one of the cats first, so that cat ate some of the food, but the other didn't. He recorded the reaction time and all the writhing of the poor hungry creature. But she survived. So he stepped up the experiments. Ground glass, laxatives."

"Ringo always was a very curious person. And smart," Lucinda interjected in desperation to add a positive spin.

"What finally got them was the lead. We didn't realize what he was doing, but I'd noticed him scraping paint from the garage walls. And he worked down at the auto shop part-time then. He was always coming home with tools and chemicals. I never found out for sure, but long afterward I saw a notebook he'd been keeping, and it had a chart comparing dry gas and paint. The days were listed down the side. I believe he gradually poisoned those two cats. We watched them get sick and weak and eventually go into convulsions and die. It was horrible. First one, then the other. Can I freshen your piña colada?"

We both shook our heads. I couldn't drink any more of the one I had. I wished it were scotch.

"That boy was a pistol," chirped Lucinda, as if she were taking part in some other conversation.

"Thank the Lord he didn't have one," George muttered back. "I'm only surprised my baby brother is still alive himself. I'd half expected somebody would have murdered him by now."

When I caught the expression on Sherele's face, my stomach lurched.

Silence hung like an icy fog, making me shiver in the hot Florida evening. Sherele and I made as hasty a departure as we could without hurting Lucinda's feelings. We insisted we couldn't keep her up any later on a worknight, apologized that we had to call our editor before the paper was put to bed, piled on one excuse after the other until it must have been obvious. Then we fled.

Back at the hotel, I ordered the double scotch I'd been craving, and drank it in two thirsty gulps. Sherele ordered a hot fudge sundae and ate it slowly, licking the spoon with loving attention. I felt sick. Sherele looked, for the first time in weeks, content.

18

Thanksgiving comes early to the *Examiner*. We celebrate it in late September, the biggest party the *Examiner* gives. Actually, *gives* is the wrong verb. *Takes* is more accurate. In Bull's incomparable style, he's an ingenious cheapskate.

Every year, the *Examiner* has a potluck buffet in the newsroom, with all the dishes except the turkey prepared by us staff members. The twist is, we have to provide recipes, so that the food section can use them for its Thanksgiving issue. And we have to clear them with Andy Mutton, the food editor, to make sure he gets the proper mix and no duplicates.

This year's pre-Thanksgiving feast was scheduled for two days after our return from Disney World, so I fell back on spoonbread. Between catching up on mail and messages, transcribing my notes and starting the week's column, I considered making even such a simple recipe a heroic effort. And the only reason that was possible was that Bull was out of town, and he'd wanted to talk to Sherele and me before we started our Disney World feature. So we could postpone that for a few days.

Washington was nearly as hot as Orlando, which in Sepember isn't unusual for our indecisive climate. I walked to work in a lightweight silk blouse, with a sweater in my backpack in case the air conditioning had been revived in our building. The temperature evoked thoughts of charcoal grilling and watermelon ice, so the newsroom's heavy smell of roast turkey and gravy was as welcome as a fur coat at the beach.

The mood was festive nevertheless. This was, after all, a two-hour holiday from work and an enormous feast. Editors and writers were trading jibes, boasting about cooking triumphs despite recalcitrant stoves and inaccurate recipes. Given that we were a bunch of cynical, jaded newspeople, this was what passed for great holiday fun at the *Examiner*.

The format of the party is designed to whip our appetites to frenzy before we're issued plates and forks and allowed to swarm the table. So for the first twenty minutes we survey the offerings, take stock, plan our strategy. Some people actually make lists of what dishes they're going to head for first. Sure, we talk to each other, but always with an eye on the buffet, memorizing the layout. Some staffers, of course, are in it for more than food. They are looking to enhance their image. They stand by their creations, encouraging upper management to try a taste.

I'd been so busy, I hadn't talked to Sherele about what we were bringing, so I was surprised to see her platter of ham rolls. I'd never known her to make them before. They looked fabulous, wreathed in parsley and red pepper strips. She'd even stuck a flag in the center, identifying them as St. Mary's County Stuffed Ham Rolls. Sherele is not ordinarily such a self-promoter. But then, I've found Sherele more and more unpredictable these days.

Being the restaurant critic, I have more excuse than anyone to be greedy. Not only do I want to taste everything, every cook wants me to taste his or her dish. Each proudly told me the origin or recipe for the dish as I eyed it.

Vince had made Indian pudding. I'd never have expected it. Cornmeal, molasses, and milk sound far too homey for his flinty character. There's no dish less cynical than this simple, long-cooked, distinctly American dessert.

Cranberry sauce came in a dozen guises, some chopped raw and mixed with orange peel, others cooked with ginger or cinnamon, one ground with apples and nuts, then molded in gelatin. The vegetables ranged from the last of the season's green tomatoes baked with a pecan topping, to canned green beans mired in mushroom soup and paved over with crumbled potato chips. Nobody owned up to that one.

I was surveying the pumpkin pies—streusel-topped, meringue-covered, and bare—when I bumped into Ringo. Literally. I hadn't seen him since I'd left for Disney World. I'd worked at burying my painful images of the young Ringo Laurenge, and managed to exorcise the adult version as well.

I jumped as if I'd seen a ghost. He didn't notice me at first, since he'd backed into me, so I had a chance to look him over unobserved. Something was wrong. From the profile I caught, he looked so pale that my ghost image didn't seem far off the mark. It took me another moment to realize that Ringo was alone in the crowd. Everyone but Ringo was talking to someone else. The people around him were facing in another direction, their backs and shoulders imprisoning him in solitary confinement. These things happen at parties, of course, but in this case it was no accident. I caught two people sneaking glances at him and turning away again, and another person approach, then swivel his head when he realized Ringo was in his path.

Ringo's misdeeds in the newsroom had finally caught up with him. He was universally loathed by now. He had become a pariah. He knew it, too. His shoulders were hunched as if he were protecting himself from a blow. His eyes looked haunted, meaner than ever. Even his lips looked gray, which made me wonder whether he was sick rather than just humiliated.

When he saw that I was the one he'd bumped, and that I was backed against the table with no escape, he latched onto me like a lifeline.

"Get a good story from your Mickey Mouse boondoggle?"

"It wasn't Ginza Sushiko, but I'll manage to spin a few inches out of it." Boondoggle, indeed. "What did you bring to this feast?"

Ringo looked confused, and ran his eyes across the buffet table. I would have taken the opportunity to turn and talk to someone else, but he lurched and grabbed onto the table behind me, his other hand grabbing my arm. It felt clammy.

"Are you all right?" I didn't really care, but the words tumbled out of me automatically.

"A touch of flu," he mumbled. Then he regained his balance and squared his shoulders. "Pumpkin pie. That's mine. You should try it. It's a family recipe. Best pumpkin pie you'll ever taste."

I recognized the pie he pointed to. It was Helen's. And he was right, it was the best pumpkin pie I'd ever taste.

Dave saved me. He was late, bringing his infamous garlic shrimp, so reeking of bourbon that one bite could make you unfit to drive. He'd probably been sampling and chosen to walk.

"Hey, darlin'," he said with a sloppy leer as he

leaned over to kiss me. He never does that in the newsroom. He must have sampled half the batch.

The people around us were amused, some slapping him on the back and one reaching to grab one of the shrimp from his bowl.

"Dave's here. We can eat," a loud voice suggested.

"You're right. Dig in, everybody." Bull was out of town; Helen had taken charge.

It was the wrong time to be backed against the table. I was being smothered by arms, shoulders, and bellies of my colleagues.

"You deal with the desserts," I told Dave. "I'm going to edge over to the entrees. I'll get food for you, too, and meet you at the National Desk punch bowl."

For once I was glad to have Ringo around. He forged a path, and I followed in his wake. Even with the flu or whatever caused his pallor, he wielded the fastest fork in the newsroom. But I'm no slouch. I grabbed two plates—one for Dave—and kept pace.

Ringo snacked as he went. A slice of fennel bread, a stalk of stuffed celery, a chunk of pâté. He piled his plate with potato salad, spinach quiche, carrot mousse, and three kinds of stuffing, laying slabs of roasted and smoked turkey on top. When he reached Sherele's platter, he slowed down, never one to pass up a chance to infuriate her.

"How could you call that St. Mary's ham?" he

said. Weak beginning. He definitely must be feeling poorly.

"It's revisionist ham. A new dish inspired by you."

I couldn't believe Sherele would flatter Ringo that way. Give him credit for something. Once again the girl surprised me.

Ringo's dulled eyes brightened a few watts at that. "Interesting. What did you do?"

"You know me, I wanted something more dramatic. A sexier presentation."

Ringo managed a leer. I managed not to upchuck.

Sherele managed to keep talking as if she considered Ringo a normal human being. "I simmered the greens in a cheesecloth bag alongside the country ham, then sliced the ham thin and put a spoonful of greens on each slice, then rolled it up and baked it together."

"Clever idea. It does sound like something I'd have thought up. Give me a taste and I'll let you know how it works."

He held out his plate, but it was full. Sherele didn't hesitate.

"There's no way you can taste my ham mixed up with all the rest of this. I'll just hold your plate here for you until you've finished the ham."

He wasn't about to trust his food to her care, so he held tighter as she tried to take his plate. She shrugged and handed him another, already filled with two of her ham rolls. She must have been saving them for her own lunch, or set them aside for a friend.

Ringo didn't even offer a thank you, he just greedily stepped away from the table and found a ledge on which to rest his plates so he could cut the ham rolls and scarf them down.

Sherele had no qualms about piling her ham rolls on Dave's and my overburdened plates, so I was right behind Ringo. And since he—with me following—had stopped for samples of nearly every dish, by the time we left the table many of our colleagues were well into their meals. Even Dave had finished his dessert-foraging and arrived at my side.

"The punch table is jammed, but I managed to grab these before the crowd discovered the wine bar," he said, handing me a glass of red. He'd thought ahead to retrieve from his desk two gadgets I'd brought from a food convention—plastic wineglass holders that snap onto a plate, in case you have no hand free for drink. Serving wine at an office lunch was unprecedented, probably Helen's inspiration carried out without consulting Bull.

Dave, who employs his investigative skills to deal with all life's problems, great and small, reached under a nearby desktop and pulled out an empty keyboard tray. He deposited our dessert plates on it and took his lunch plate from me. I couldn't wait; curiosity triumphed over politeness, and I picked up a ham roll and took a bite.

Sensational. The salty aged ham enclosed a pungent coarse green paste in which I could identify kale and cabbage, then the spices hit. First the black pepper, with its warm dark smell, then, like the burst of a firecracker, the red pepper. It tasted like warm earth and a starry sky. My mouth full, I signaled with my eyes to Dave. He was going to love this dish.

Dave met my eyes not with hungry complicity, but with alarm.

At the same time I heard a muffled yelp. Or a stifled roar. Whatever it was, it was a noise I'd never heard a human make before.

Dave dropped his plate and reached past me. My eyes followed, but I was slower than Dave. Too slow to be of any help.

Ringo was right behind me, in deep trouble. He was gasping and groaning, doubling over and clutching his stomach. Dave and several others were trying to hold him up, but his writhing made it hard for them to keep a grip. It must have been only a matter of seconds, but the process seemed to take hours, in slow motion. Ringo was shaking and making dreadful guttural sounds. Then he started vomiting. His helpers instinctively jumped back, and Ringo buckled to the floor, landing with a thud, a sound never to be forgotten. His entire body began to jerk in convulsions as the heroes of the newsroom did all the things one is supposed to do in medical emergencies. They protected his head, they restrained his flailing arms, they checked his mouth to keep his tongue from choking him. The sight, the smell were enough to send even the stouthearted fleeing, but compassion overcame disgust.

The room was eerily quiet, except for the thrashing of Ringo's limbs. I could hear someone talking on a phone, demanding an ambulance.

All was still. Ringo stopped thrashing. Stopped moving altogether. His eyes were open, staring at some other world. His mouth was pulled into a grimace, a kind of ghoulish open-mouthed laugh, white teeth against blue-gray gums as if he'd been dead for a week. I couldn't stand looking at him, but I couldn't tear my eyes away. I'd never seen anything so horrible.

Vince, of all people, sprang into action. He started pressing Ringo's chest and breathing into that reeking, discolored mouth. I never would have expected such strength from such a scrawny man, such resoluteness from the squeamish Vince.

He kept it up while dozens of us stood by riveted, in silence. We could hear sirens in the background.

Let the elevators not be slow today, I prayed.

In the end the paramedics left Ringo where he was. Dead, of course. Their high-tech rescue equipment couldn't bring him back to life. Besides, it was obvious to the medical team if not to us civilians that a heart attack wasn't his problem.

He'd been poisoned. This was a job for the homicide squad.

They would have come to that conclusion, I learned, even if Sherele hadn't hurried them to it.

In the rush of events I hadn't noticed Sherele at all. She'd stayed out of the thick of the action, moving from the buffet table to a desk far behind it. She was all alone, sitting outside the periphery of the mesmerized crowd. As I heard it reported later, her first reaction when Ringo let out a yelp was to laugh.

"Young firebrand can't take it," she said, at least that's what two reporters remembered.

"The guy's really sick," one shot back at her, appalled by her reaction. Sherele didn't respond, but she stood on a chair to take a look for herself. After a minute she climbed down and walked away. Nobody seems to have noticed her after that, until she made herself noticed.

After the paramedics had worked on Ringo for minutes that seemed like hours, the words rippled through the crowd:

"He's dead."

"They can't revive him."

"I can't believe it. He's gone."

"I've never seen a dead body."

"The smell, oh, God, the smell."

Then a scream, endless and excruciating, a sound filled with blood. I didn't even recognize the voice. It was a shriek, far too long for one human, one breath. It disintegrated into a blur of words.

"He can't be dead! He can't be! He can't! I didn't mean to really hurt him! I didn't!"

Like a wave, the crowd turned and rushed toward Sherele. One of the medics shouldered his way through the tightly packed voyeurs, another picked up a phone and dialed.

By now I'd recognized the hysterical voice as Sherele's, and I saw that I could get to her faster if I avoided the press of bodies and ran down an outer aisle to come from behind.

I still had to muscle my way through part of the crowd, but once they realized who I was, people edged aside and made room for me. When I got to Sherele, she was hunched over with her hands covering her face, sobbing so that her shoulders shook and her body lurched from an occasional gasp. I knelt in front of her and tried to wrap her in a hug, but I couldn't reach her, certainly not emotionally. Sherele was too hysterical to acknowledge anyone. So I stood and leaned protectively above her, first rubbing her back, then patting her hair. I felt at a loss. I didn't know how to calm her, to comfort her, even to get her to hear me.

"Sherele, c'mon, sweetheart. Calm down, sweetie. Tell me what's the matter. Let me help you." Help her? I felt totally helpless myself.

Time was no longer at a crawl, it felt as if it had stopped altogether. Sherele was a huddle of quiet sobbing, I was trying to soothe her and shield her from—I didn't know what.

Between sobs, Sherele was mumbling. It was hard to make out the words, so I leaned in closer.

"Just tell me what's happened, honey. Let me help."

"It was only pepper."

Sob.

"I didn't think I used that much."

Sob.

"Just pepper."

Sob.

"I didn't mean to kill him."

I thought only I could hear what Sherele was saying, but that wasn't so. A murmuring spread through the crowd. Our colleagues—our friends— retreated some distance, a loose mingling of people whose attention kept shuttling from one horror to the other, from the dead Ringo to the distraught Sherele.

This frozen agony threatened to go on forever, it seemed to me, until an elevator opened and a bustle of suited men hustled out of it. The homicide detectives had arrived.

I couldn't actually see them, but I could hear their businesslike buzz, and stage whispers spread word of their identity across the room. Their appearance was like a switch, turning on the motor of the *Examiner*. Editors marshaled their troops to return to their desks and leave the police and the medical examiner space to do their work. Besides, deadlines were looming, and nothing stops a newspaper. Secretaries and news aides were commandeered to dismantle the buffet and make the aborted party disappear. The owner of

Sherele's chair approached, then thought better of it and walked away.

"Sherele, let's go to the restroom and put some cold water on your face. Or would you like me to take you right home?"

She nodded, which was her first acknowledgment that I was there. But she didn't look up.

I was making progress. "Good. Let me help you up, and we'll get our things. Can you do that?"

She nodded her head again, at least I thought she did. I reached for her elbows to help her stand, and Dave arrived to assist me. He was too late.

"Where do you think you're going?" The voice sounded like gravel.

Wedging between Dave and me was a guy the size of an SUV. "Leave her alone. She's mine. You people just get back to work and let me do my job here."

That voice left me feeling like a skinned knee. It was a voice I knew. One nobody'd ever forget. Randy Mason was a homicide detective, a guy so mean and dangerous that I always figured he had to be the city's main deterrent to crime. I couldn't imagine a worse punishment than being at the mercy of Randy Mason. Even hearing him read you your rights could send your heart pumping a gusher.

I looked up and caught his cold weasel eyes.

"Well, well, lookee who's here. It's Miss Fancy Fork."

We'd met before, more times than I'd have

wished, mostly when I was with Sherele and Homer. Randy and Homer, who both worked in the same office, were natural-born enemies. Randy was cruel, Homer was compassionate. Randy cared little for the fine points of criminal justice, Homer was scrupulous. Randy was a redneck, Homer was an African-American—not that Randy would ever use the term.

"Move on, Wheatley. You're in my way. This is the one I want."

He reached for Sherele's arm and yanked her from her seat.

Dave and I both yelled in protest, but Randy didn't flinch. His life was probably an unending stream of yells and curses.

Once Sherele was on her feet, he jerked her hanging head upward and took a look, making her yelp.

"Whoa! Who've we got here? Looks like I caught me a big one."

Sherele went quiet. She became rigid and still except for a series of shudders left over from her sobbing. After a pause of countless seconds, she jerked her arms from Randy's grip.

"Keep. Your. Hands. To. Yourself."

"Not a chance. You're in my hands now, lady," Randy said with a leer. His mouth was grinning, while his flat gray eyes had the glint of a switchblade. "Your friends tell me you poisoned that man lying there, your very own coworker. Imagine that, Sherele. One would think Homer would have taught his girlfriend better."

Randy whipped out a pair of handcuffs and locked them on Sherele's hands before anybody else realized what he'd been reaching for.

"Sherele Travis," he said, making the name sound like a disease, "you are under arrest. You have the right to remain silent . . ."

The words droned on like a march without a tune. They were so familiar, yet I'd never heard anybody recite them in person. They were the stuff of movies, of television, of fiction. Not of real life.

Randy turned Sherele toward the door and began to tug her in that direction.

"Let me go along," insisted Dave. "C'mon, Randy, you'll be better off with me to vouch for the way this has gone down."

"I don't need your help, Zeeger. We homicide detectives can take care of ourselves without the help of the media. You just stay here and keep your girlfriend under control."

"Don't worry, Sherele, we'll take care of this," I crooned to my stupefied best friend as I hurried alongside her. "Keep cool, baby. We won't let anything happen to you. I'll call Homer."

Randy picked up his speed, making Sherele lurch and stumble. "You do that, Wheatley. I can't wait for Homer Jones to stick his black nose into this."

Helen was at the elevator door, with the *Examiner*'s attorney. "He's going with you," she told Randy. She wasn't asking, she was calmly, assuredly certain. The woman knew how to issue a command with more quiet power than anybody I'd ever seen.

Even Randy was slightly tamed. "Sorry, ma'am, but we can't do that."

"This is Miss Travis's lawyer. You certainly can take him along."

"Is this your lawyer, girlie?"

The "girlie" did it. "You mean 'Miss Travis,' don't you? Yes, he's my attorney. And I've said all I'm going to say."

This small contingent of stony faces disappeared behind the sliding metal doors.

19

Homer couldn't sit still. He couldn't stand still. He kept walking into walls as he paced my living room. Every once in a while he shook his hands as if to revive their circulation. The rest of the time he kept them clenched.

His voice sounded clenched, too, as he rattled on to Dave and me, trying to make sense of what had gone on at the *Examiner* a few hours ago and afterward at the city lockup.

"It was too late. By the time they'd photographed and fingerprinted her—which I'm sure Randy managed to get done as slowly as possible—it was too late for an arraignment. Now she's got to wait 'til court opens tomorrow morning. I'll make sure her case is handled first thing, at eight A.M."

"Did you see her?"

"That bastard managed to keep me away. Thanks to Randy, my boss is very concerned about my appearing to meddle in this case. He won't let me touch it. But I managed to deliver a message to somebody I know in the cell block, and I'm assured they'll treat her the best they can."

"What did they charge her with?"

"Second-degree murder. Thank God, Helen sent a lawyer with her. At least that got her to stop talking. So they didn't get a confession on videotape. I have no doubt she'll be out on bail tomorrow, and we'll take it from there." He paused with his back to us, making a pretense of looking out the window. "How could she have been so . . . I don't know what . . . stupid?" Homer's voice broke. He clearly didn't want us to see his face following suit.

"Homer, she didn't mean it. It was a prank. Anybody might have done it."

"Not after they'd threatened repeatedly to kill the guy."

"Nobody takes those threats seriously. We all say that when we're pissed off at somebody."

Homer got himself under control and turned back to face us. He was once again the detective.

"Tell me again what she said to you."

"I wish I had more to tell you. She was mumbling, and I had a hard time making out what she was saying." I'd had a shower and washed my hair before Homer arrived, and so had Dave. I was in my robe, Dave in jeans and a sweatshirt, but I still imagined the smell of death on us. Homer was, as ever, in a suit that looked as if it had just come from its plastic cleaners' bag. But his expression reflected that same aroma.

"I know, I just need to hear it again."

"She said it was only pepper, and that she didn't think she'd used that much."

"They confiscated Ringo's plate?"

"That and more, I'm told. Apparently they walked off with some of the desserts."

"Evidence, eh?" Homer sneered, then continued his questioning. "You said she used the term 'murder.' "

"Something like that. She didn't mean to murder him, or to kill him. Words to that effect." Homer's pacing was making my head hurt. More precisely, it was making my head hurt more than it already did. I felt stapled to my red velvet platform rocker. Nothing could have made me move.

"Who else heard her?"

"A lot of people."

"The actual words?"

Dave took charge of this question. He was on the sofa, moving nervously, as much as a body could while sitting in one place. He crossed his legs and uncrossed them. He swung whichever foot was on top. He tapped his fingers, cracked his knuckles, balled his hands into fists, wrapped his arms across his chest and unwrapped them, then rotated his shoulders and neck. His voice sounded fidgety as well.

"I don't think anybody but Chas could hear exactly what Sherele was saying. I was the next-closest person, and I couldn't. But her voice was rising and falling, so some words stood out. The word 'pepper.' And 'kill.' I think people filled in the intervening words for themselves."

Homer crossed to the sofa and sat beside Dave. Thank goodness. I was getting dizzy watching him stride back and forth.

"Tell me your version of what you saw before Ringo died."

People have their own ways of dealing with a crisis, their own rituals that let them incorporate a trauma and calm their system so they can go on living and breathing. Homer's and Dave's, as I should have anticipated, were similar. They are both investigators. They ask questions. They look for the pieces of a puzzle, then twist them and turn them, until they see how these peices fit together.

Sherele's being charged with murder was nothing Homer could face straight on. He could only approach it one puzzle piece at a time. Now he was examining every piece carefully, thoroughly, over and over again, hoping to get to know them all so surely that he could begin to place them in context.

Dave had a different set of pieces, which he, too, had been turning over and over in his mind. He talked of them haltingly, still looking for new knobs and curves in each one that might connect to some other bit he knew.

"I couldn't see much of what was going on around the main buffet table, since I was hanging around the desserts and the drinks. So most of what I know is hearsay, at least until Ringo started eating."

"I don't want the hearsay," Homer said, his voice steadier and stronger than it had been while he'd been pacing. "Not yet."

"I'd just met up with Chas and was about to start in on my plate of food." He stopped to think, to position the scene precisely in his mind. "Ringo was behind her. I was noticing how high his plate was piled. The guy was a pig, always a pig, stuffing himself even when he looked like he had a hangover. Then I noticed that he had two plates. Even more of a pig today, I said to myself."

"Two plates?"

"Yeah. He put one down on a ledge, and started eating from the smaller one. The one with Sherele's ham rolls on it."

"Could you see what else was on the plate?"

"Nothing. It just had ham rolls. Two of them."

"You're sure?"

"I'm sure."

I might have been skeptical about a precise recollection from someone who'd been through such a chaotic and traumatic scene, but part of Dave's talent as a reporter is his ability to see and recall the details of any experience. Homer knows that about him, too. He was taking notes. Dave was in his reporter mode, and Homer was safe in his role as detective. For the moment we had regained the normal rhythm of our breathing.

"Then what?"

"Ringo was eating the ham. The guy eats so fast you can hardly see the fork move." Dave halted. His face flushed and his voice hoarsened. "I mean ate. He always ate fast."

"Go on."

"He must have eaten about half the plate when his face went from ashy white to bright red. He yelped. Or roared. Made some awful animal sound." Dave stopped again, shook his head as if to clear the image, then continued. "He dropped his plate and looked stunned. As if he'd been jolted by a bolt of lightning or something. I reached out to steady him. I must have dropped my plate, too."

"He fell to the floor?"

"Not right away. First he kind of clutched his mouth and his stomach. Seemed to clutch everywhere. I grabbed him, and a couple of other guys helped me. We were trying to prop him up, but he was moving and sort of staggering, and it was kind of hard to keep hold of him. Then he started vomiting."

"You all backed off and he fell, huh?"

Dave looked mortified. "I didn't mean to let go. I just did, instinctively."

"And he hit his head on the floor?"

"No, the fall itself wasn't that bad, at least not

for him. His head hit my shoes. A soft landing, compared to what it could have been."

"But he was out?"

"I guess you might say that. He went into convulsions."

"It was awful," I blurted, as Dave's retelling brought back the sights and the smells.

"A lot of people at the *Examiner* know first aid and CPR and all that. Everyone did what could be done until the ambulance arrived. But it was hopeless," Dave wrapped up his tale.

I felt tears welling up, but I didn't think they were tears for Ringo. My grief was only for Sherele. The dead Ringo maintained the power to destroy her as effectively as had the live Ringo.

The three of us fell quiet. We hadn't run out of things to say, just the will to say them. This was the longest I'd ever been with Homer when there was no talk about food. I didn't even have the heart to offer to call for a pizza delivery. And all my beers were now empties.

My mind was spinning in bizarre directions. I felt guilty thinking about talking about food. I was now thinking about my thinking. I knew this was my mind's way of taking a break from the pain of thinking about Sherele.

Dave's, too.

"What have you got to eat?" he asked as he unfolded from the sofa and aimed himself toward the refrigerator.

"Not much. I just got back from Florida." As if

he didn't know that. And as if I ever had much food in my apartment.

"You've got peanut butter," Dave called from the refrigerator, where his head was nearly inside. "I'm going to make us all sandwiches. What else would you like on it?"

Suddenly, food sounded like a good idea. Now that someone else had brought it up.

"Pickles," I called out.

"I know, just like Kinsey Milhone," Dave answered. "On what kind of bread?"

"Triscuits. I've got some stashed away in that cabinet right above your head."

"I'm a traditionalist. I'm going to have jelly. I assume you have some real bread in the freezer. What about you, Homer? What's your secret peanut-butter passion?"

"Let me see." Homer got up and nudged Dave out of the refrigerator. He started rummaging through the oddments scattered on my shelves. "I'm not in the mood for jelly. Maybe mustard, if that's all you've got. What's this?" He held up a flat plastic container.

"It's Burmese. *Balachaung*. Fried onions and garlic with dried shrimp and chilies."

"Sounds lethal," Dave said. Then he reddened in embarrassment, belatedly making the hot-pepper connection. "Sorry."

Homer opened the container and smelled it, then dipped in a finger gingerly and licked it. "Wow! That's potent! Where can I get some of this stuff? I think I'll make me an Asian-fusion peanut-butter sandwich. I wish you had a little duck sauce. That would smooth out the rough edges."

"Drawer on the far right. Next to those little packets of soy sauce."

Either we were starving or the food was comforting. Each of us sat in a different corner of the room, and conversation stopped altogether while we ate our peanut-butter concoctions as if they required total concentration.

My snack turned out to be an inspiration.

"I've got a bottle of cognac in the bottom of my closet." Food had brought to mind drink, which led me to remember the Courvoisier I'd bought on sale for Lily's birthday.

Dave usually turns up his nose at such posh stuff, but not when the beer's all gone. He went for the glasses while I dug out the bottle.

We didn't bother to make a toast.

Two snifters later, Homer was ready to play detective again. He leafed through his notebook, turning pages back and forth, then scribbling a few more notes.

Without looking up, Homer directed a question to me. "Pepper. You said Sherele specified pepper. Right?"

"She was mumbling, so I'm not a hundred percent sure. But that was the impression I got. She was saying that she didn't mean to kill him and she was sorry and it was a mistake, and I think she repeated 'pepper.' I put it together that she had intended to punish Ringo with a painful jolt of hot pepper in his ham rolls. But I'm sure, absolutely sure that she didn't mean to inflict serious damage."

Homer was quiet again. Dave and I stared as if we could watch wheels turning inside his head. After what seemed like a long time, he looked up, and we looked away, uncomfortable at having been caught staring.

"I'm not clear on one thing here." Homer tapped his notebook. "If Sherele had poisoned the ham rolls, how come nobody else got sick? Lots of people ate that ham, am I right? Even you."

I was the first to speak up. "I didn't really have much chance to eat mine. Just a bite. And it was good. Great, in fact."

"Not too much pepper?"

"A lot, but certainly not too much. It's a dish that depends on a certain amount of hot pepper."

"Did anybody else complain or get sick?"

"No, but I'm afraid there is an obvious explanation." I'd been worrying over this.

"Give it to me."

"Sherele had a separate plate set aside, with two ham rolls. That's what she gave Ringo."

"Anybody else see that?"

"Everybody."

"The woman's never learned a thing from all the plays she's seen." Homer went back to his notes.

A few moments later he started again. "Okay,

here's another thing that makes no sense to me. How can you kill someone with pepper? Make him feel pain, sure. But how can peppers kill?"

Again, I was the one to answer. "It's not common, certainly. And I really don't know much about this, but food can do some strange and terrible things. Someone could have an allergy or a sensitivity. Or maybe if someone was already sick or weakened in some way—"

Homer held up his hand to stop me, and started leafing through his notebook again. "Hangover. There it is. One of you said something about a hangover. What made you think Ringo was suffering from a hangover?"

I thought Dave had used the word, but Dave seemed lost in thought. So I took on Homer's question. "He looked wretched, and he wasn't even bothering to hide his foul mood. I was surprised he could even eat, although I never knew anything to slow down his insatiable appetite."

Homer turned to Dave, intent on drawing him out. "You used the term 'ashy,' something about his face turning red from ashy white."

Dave roused himself. "I didn't think about it at the time, but he did look pale. I guess I registered it without considering what it meant."

"It sounds to me as if Ringo was already sick."

"You've got a point," Dave said.

"And maybe that's why Sherele's pepper killed him," I added.

"More than that," Homer said, the power of his

conclusion propelling him to rise. "Maybe it was something else entirely that killed him."

We all stood up, as if the idea gave us something immediate to act on.

"How long does the toxicology take?" Dave and I threw Homer the same question.

"Ordinarily, the lab tests take a couple of weeks. Or even longer. In fact, our medical examiner's office has been such a disaster that last year I would have said there'd be a good chance of never getting the results at all. And even when we got them, they couldn't be considered reliable."

"I remember the stories we did on that," Dave said.

"Those stories were a help. The office has been cleaned up, at least some. And for a high-profile case such as this, particularly when the press is so closely involved, they'll definitely put a rush on it. You can bet the medical examiner's going to do the best he's ever done in his life. And the fastest. I wouldn't be surprised if we got the blood work back by the end of the day tomorrow."

"He's going to have the press corps from everywhere in the world camping out on his doorstep." Dave sounded as if he'd be among them.

20

After Homer left, Dave might have started his vigil immediately if Helen hadn't called first. Her stated purpose was to check on how I was doing, but she talked longer to Dave than to me. With Bull away and apparently unreachable, she was running the show, and there was no journalist whose instinct she trusted more than Dave's.

"Obviously, since it's our story, we've got to come out on top of it," he argued gently with her. "No, I don't think we should hold back one bit. The hell with modesty, or propriety, if that's what you want to call it. If you could get in touch with Bull, he'd throw everything we have at it, and you know he would."

Dave's brows drew tight, his left hand twiddled a pencil. He looked as if he were trying to contain an explosion. He started to raise his voice,

then dialed it down. I knew what he was thinking:
Helen was so decent it was hard to fight with her,
and she certainly must be under crushing stress.

"Helen, I know you've got to do what feels right
to you, but stop and think about how Bull—and
you—are going to feel when every paper in the uni-
verse plays this above the fold." He momentarily
lost it, and his voice rose again. "While the *Examiner* treats it like a fucking everyday urban irritant."

He looked over at me and his expression grew
contrite as he continued. "I'm sorry, Helen, I know
we're all under a lot of pressure. But I feel very
strongly about this. Thorough isn't enough. We've
got to play this big."

He listened for a minute.

"I'm going to come down there. No, it's fine.
Chas will be okay without me. I'll be there in a
half hour. Let me help you out."

He listened a few moments more and said that
yes, he understood. "You're a great journalist, Helen. One of the best. Whatever you do is going to
turn out to be the right thing."

When he hung up, he looked sad from head to
toe.

"You're off to the office?" I asked.

"No, she made me promise I'd stay here with
you. Said she'd rather handle this without me
looking over her shoulder. I'm afraid I came on
too strong."

"Next time she'll know enough to switch it
around—check on your well-being and ask me for

advice instead. I side with Helen on this. My opinion is that it would be just too self-serving to play this as if it were World War Three."

Helen, like me, was undoubtedly dreading seeing Sherele's arrest as a six-column headline.

I'd said my piece and stopped there. Dave and I both knew enough to drop the subject. We were too drained to look for anything but comfort in each other. We draped ourselves across the sofa as if we were one limp body and watched the late-night news.

Details had been sketchy for the six o'clock reports. And we'd been too stunned to turn to the early-evening news until it had been nearly over.

By eleven o'clock, the stations had time to organize the facts and rev up the rhetoric. Washington's best-known talking heads were shaking themselves sadly and summing up the short but profound life of "the most extraordinary journalist of the electronic age." With each interview Ringo climbed closer to fourth-estate heaven. If he could have heard the praise, Ringo might have considered his death worth the trouble.

Even worse, Sherele was found guilty in the court of Washington's theater owners, particularly the very ones who'd been loudly and frequently questioning her right to judge them. The *Examiner* management refused to comment on Sherele's arrest, so the reporters sought out people who would—mostly those who had been the victims of her pen.

I'd seen enough of my fellow vultures. We turned off the TV and dragged ourselves wearily and miserably to bed, then stared silently into the dark through most of the hours until Sherele's arraignment.

The *New York Times, USA Today*, and the *Washington Post* hit my door before the *Examiner* the next morning. Just as I'd feared and Dave had predicted, Ringo's newsroom collapse and Sherele's arrest were played with as much noise and glare as the downing of a jetliner. This was one death, not hundreds, but for newsmen it was one of theirs, in a place that looked like their home. The papers had had to make do with stock photos of the victim and the accused, since the *Examiner* hadn't allowed any outside photographers on the scene. But that seemed to make them redouble their efforts to paint the picture in words. Again, Ringo had been elevated to somewhere up around Bob Woodward in the annals of journalism.

The *Examiner* arrived an hour late, and when I picked it up I could see why. The paper couldn't have played the story any bigger if it had been announcing Armageddon. The headline screamed and the full-color photo bled. Almost literally. Ringo's corpse sprawled across three columns at the top of the page.

Even Dave groaned.

"I'm beginning to wish I'd kept my mouth shut," he confessed. "I never guessed that Helen had this in her."

"She didn't," I said. I'd unfolded the paper and seen the black-bordered box that was an Appreciation—the personal summing-up newspapers run as a feature when someone famous dies. The byline was Bull Stannard.

"No wonder the paper was late," Dave said as he turned inside to find two full pages on the life of the most influential and accomplished reporter to ever die in the *Examiner*'s newsroom. "Bull must have gotten back in time to tear it apart and remake it. Nobody else could achieve quite this level of crass commercialism."

"Let me see what it says about Sherele."

Dave shuffled through the pages. "On that subject he managed commendable restraint." He handed them to me.

"It looks as if the paper said the least that could be said without it being open to the charge of whitewashing."

"He must have left that part to Helen."

When I arrived at the *Examiner* building, I found it under siege. The outer perimeter was a phalanx of trucks and vans with television logos. Inside that was a thick wall of bodies—reporters, cameramen, and police to keep them behaving. I flashed my press pass left and right, staring at the ground as I elbowed my way without making eye contact or answering any of the questions thrown at me.

When I reached the steps, I had to look up, and the sight stopped me short. At the top of the staircase stood Bull, our official leader, giving a god-damn press conference.

You'd think, his having been out of town for nearly a week, he'd have better things to do with his time. But there he was, letting his deputies keep the traumatized newsroom running while he grandstanded with the outside press.

I turned my head away as I climbed past him. I didn't want to have to exchange pleasantries in front of the eyes and ears of the world.

"That's it for now, boys. I've got a paper to run," he said as I reached the door. Then he lumbered up behind me and followed me in.

"You making it through all this?" he asked as if we were colleagues exchanging comments on the weather.

"Not as well as you, I'd guess. There's no profit in it for me."

An elevator door opened and I stepped in. Two women were about to follow me, but Bull turned and held up his hands to stop them. "Sorry, ladies, but this is an express elevator. I hope you won't mind taking the next car." Then he joined me, and side by side we watched the doors close in front of their grimacing faces.

"It's all going to work out, Chas," Bull said placatingly.

"You mean once you've washed the vomit from the floor and hired a new black female theater critic?"

He didn't bite back, which surprised me. Bull never misses a chance to extract a hunk of flesh.

"Sherele's going to be all right. I'll see to that. She won't go to jail. I promise you."

"You're too late. She's already in jail. And you weren't here in time to make sure she kept her mouth shut, so she's likely to stay there."

The door started to open on our floor, but Bull hit a button to keep it closed.

"I wish I had been here. Then none of this would have happened. But I'll get it taken care of. And I'll make it up to her."

Just like Bull, to think he could control the judicial system as well as the elevator door.

My phone was ringing when I reached my desk. After three rings it switches to voice mail, so I lunged for it. Too late.

I looked over at Sherele's empty desk, where her screen saver made my heart thump. For a moment I thought Sherele must be here if her computer was on, then the thump became a thud when I realized she must have left it on yesterday.

The tiny red dot on my phone was lit, but I booted up my computer before I dealt with my voice messages. I wanted to leave time for the most recent one to be included. I picked up the phone and dialed, then started listening to the recorded calls. Today I was too impatient to wait through the requests for restaurant recommendations, the complaints about overcooked fish and overbooked tables, the publicists bragging that their clients were invited to cook at the James Beard House in New York.

I was waiting to hear from Homer.

Instead, it was Dave's voice on that last message.

"She's out on bail, sugar bun. That's the best we can hope for at the moment. Homer called me because he couldn't reach you. Busy signal or something. He's taken her to his place, since hers is under siege by that pack of dogs we call the press. He says she's doing as well as can be expected under the circumstances. Looks like hell, but no serious damage. She says all she wants at the moment is a shower and a good sleep. She told Homer to let you know that, so you don't try to call her. She'll call you as soon as she gets her head back in shape, sometime this afternoon. She wants to talk to you, but she thinks Homer's apartment would be a bad choice for that. She feels she ought to leave there as soon as she's able, and is worried about the place being bugged. Which might not be as paranoid as it sounds. She would like you to think of a place to meet that nobody will be staking out. She doesn't want to impose on you—you know Sherele—but I think she would be grateful if you could think of a place where she could stay for a short while until she's ready to face the public. I'd offer my apartment, but too many people in the building know her. Yours, too. Anyway, I'll be in later and maybe we can figure out something together. Stay cool, Hot Lips."

Newspapers are used to crises. In fact, crisis is their business. I've never seen a newsroom as immobilized by trauma as ours was. On the outside that day, the *Examiner* was what stirred the world's news. Inside the building, though, it seemed less a newsroom than an intensive-care waiting room.

Computers remained idle. Reporters, editors, and copy aides clung together in small groups, talking just above whispers. Wit and repartee were on vacation.

I exchanged a "How are you feeling" with a group or two, and I had a sit-down with Helen that was more unspoken reassurance than real conversation. Even Bull, crisscrossing the newsroom for a round of shoulder-thumping, couldn't rouse any vitality from stunned colleagues. He finally retreated to his office and his telephone.

For a while I thought about calling Ringo's mother and sister. Part of me felt I should, but as soon as I considered what I would say, the more cowardly part of me took charge. What could I do? Call and thank them once again for the dandy piña coladas and tell them that the nice theater critic they'd hosted had accidentally poisoned their son? No, not I. They could get their news elsewhere, and surely they had by now, given the press saturation and Ringo's martyrdom.

I can't tell you exactly how I passed those hours. I think I spent a lot of time tapping one foot, and every once in a while it seemed as if I needed to remind myself to breathe. I couldn't

write. I couldn't work. I couldn't surf the Internet.
I could only stare at the phone and will it to ring
with Sherele's or Homer's number on the caller
ID. I wasn't answering otherwise.

"Wheatley, pick up your phone!"

That was one of the *Examiner*'s receptionists,
shouting to me across the funereal quiet of the
newsroom.

I stared at my space-age telephone console.
Nothing was ringing, but I was startled to note
that the time read four o'clock. Then the phone
did ring, displaying a number I didn't recognize. I
picked up the receiver.

"She's out! She didn't do it. It wasn't her."

The voice was Homer's, though it took a few
words for me to recognize it. He was hoarse and
breathless.

"How do you know? Who did it? Homer,
where are you?"

"I'm at the courthouse, and I can't talk, but I
just found out. The toxicologist, bless his bureau-
cratic soul, put a supersonic rush on the job, and
he found that Ringo didn't die of chili-pepper poisoning or anything like that. Sherele couldn't
have killed him."

"Who did? Or what did?"

"It was lead poisoning. The guy had a ton of it
in his blood. Enough to kill an elephant—or at
least a journalist pig."

"But how?"

"There's no way of knowing. Everyone's wondering where a man could acquire such a lethal dose, but it was probably an accident. Lead accumulates in the body, so it could have been building up for years. And it takes time to act, so he would have had that toxic level for a while, at least a week."

"What happens next?"

"The medical examiner is no longer ruling it a homicide. Sherele's charges have been dropped. In fact, it looks like the whole case is being dropped. It's not a natural death, but since there's no way of proving whether or not it was an accident, it's just listed as a poisoning from an unknown source."

"It could have been suicide."

"Naw. Pretty gruesome way to die, and I can't imagine someone waiting around to die for a week."

"It still could be murder."

"With no way to tell when the poison was administered, and no apparent motive or means, that's a pretty unlikely ruling. Not enough to go on. Nobody's going to look for that kind of trouble."

"So it's all over?"

"All but the shouting."

I was elated. I was relieved. And I was curiously deflated at the same time. Sherele was free, but Ringo was still dead. And much as I might have thought I wished for that very event, witnessing it made me realize how little I meant that wish.

Besides, it's very unsettling to watch someone die and never know why he did.

I figured Homer had already called Sherele, so I wouldn't be waking her if I did. I had to hear her voice before another moment passed.

She sounded drained, as listless as I've ever heard her. But now she had every reason to get better.

"I spent the night making lists in my head of the reasons I wanted to die. I couldn't figure out whether it felt worse that I'd killed someone or that I could be spending my life in jail. I argued about it in my head all night. It made no sense, but it helped to shut out the terror and the smells and the sight of Ringo's convulsions. Oh, Chas, I so much wanted to die."

"You don't need to think about that anymore. It's all right now."

"It will be. It's not yet, but you're right, it will be."

"I'm coming over there. It's too soon for you to go home, the press will be all over you. So just stay right there. I'm bringing dinner."

By the time I got off the phone, Bull obviously had the news. And it had spread through the newsroom. The proper late-afternoon buzz had returned. The air felt like a vibrating electrical wire, pulsing energy. Bull was going from desk to desk, reading over shoulders and issuing orders. He was the commander-in-chief once again, and the *Examiner* was charging into the story.

21

In the end, it was Sherele who called Lucinda and George but, of course, they already knew about Ringo's death. They'd even called the *Examiner*, they said. They'd tried to call me, but in Lucinda's rambling request to be transferred to my extension she apparently mentioned that she was Ringo's mother, so the astute operator had put her call through to Bull.

"He was a very nice man, even if his voice was just like his name," Lucinda started to spin out her story.

Sherele nodded for a while and muttered an occasional "uh-huh." She wedged in some apologetic words that apparently were being cut off by Lucinda's continued narrative. Finally she got in a complete sentence: "Are you coming here for the funeral, or are you having it there?" She nodded and muttered a few more times, and added, "And bless you, too."

She hung up and stared at me with disbelief in her eyes.

"She told Bull just to cremate him or bury him any way he wanted," she reported. "She said she is saving her vacation time for a trip to Memphis, and since she hadn't seen Ringo for years, she is going to just go on as if he were still alive, which he is, in her head. Besides, she wouldn't feel comfortable around all the big-wigs who were Ringo's friends."

We both shook our heads, as if a swarm of gnats had been released by the phone.

"Poor mom," Sherele said.

"Poor son," I added.

"Poor sister, poor father, poor entire strange family."

"Knowing Lucinda explains a lot," I concluded.

"Not enough," Sherele finished with a note of reality.

Nobody does memorial services like the press. First of all, they're big. Enormous. Any person who wants to be looked on favorably by the press finds an excuse to come. Anybody who wants to be in the limelight sees a memorial as an opportunity to be photographed and quoted. And newspaper people from everywhere take a colleague's memorial service as a chance to network, often with travel expenses paid by their employers.

Those colleagues who travel the distance need to justify the expense, of course, and being as competitive as journalists are, they send home stories dripping with poignancy and color, hoping to make the front page.

Thus the *Examiner* continued to lead the news, even though nothing was happening except that Ringo was being deified.

Even those of us at the *Examiner* participated in this rampant emotionalism. We had to pretend to go along, to mourn his passing. That became harder to do as the ghastliness of his death receded and the residue of his vicious nature remained. Not that we'd wanted him to die, we just wanted him out of our newsroom and our lives. We felt hypocritical honoring him, eager to have the whole miserable incident over.

Our hypocrisy made us more uncomfortable once we found that we were reaping rewards from Ringo's death. The *Examiner* was booming. Ads were pouring in, particularly for a pull-out memorial section Bull planned—much to everyone else's disgust. Reporters from the *Examiner* were sought for interviews, first about Ringo and then in their own right. Even some job offers arrived for my more visible colleagues. I turned down one from a high-powered New York magazine, and Dave rejected nibbles from Chicago and L.A. Sherele had no such luck, thank goodness. I was afraid she'd jump at a chance to leave town.

The job change that did please me was that

Linda was elevated from Prince George's County to Ringo's job. I was surprised; I'd have thought Bull would look outside the paper for another star. Maybe in the long run he, too, had learned a lesson from Ringo's tenure. Both living and dead, Ringo had brought glory and financial gain to the *Examiner*, but the cost had been great. I'd been afraid Bull had never noticed that cost, but maybe he had.

He was a chastened man. Once the noise over Ringo's death died down, Bull, too, seemed quieter. Even nicer. He spent more time than I could recall roaming the newsroom rather than holing up in his office and expecting us to come to him. Not only did he make an uncharacteristically popular decision in promoting Linda, he started complimenting reporters on their stories.

"Bull must be in love." Such was the incredulity in the newsroom.

I thought the explanation was simpler and more obvious: Bull loved money, and the *Examiner* was making it. Ringo had served his purpose and the momentum was continuing.

What astounded me, though, was the realization that none of us was acting in character.

Bull was nice.

Dave was content.

The newsroom was peaceful.

And Ringo was dead.

Most amazing: nobody seemed to care how that happened.

I didn't think I cared all that much either, until I started having nightmares. In my dreams, I saw Ringo gasping and retching. I stood by helplessly as he was flung off a cliff. I watched him abandoned in a desert.

I didn't dare talk to Sherele about my disturbances. Dave was sympathetic, but only up to a point. He tried, though. In the middle of the night he rubbed my back until I could talk calmly.

"Why can't I just let it go, like you do?" I wondered, snuggled up to his bare chest.

"You're the one who was closest to it," he said. "We were right there when he fell. And over the long run, since the time when he came to the paper, you probably talked to him more than anyone else did. He was a presence in your life because of his obsession with food and because he hurt Sherele and those restaurant guys you liked. And you were the only one, outside of Sherele, who met his family. Or even knew he had a family."

"You think because of all that I see myself as responsible for him?"

"In a way. Nobody else seems to care about him, either positively or negatively. Not even his family."

"I guess I do feel that I'm left holding the bag."

"Not that there's much you can do about it. What is there still possible but to mourn him, or at least to mourn the fact that a young man, any young man, died so prematurely?"

"And painfully. But it's more than a matter of mourning."

"What, then?"

"I need to find out how he died."

"Aw, Chas, that makes no sense."

"How can you say that? You're an investigative reporter."

"Exactly. I know by now that not everything is worth investigating. What is there to gain?"

"Maybe it could keep someone else from dying the same way. If it was an accident. Or maybe it wasn't an accident."

"There are hundreds of other unsolved murders, thousands of accidental deaths in this city. Many that are more worth investigating than this one."

"But this is the only one where I knew the victim."

"Maybe what this really is about is that you're hankering after the police beat." Dave said this with a kiss to the back of my neck. It had a definite let's-get-back-to-sleep flavor.

Dave wasn't going to whip up any enthusiasm for this venture, and I couldn't really blame him. It was probably a waste of time. But I had to try.

"I think I'll stick with restaurants for the time being," I said, fluffing my pillow into sleep mode. If I'd let him know I wasn't deterred, he'd feel he had to stay up the rest of the night dissuading me. "Time to get back to sleep. I'll try to dream about chicken soup."

And I did.

The next day, I swiveled my computer screen slightly so that Sherele wouldn't catch sight of it, and I started playing out my obsession with Ringo's death. I searched the Internet for whatever there was to learn about lead poisoning.

Its first symptoms are flulike, with headaches, muscle aches, weakness, and sluggishness. Diarrhea, pallor, vomiting.

Check.

Aggressiveness.

Nothing special for Ringo.

Loss of appetite.

Nope.

Discoloration of lips, a blue-gray line along the gums.

Interesting. I'd noticed his gums looked bluish.

Convulsions.

I shuddered just thinking about them.

Where could Ringo have come across lead? Paint, of course, at least old paint. Lead-based paint had been banned for many decades, but really old houses still had layers of lead paint under their new coatings. I'm sure if I scraped away the persimmon and mustard and ochre tints I'd slathered in my loft, I'd unearth some aged lead layers. Fortunately I've always made a point of keeping my walls freshly painted, mostly because I love trying new colors.

Once I'd exhausted the paint sites, my search engine brought up something called tetraethyl lead, a gasoline additive. Sounded interesting, though it, too, has been outlawed. Of course— now we're required to use unleaded gasoline.

It wouldn't have taken much lead to cause death. Nor would the stuff be too obnoxious to ingest: a sweet odor, according to the website. What struck me as most interesting was that the symptoms—and death—wouldn't show up for a week after it had been consumed.

Maybe Ringo accidentally spilled old paint into his bowl of cornflakes, or his ceiling was flaking lead-based paint right over his kitchen table and regularly contaminating his coffee. Someone could check that out. But if the poisoning was intentional, I'd never find out. This had the elements of a perfect crime: nobody could track down a week-old poisoning. The evidence would undoubtedly be gone. And since the time or place couldn't be pinpointed, checking alibis would be irrelevant. But I'd try.

I needed Homer. Homer needed lunch.

He always does.

The smell of my package brought Homer to his feet. "To what do I owe this honor?" he asked, looking at the oyster po' boy I'd brought him from Johnny's Half Shell, where they know how to fry an oyster to its finest crackling moment.

I closed his office door and sat in the molded plastic chair in front of his desk. "I wanted to talk to you about poisons."

He looked warily at his sandwich and lifted an eyebrow at me.

"I didn't say I wanted to test poisons, just talk about them."

Homer winked and took a bite. And another. A gleam of remoulade touched his cheek. His mouth full and his hands occupied, he signaled that I should go on.

"I know this isn't my business, but I can't stop thinking about Ringo and how he died."

"You're right. It's not your business." The words were muffled by French bread.

"I won't make a big deal of this, I promise."

Homer looked skeptical. I didn't blame him, given my track record for meddling in murders. But since his mouth was still busy with oysters, I continued before he could seriously interrupt me.

"I just want to satisfy a few minor points of confusion. Just to feel I've done something about it so maybe I can sleep better. Maybe reassure myself that it was an accident."

Having finished his sandwich, Homer was at his most agreeable. I'd known my timing would be good. "What would it take to reassure you?"

"I want to see his apartment. Old lead paint, or something, you know."

"Save yourself the trouble. I've already seen the photos. In fact, don't spread this around, but I did more. For Sherele's sake, I unofficially went over to Ringo's apartment and took a look around. It's clean. Newish paint job. No cracks, no flaking. All shipshape. I poked through his cupboards and drawers. Nothing. *Nada.* I can guarantee you that."

"So how could he have been poisoned?"

"Maybe it was in his system for a long time. Or it was a freak accident from something he ate that got contaminated in some weird way. We'll never know. I do know the guy had plenty of enemies and you think one of them slipped him a doctored doughnut or something. But people have enemies. Most of us. That doesn't mean we're going to get murdered. Give it up, Chas, before it becomes a major crusade. Not every death reveals its cause."

He was right. And the more I thought about it, the more reasons I found for not pursuing the cause of Ringo's death. One thing Homer said hit home. Enemies. We all have them. And as I reflected on Ringo's, I was reminded that I much preferred his enemies to him. Would I really want to discover that Ben or Kirk had doctored his kir royal with a few drops of lead? Or that Linda had obtained her new job by slipping powdered paint into his vending-machine snack?

Ringo was dead. Nobody was much the worse off for that except Ringo himself. I'd just go buy a supply of Tylenol PM and get on with my life.

Sure.

22

As soon as I finished my column that afternoon, I returned to the Internet. I tried Mamma, Dogpile, Google, AltaVista, keywords: lead poisoning. I read monographs from the Centers for Disease Control and diatribes from health activists. I exhausted the search engines' resources and wound up with a headache.

My aspirin bottle was empty. I'd live with the ache until it was time to go home.

I hadn't realized, but it turned out to be long past time to go home. I'd wasted half of one of my rare unscheduled evenings, and forgotten I'd planned to use it to test a new neighborhood delivery service. Homer had warned me against making Ringo's death a major crusade. It wasn't too late to listen to him.

"I'm done," I vowed to myself. To prove it, I

shut down my computer and reached for my bottom right-hand drawer, where I kept my purse.

Instead, my hand went to my bottom left-hand drawer. I'd just remembered a travel kit I'd stashed there. If I remembered right, it had a foil packet of aspirin.

It also had a prescription bottle I didn't recall. Penicillin, from four years ago. I couldn't remember why it was there. What was more puzzling, the travel kit was less than a year old, a party favor from a fund-raising dinner Sherele had roped me into. I opened the bottle, and it wasn't pills at all. It was dark orange powder—on second thought, flakes, and not quite dark orange but persimmon. One of my favorite colors, the exact shade of my bathroom walls.

I poured some into my hand, and my heart jolted as if the stuff were electrified. I bent my head to smell it. I stirred it around with a finger. This was paint, I felt sure of it. Powder and flakes of paint, a little grimy and gray, but mostly the color of my bathroom. What the hell was my bathroom paint doing in a penicillin bottle in my desk? I massaged my eyes and saw the image of a vitamin C bottle filled with sleeping pills.

This bottle of paint smacked of Ringo, but the only connections that came to mind were too bizarre.

Was Ringo poisoned by paint? By my paint? How? By whom? And what was my paint doing in my desk?

I started to call Homer, but pulled my hand from the phone. This was trouble, and Homer could mean more trouble.

I called Dave, but when his answering machine clicked on, I remembered that he was out drinking with one of his old FBI buddies. Best not to bring the FBI into this yet.

Whom could I call? No one. I'd better play this cautiously. Think it through. Sleep on it. Keep it to myself until I could talk to Dave, not rush into something that could incriminate me.

I put the bottle in my purse, feeling like I was packing a loaded gun. I got up and headed through the near-empty newsroom toward the elevator.

Thoughts were churning faster than I could organize them yet they guided my action. I turned left and barreled into Bull's office.

"This is just between us."

"Hello, Chas, what's on your mind?"

"Can this be off the record, totally off the record, no matter what?"

Bull looked wary, leaned back in his chair in that superficially relaxed way that really means he's wound tight but doesn't want it to show. "Absolutely. Off the record. May I ask what the topic is?"

"Lead poisoning."

Bull dropped the casual pose and leaned forward, his arms crossed on the desk, his eyes blinking nervously.

"Ringo's?"

I nodded.

"You want this off the record?"

"Absolutely. No matter who asks, even the police."

"You mean both of us are off the record?"

"Yes. This conversation never happened."

Bull got up and walked around his desk. He stood for a moment, seemed undecided whether to play this at attention or at ease. Suddenly he stuck out his hand. "Okay. In fact, let's shake on it."

We did, Bull making it a two-handed shake, clutching firmly to my wrist with his left hand. It was sweaty. So was mine.

He opted for the at-ease mode, sitting on the corner of his desk. "Go on," he said.

Even though Bull had promised secrecy, I wasn't sure I'd done the right thing by coming to him. That small jar in my purse made me feel vulnerable and wary. I started by beating around the bush.

"Did you ever hear of a journalist named E. G. Lansing?"

"Sure. Talented guy. Suicide, apparently. A damned shame."

"They say Ringo might have had something to do with it."

"Not the kind of thing you can prove. Unfortunately."

"Did you know that Ringo, when he was a kid, used to experiment on cats by feeding them lead paint until they died?"

"It doesn't surprise me."

"Why not?"

"He never lost that obsession."

"How do you know that?"

Bull looked increasingly relaxed. He'd always been a storyteller, and he answered my question by taking his time and spinning a tale.

"The late unlamented Mr. Laurenge was an obsessive in every way you might measure. It was never enough for him to write a story; it had to be a series. He couldn't stop with one interview, or five; he had to interview everyone who could possibly relate to his subject. He was never just an acquaintance, he was a friend—or an enemy.

"You saw it at its most basic: when he ate, he ate it all. He was greedy, hungry. He not only wanted everything, he would go to endless lengths to get what he wanted."

I wasn't surprised to hear this about Ringo, but I was surprised to hear it from Bull. He'd always excused everything Ringo did.

He had more, and worse.

"In a journalist, that's a good trait. A journalist needs to be tenacious and to pursue a story to its limits. That's what made Ringo such a successful reporter and a star at such a young age. I wish it had stopped there."

"How do you mean?" I couldn't identify the tone Bull was taking. It was dark, angry, but muffled by something else. Poignancy? Regret? Grief? I wished I could call a time-out to pull my thoughts together.

"It wasn't enough for him to uncover secrets for his stories. He became drawn to uncovering secrets for their own sake. And revelations alone didn't satisfy him any longer. He was fascinated with destruction."

Now Bull was losing me. "You mean Two Views? Or because he stole his colleagues' thunder?"

"Thunder wasn't enough. He moved on to lightning bolts, tornadoes, hurricanes."

Bull must be tired, I realized. His metaphors were getting out of control.

I needed to focus my thinking. Start from the beginning. I reached for my purse. "Lead poisoning. Let's get to that. I came to talk about the source."

"You've got to understand that the source begins with Ringo and his obsessions."

"That's what I don't understand. What was the point?"

"The point was that Ringo had been supposedly doing a story on lead poisoning, but if he really had been, I would have known. He never could resist bragging about the stories he was digging up. So when I discovered his notes, I knew they weren't for a story. But there's no way he would have spent so much time on literature searches and medical studies without some sort of goal. What I had to face was that it certainly wasn't a journalistic one."

"Ringo had been doing research on lead poisoning?" I felt more alarmed than ever. Why would Ringo have planted a sample of my paint in my drawer? I'd already realized it must be contaminated with lead, but I didn't understand how Ringo was connected. Surely he wouldn't have poisoned himself just to pin the murder on me.

"It was more than research. It was a whole plot. A convoluted scheme of destruction and blame, a game that he played in his head that he was inexorably tempted to play in real life, like those kittens."

This was too far-fetched. Wasn't it? "It's a big leap from poisoning cats to poisoning people."

"It was more a matter of edging closer over a period of years. Probably from childhood. At his age it was just one more step rather than a leap."

"You're saying Ringo was on the verge of killing somebody?" I started to protest, but then there was E. G. Lansing to consider. "Who would he have killed?"

"That probably didn't even matter to him. The point was that he could do it and get away with it. And he could direct the blame to someone else, his real intended victim."

So my bottle of lead paint wasn't news to Bull.

"You knew about it."

"I did, though rather late in the game."

"And Ringo was killed by his own scheme."

"You might say that."

"Cause of death, arrogance. Administered by lead paint."

"Too obvious. Tetraethyl lead."

"The gasoline?" I remembered coming across that on the Internet. Bells were ringing in my head, but I couldn't catch the tune yet.

"Gasoline additive. Improves performance, keeps the engine from knocking. Or at least it used to, until it was banned for cars and we all started using lead-free fuel."

I couldn't make sense of Ringo's demented scheme. If he was playing around with—and somehow killed himself with—a gasoline additive, why had he planted lead paint in my drawer?

"I don't get it. Where did the tetraethyl lead come from?"

"Ringo discovered a source on the Internet."

Another chord resounded. How could Bull know what Ringo discovered?

"You knew what he found on the Internet?" The implications were making me feel sick. I started with the most obvious. "You monitor our Internet use?"

Bull's eyes twitched slightly. I'll bet he didn't mean to let that seedy little fact leak out. But he pretended insouciance. "Everyone knows that Internet use is about as private as cell-phone calls."

I braced myself for the answer to my next question. "And our e-mail?"

"Chas, you can't show me a company that doesn't keep a copy of every piece of e-mail that its employees send."

"Your investigative team would be glad to check that out, I'd wager."

"Don't forget our pledge of secrecy here."

He was right. I couldn't even tell Dave. We were off the record.

The privacy issue, though, was only a smoke screen for my more dreadful suspicions. I returned to the reason I'd come in the first place. Or I tried. I couldn't seem to find the will to pull out that bottle from my purse. I procrastinated with another question. "As you said, tetraethyl lead was banned. If that's true, how could it be sold on the Internet?"

"It's banned for road use. On the Internet it's sold for off-road use. Racing cars. For thirty bucks you can buy enough to poison the whole newsroom."

I shuddered. Had Ringo volunteered to bring the punch to the office Thanksgiving potluck? No, ridiculous. Too easy to trace. And I said so.

"If Ringo ordered it and poisoned someone, it could be traced to him. A murderer would know that. The company would have records. The post office or FedEx or whoever delivered it would have records. His credit card company would have records."

"Exactly. It was brilliant, wasn't it, even if I do say so myself?"

I started to agree, as one tends to do automatically when Bull demands our adulation, but then I thought about what he'd been boasting. The bells were meshing into a tune. "*You* ordered it!"

"You don't think Ringo would have been stupid enough to have ordered a poison that would be traceable to him?"

I felt that I'd entered Bull's office under a gray cloud and there encountered a gathering storm. I wanted to run for shelter.

I made one last try to piece together what Bull was saying in different ways. But they only fit into one horrifying picture. "You ordered tetraethyl lead under Ringo's name. So it wouldn't be traceable to you. How could you?"

Bull took my question literally rather than rhetorically.

"It actually wasn't hard. I just used his computer and his credit card number. Easy, in fact. And the mailroom has a record of it being delivered straight to Ringo's desk."

Ringo usually came into the office late, and Bull is often here early. The best schemes are the simple ones.

This conversation wasn't the one I'd been expecting. I'd come to talk about Ringo's scheming, and found another layer of menace applied by Bull. My scalp began to tingle, and an ache started between my eyebrows.

"You're telling me you secretly ordered this tetraethyl lead and left it traceable to Ringo." Maybe Bull had planted that lead paint in my drawer. "And what did it have to do with this?" I pulled the bottle of paint from my purse and shook it in his face. The cover flew off and paint flakes spewed across his desk.

"What's that?" Bull asked, scrambling out of the way.

"It's paint. From my apartment. Probably laced with lead. That's what I came in to tell you about. Ringo planting lead paint in my desk."

"Yours, too?"

"What do you mean, 'too'? Who else found lead paint planted in a desk drawer?"

"Sherele. I found it, actually, weeks ago, back when she was freaking out. It was in a prescription bottle. Sleeping pills. I was afraid of what she might do with them. So I checked the bottle out, and instead of pills I found leaded paint chips. Probably from her apartment, the same as yours. I got rid of it."

Too much was being thrown at me. I wanted to walk out and pretend I'd never detoured from the elevator. My headache was spreading in every direction while my thoughts were trying to unravel the conversation. I started pacing Bull's office, watching him only out of the corner of my eye. He had fallen silent, too. He retreated behind his desk, as if to reestablish his authority as the boss and remind me I was the underling. When I stopped pacing and faced him squarely, his eyes darted away. He looked down at his desk and slowly brought up his hands to massage his forehead. He couldn't meet my gaze. The silence had an ominous quality.

Our conversation came together in my head, all the notes in place. I probably should have kept my thoughts to myself and retreated before things got out of hand, but I've never been one to keep my mouth shut unless it was chewing.

"You knew—or suspected—that Ringo planted poison in Sherele's desk, something that could be easily traced to her."

"I didn't know about yours."

"I realize that now, but that's irrelevant. The real issue is that you bought poison and made sure it would be traceable to Ringo. That's what I'm trying to understand."

Bull invented a smile and pasted it on his face. That's how unnatural it looked. Bull was back-pedaling. "It was just a prank. A practical joke."

Sure. Fun and games with poisons. "I know you weren't going to poison someone else in the newsroom and blame it on Ringo. That's his sort of evil. But you poisoned him." There, I'd said it.

Bull stopped rubbing his temples and pinned his eyes to mine. I thought of deer caught in head-lights, though grizzly bear would have been more apt. His stare was not at me, but through me, to some imaginary bullet speeding toward his heart. His hands roamed the desk looking for safe harbor. He picked up a napkin and began twisting it.

Bull, the gracious host. Linen napkins at his desk. "You fed him poisoned madeleines, didn't you." I wasn't asking, I was stating it. The words switched on a scene in my mind. "A poison that takes a week to work. You were feeding him those

madeleines when I was supposed to be in Florida.
That's why you seemed so nervous when I came
into your office and told you my flight had been
canceled."

I could see Ringo with his feet up on Bull's
desk—Bull never would have stood for such behavior under normal conditions. There was
Ringo, acting as if he owned Bull's desk and getting away with it, while Bull was feeding him
toxic madeleines.

"How did you dare? You could have poisoned
me, too." My voice was cold and calm. Inside my
head, thoughts were screaming.

"You hate anise."

I laughed. His solicitude sounded so unexpected. Then I realized what he meant. Bull had
counted on the fact that Ringo's palate was all pre-
tension. "They weren't really anise, were they?
You just said that to warn me off."

"They were cardamom."

"He wouldn't have known the difference."

"Best he ever had, he said."

Once I started laughing, I couldn't stop. And
Bull joined me, until his bulky shoulders were
shaking and his eyes were leaking hysterical tears.

It got worse. Bull's tears turned into sobs. He
put his head in his hands and struggled to get control. I felt embarrassed for him, and my eyes
darted to the window that overlooked the newsroom. Few people were left in the office, just a
huddle of editors and reporters in the far corner.

It dawned on me to feel relieved that those coworkers remained. Here I was with a murderer, and I was the only one who could connect him with his crime. Far-fetched as it felt to consider Bull a danger to me, it was no more bizarre than his being a killer in the first place. I might be glad to have some help within shouting distance.

Bull wasn't the only lunatic in the room. My next reaction struck even me as demented. I had a strong urge to interview him. It's not often you have a chance for a quiet chat with a murderer, especially a man who's long had your respect, admiration, and personal loyalty. Not to mention one whom you've pissed off from time to time. What pushes a man who's long been used to enormous stress and a newsroom of difficult employees into offing one of them?

"What about the paper? How could you have done this to the paper?" I decided to start with what I knew was closest to Bull's heart.

"Look at the circulation figures. The worldwide news stories, the television. The *Examiner* has never been so hot. Amazingly, Ringo's been worth even more to us dead than alive."

"But surely you didn't murder him to increase circulation."

"Chas, you knew only that he was making life difficult for your colleagues, and that he had hurt your friends. You didn't know the more serious mayhem he was planning."

"You could have just fired him."

"He was planning to leave anyway. And I could have let him go in peace, even though that would have been a blow to the paper. But he was taking steps to buy his new job with the blood of his colleagues. He had dossiers. He'd been collecting details on every reporter and editor whose foibles might be considered news."

"How much could there have been? None of us has that much dirt to dig."

"Innuendo can make even a little dirt grow pretty showy blossoms. A sexual encounter one would like to undo, a gift from a source that one didn't bother to send back, those free books your colleagues have sold, a plea for leniency that a traffic cop honored but didn't forget—these are so small and relatively innocent. But when they're presented as the tip of the iceberg, their innocence seems deceptive. And some of us have made some more serious mistakes that have escaped consequences. Nobody you care about would have been left unscathed. Not Sherele, not Helen, not Dave—"

"We could have dealt with it."

"Believe me, Chas, Ringo would have made the *Drudge Report* seem like puff pieces."

I believed him. After all, I'd seen how Ringo had been able to destroy a restaurant with merely the power of suggestion, how he'd attacked Sherele and then set out to further disable her. He'd had no conscience, no qualms, no scruples. But he did have extraordinary intelligence.

Yet the pieces didn't quite fit.

"If Ringo had been studying lead poisoning, he obviously knew what the symptoms would be. How come he didn't figure out that he had been poisoned, and get himself some treatment in time?"

"He could have," Bull answered. "And I'm somewhat surprised he didn't, though it might not have helped. I've thought a lot about this, and my best guess is that his arrogance was his downfall.

"Ringo considered himself above the law and beyond morality. Rules didn't apply to him. He thought he was invulnerable, even physically. Therefore, when he began to feel ill, he probably dismissed it as the flu, or the results of working too hard. He couldn't imagine he could be a common victim, or that someone could achieve with him what he'd planned to impose on someone else. Maybe I'm wrong, but that's the way it seemed to have worked. Unless he really just wanted to die. We'll never know."

Of all the stunning things I'd heard in the office, none surprised me more than Bull uttering the words "Maybe I'm wrong."

I couldn't stomach any more. I had to get to Homer. Let him deal with the rest of Bull's sordid confession. "I'm leaving," I said, as if I needed Bull's blessing for doing so. I half expected him to stop me, or to pull a gun on me and silence me forever. But certainly not with people outside the window. Maybe he'd accompany me out the door and take me to some desolate place to shut me up. I didn't know how or why he would let me go, now that I knew about his crime, but I was going to try to take advantage of this weirdly chatty moment to escape while I could.

"If you need to talk about this any more, I'm always here for you," Bull said as if we'd been talking about a story that had me stumped.

Insane. Nuts. Thank goodness, Bull didn't seem to recognize the seriousness of what he'd revealed to me.

"Chas, I always said you were a credit to journalism. One of those who understand the sacred value of honoring what's off the record."

That stopped me in my tracks. I should have kept going, and just left Bull to believe whatever he believed. But as I've said, I never could keep my mouth shut.

"You expect me to keep murder off the record?"

"Of course I do. You committed yourself to that. If I didn't know you to be a journalist of such integrity, I never would have agreed."

"Wait a minute. Journalism isn't God. There are ethics higher than journalism." Maybe I should have just humored him and escaped, but I couldn't separate this Bull from the one I'd known and worked for all these years. I'd sometimes adored him and often been infuriated by him, but he'd been a mentor ever since I'd walked through his door straight from a restaurant kitchen and fresh from a divorce. I couldn't turn my back on him, even as I feared that I should be watching my back.

He looked intently into my eyes. "What you gave me was a promise, a sacred trust."

"Within the limits of journalism. But there are higher ethics to answer to. I have to answer to society's laws. I can't abet a crime. That would turn me into a criminal." This was unreal. I was standing in the office of a murderer, arguing ethics with him. Yet, with those computers lined up on desks outside his office window, this still felt like a workspace, my familiar home away from home, and Bull its leader.

I was driven to continue talking. Why? To get his blessing, his permission to turn him in? I didn't know, but the session hadn't yet reached a conclusion, of that I was sure.

"Look, Bull, you shouldn't even be arguing with me. You know it will go easiest for you if you turn yourself in. Talk about the mitigating circumstances. Control the way it comes out. If I was getting this close to unraveling the truth, someone else will, too, before long."

"Ha!" Bull's laugh, more a bark, startled me. "You give yourself too much credit, Chas. You didn't even begin to suspect anything. You never would have come close. You just marched in here and stumbled into an unanticipated conversation. There's nothing for anybody else to discover."

"It doesn't matter how I happened onto this.

Somebody else will, too, in an equally accidental way."

"Then leave it to somebody else. Not you, not after we've been friends for so many years."

"You ask too much."

"It was your idea, Chas. You came in, insisting we keep this conversation absolutely secret."

"That was when I thought we were talking about the paint planted in my desk."

"Oh, so you think such rules apply only to what's dangerous to you? Your morality extends only to my protecting you, not your protecting me?"

"Yes, but I didn't kill anyone."

I would have expected Bull to be growing ever more nervous. Certainly I was. But he seemed to be melting into a state of repose. His voice became deeper, more resonant and, I must admit, more compelling. He sounded less the journalist, more the professor.

"I trust you, Chas, to see what is best, to weigh the death of a cunning and dangerous man whom nobody mourns, against the good of your dearest friends and the good of the newspaper, to which we have both devoted our lives for a very long time. As for your endangering yourself, you certainly know by now that you can trust my strength to protect you as it would any of my staff. Nobody can or will find out what has passed between us here."

I wanted to shout, "Bullshit!" But I thought bet-

ter of it. The potential for danger had begun to
sink into my numbed brain. Instead, I decided to
humor Bull. "You're right. I hadn't thought of it
from that point of view. You've committed the
perfect crime."

Bull was obviously rethinking his tack, too. "I
haven't said I committed anything, Chas. As a
reporter, you know the difference between state-
ments and suppositions. You've drawn conclusions that have no basis in fact."

"Maybe you're right. But neither you nor I is
the person to decide that. The fact is, Ringo is
dead. What do you do with that absolute irrevoca-
ble fact?"

"You see it for what it is. Ringo is now more
revered than he ever could have hoped to be. A
martyr. An international hero. Beloved by all who
would have loathed him were he still alive."

"Why couldn't you just have fired him? I know
you were worried about what he knew, but we're
all grown-ups. We could have defended ourselves
from any threat Ringo could pose. And the paper
could have thrived without him. As it is obviously
doing."

"He was not just useful to have on our team. He
would have been a danger to us if he left. Look
how he used the paper to try to destroy that
restaurant, Two Views, and he only failed because
a few of its prominent friends decided to make a
show of returning to dine there."

"Including you." In fact, Bull had gone twice,

once with the secretary of state and next with Oprah Winfrey. I knew he'd been making amends.

"But no number of friends would have been enough to resuscitate a newspaper after Ringo had disemboweled it. He had the weapons to destroy us. Instead, his death has been a great boon to the *Examiner*. Look at the sales. Look at all the attention. We've been noticed. Everywhere."

"But at what cost? Bull, was it worth killing him?"

Bull paused and swiveled his chair so it faced the newsroom. He didn't look at me when he answered. "Who says I did?"

"I do. You said so." I stopped to think over what he'd been telling me since I arrived. "More or less."

"Never. You drew your own conclusions."

I wished I'd had notes, or a tape recorder. I frantically tried to reconstruct our talk, but like many reporters, I'm not good at recalling conversations without the notes I've learned to use as a crutch.

Did Bull actually tell me he'd poisoned Ringo? Probably not.

He'd as much as said he'd ordered the poison. I think.

"Maybe I don't have enough evidence to harm you. I'm not looking to harm you anyway. I just have to do my job, whatever that job is. As a citizen as well as a journalist. What I wish I could understand is how you could have seen murder as part of your job." I felt bewildered, and grief was beginning to thicken my voice.

"You know, I think Otis Chandler put it best. He'd been a great publisher at the *Los Angeles Times*, then after he left, the new management nearly destroyed the paper. He wrote a letter to the newspaper staff denouncing the management, and in it he said, 'The trust and faith in a newspaper by its employees, its readers and the community is dearer to me than life itself.' "

"If that's true, then you must already be reconciled to your punishment, and you must have known from the beginning of our conversation that I'd have to turn you in."

"Just imagine how that's going to boost the *Examiner's* sales."

Bull came around the desk faster than I expected he could move, and he grabbed me. I started to defend myself, ready to knee his crotch or scrape his face with my nails, but realized it wasn't an attack. It was a hug.

"Go have dinner. You have your job to do. Say hello to Homer for me. I've got to get out of here, or I'll be late for my dinner date."

"Who're you having dinner with?"

"Johnnie Cochran."